CONTAINMENT

Anarchy hits Dunedin when a cargo ship runs aground on Aramoana Beach amid a crowd of onlookers. One of them discovers a skull in the sand while desperate scavengers fight each other for the best of the bounty. Waking up to the chaos and hurrying outside to give the police a hand, Detective Constable Sam Shephard cops a wallop before her attacker is himself beaten senseless. Returning to work, she is sent to help recover a body submerged in the water, the autopsy revealing that this was no accidental drowning but a lethal assault. The undercurrents from one morning's madness turn out to be far-reaching as Sam begins to tie events together. Who else will be caught in the backwash, with a killer on the loose? Can Sam stem the tide?

Books by Vanda Symon
Published by Ulverscroft:

OVERKILL
THE RINGMASTER

VANDA SYMON

CONTAINMENT

Complete and Unabridged

AURORA
Leicester

First published in Great Britain in 2020 by
Orenda Books

First published in New Zealand in 2009 by
Penguin Books (NZ)

First Aurora Edition
published 2020
by arrangement with
Orenda Books

A catalogue record for this book is available
from the British Library.

ISBN 978–1–78782–312–9

Published by
Ulverscroft Limited
Anstey, Leicestershire

Set by Words & Graphics Ltd.
Anstey, Leicestershire
Printed and bound in Great Britain by
T. J. International Ltd., Padstow, Cornwall

This book is printed on acid-free paper

For Mum

Prologue

What started as a small crowd of bewildered residents, huddled against the seeping chill of a dark Dunedin winter morning, had grown to a string of awed and silent spectators leading from the tip of The Mole to the end of the spit. Their vehicles occupied every conceivable snippet of vacant real estate, while those arriving attempted absurd turning manoeuvres in streets never designed for heavy traffic. On the other side of the harbour entrance the distant play of car headlights winding from Taiaroa Head to Harrington and beyond held testimony to similar scenes.

August's watery sun was rising on the horizon, pushing back the vestiges of an eventful night, revealing an unlikely tableau. Shafts of lemon light struck the bridge of the *Lauretia Express*, accentuating the unnatural tilt of her peak. Fingers spread along her container deck, the play of light and dark giving it the appearance of a decayed jaw studded with random teeth. The hulk of the stilled ship dwarfed the buzz of tugs, pilot boats and inflatables that strafed the stricken hull with spotlights.

The scale of the accident was all too apparent to the shivering crowd stretched along The Mole. The ship towered above them like an eight-storey building, marooned at an impossible angle. The strobe of camera flashes added to the

1

eerie atmosphere, creating a stilted cinemascope of the *Lauretia's* demise.

Those further down on the spit huddled in clusters, staring at the incongruous sight of iceberg-like containers, some beached upon Aramoana's sands, some not so fortunate to find dry land. People moved in slow-motion swarms, circling, pointing, whispering in reverent tones at a respectful distance. The whispers were silenced as three young men approached one of the metal boxes. The low sun bathed them in hallowed light as they ran their hands over the surface, and then grasped the door handle and pulled. The security seal was no match for their determination. The creak of metal grating on metal cut through the tense air, puncturing the silence. A held-breath stillness followed, then there was a collective gasp from the crowd. An invisible line had been crossed, and as if upon a signal, the masses descended, as vultures upon carcasses. Eager hands grasped at doors, greedy arms lifted out cartons, motorbikes, furniture, tossing aside that deemed unworthy, plundering that deemed treasure. Fights broke out among those determined to have the best of the bounty, while the moral minority stood back, appalled but helpless. Anarchy had hit Dunedin.

Soon the detritus of pillage was strewn across the beach; ornaments, books, papers, clothes. Those not actively emptying containers poked through what had been cast aside, pocketing the desirable. An elderly woman, wrapped up against the cold, shoulders draped with her newly found bounty — a red woollen coat — poked another

2

pile with a piece of driftwood. She bent over closer to examine the glimpse of shiny white that tantalised from beneath a pile of garments, and then reached out a hand to push aside the coverings. It took several moments before her mind took in the eyeless sockets of the human skull and another five seconds before her lungs sucked in enough frigid air to unleash a scream.

1

'Jesus bloody Christ.'

Beaches were supposed to be pristine stretches of white sand dotted with colourful shells, artfully strewn scraps of seaweed, cast up driftwood, the only sound the waves gently lapping the idyllic shore. Beaches were supposed to be havens of isolation and tranquillity. Beaches were supposed to be . . . well, anything but this. The sight before my eyes made me promise to God I would never complain about finding a dog turd on a beach again. A dog turd would be good, a dog turd would be easy. This was . . . where did I start?

I stood at the top of the wooden steps that led down to the spit. There must have been two hundred people roaming along the sand, and it looked like even more were up on The Mole, going by the number of cars parked stupidly and illegally anywhere and everywhere. It was as if half of Dunedin had simultaneously chosen to take an early Sunday morning joyride to Aramoana. Except that it wasn't a joyride — looking at people's faces, there was nothing joyous about it at all. There was awe, anger, disgust and straight-out greed on those faces, but not joy. There was only one reason they were here, and that reason was so vastly out of place, so incongruous, that my mind was trying every trick it could to try to convince me that, no, that wasn't a bloody great container ship stuck up by the end of The Mole, and no, those weren't shipping containers stranded on the beach.

How the hell could this have happened? There hadn't been a storm to wreak havoc and drive the ship off course. And anyway, when the weather was that severe they closed the Taiaroa Head entrance to shipping. The lanes were too narrow and convoluted to risk it in poor visibility or high winds. Sure, the breeze had been up in the night, but it hadn't been that bad. Normally if the wind was getting serious, the tree outside my bedroom window did a bit of a creak and scrape on the glass, not that I'd have heard it over the noise from that bloody party at the neighbour's. I'd spent the long hours of darkness enduring someone else's bad taste in music at make-your-eardrums-bleed volume. So much for my hopes of a restful weekend in Aramoana at the crib. Under any other circumstance I'd be grateful for the chance to get away to my folks' friends' holiday home to dog-sit their fluffy mutt. Today, not so much. My eyes scanned the warped scene before me. I didn't think the weather conditions could be blamed for this. No, surely all this had to be human error, or mechanical failure. One thing was for sure: heads would roll. The carnage here on the beach wasn't the result of nature's fury; this mess was entirely man-made.

I stumbled my way around the debris. There were books, clothes, furniture, loose papers wafting around like oversized confetti, toys, smashed ornaments, candles, wine barrels, nondescript cartons, unidentifiable tat and people — people everywhere, sifting through the goods casually like they were searching through the titbits on offer at their neighbour's garage sale.

My eyes kept darting to the ship and its precarious lean. I don't know if it was an optical illusion, but it looked huge and close; my pre-caffeine brain grappled with the spectacle. It was hard to figure what was stranger in this catalogue of the bizarre — the ship, or the car, on its roof, in the drink, with its wheels saluting the sky. I took it from the presence of the fire engine and a few blue-uniformed officers that the car situation was under control. It was hardly surprising, given the number of cars and the number of their drivers doing dumb-nut things, that someone eventually got shunted off the narrow little road to The Mole car park and into the water. I was amazed there weren't more of them testing out their vehicle's buoyancy, or lack of. The driver's owner was lucky it was shallow there and even more lucky tides and weather had dumped sand over the jagged rocks.

The police presence was small; it was early and a Sunday, and I was guessing there hadn't been time for the Dunedin Central Police Station to mobilise more staff and get them out here to Aramoana. There was a group of police officers ahead of me trying to maintain a cordon around what must have been some fascinating booty; despite the tape and officers, people were still trying to get to the choicest bits. I recognised the Port Chalmers community constable. He would have been, geographically speaking, the officer stationed closest to Aramoana, if you didn't count me on my supposed peaceful weekend off at the beach.

'Hey John, what's happening?' He was a big, burly kind of a bloke, much like my partner Smithy; they seemed to breed them big down here. The extra layers of clothing needed to ward off the cold didn't do anything to slim his silhouette.

'Bloody mayhem, that's what's happening. The sooner we get more back-up out here the better. I don't know what the hell's taking them so long. In all my years I've never seen behaviour like this. So much for us being a civilised people.' It was quite evident John Farquhar had done a drop-and-run to get out here this morning: his face bore five o'clock shadow — five a.m., not p.m. — and his dark, time-for-a-trim hair hadn't seen any attention either. Not that he probably gave a damn; he had a scowl that looked permanently engraved.

'Where can I help?'

'Further up the beach would be good.' He pointed in the general direction of the cribs down the end of the spit. 'Make sure no one's doing anything too dangerous. There aren't enough of us to stop the looting, just do what you can. At least we've got this patch contained, finally.'

'What happened here?' I asked, moving towards the taped-off area.

'Old lady found a human skull in among the piles of crap. We've cordoned off as much as we can until the SOCOs arrive.'

And it just kept getting weirder.

'Does it look like it came from a container?' I asked. The SOCOs, or scene-of-crime officers, would have their work cut out for them. No neat and tidy little crime scene here. It was probably contaminated in every way known to man.

'Appears that way, but who could tell in this bloody great mess.'

Even with the police presence, people continued to drag objects out of the containers. They probably figured the few police there had bigger things to worry about than their pilfering. But still, I'd never seen such blatant audacity before. They were clearly letting greed outweigh brains, because if they'd bothered to think about it, there was only one road in and out of town, and it would likely be jammed up as hell — with a checkpoint on it. So unless they were prepared to swim with their booty, all it was going to achieve was a criminal record and public humiliation. Not to mention dealing with some very tetchy officers.

My eyes couldn't decide what to rest on as I walked further along the beach. They flitted from boat to beach to boxes. The sight of the ship across from The Mole was straight-out freaky. The scale of something that big blocking the harbour made the surrounding land, houses and cars seem Lilliputian. It looked like someone had Photoshopped a bloody great leaning tower onto an otherwise unsuspecting landscape. Then there was the beach, strewn with pillaged containers, junk, damaged goods, motorbikes, toys, furniture, packs of disposable nappies — you name it, it was here. God give me strength, and coffee.

The sound of raised voices induced me to break into a trot. The tone and volume indicated things were getting a bit heated. I came around the edge of a container to see a tug of war going on between a guy in his twenties and another man in his fifties. The object of their desire was a sizeable cardboard carton that rattled with a suspiciously non-intact sound as it jerked from one combatant to the next.

'Get your hands off it, you thieving little bastard.'

'I got it first. Let go, you stupid old coot.'

'Excuse me, what's going on here?' I said, although it was pretty apparent. With all this stuff strewn everywhere and cartons as far as the eye could see, they'd decided to fight over the same box. How very adult. How very illegal.

The older guy filled me in on the details, speaking through gritted teeth and the overhang of his grey walrus moustache. The strain of the tussle was very apparent on his face.

'This little shit is trying to take off with the box, and I'm buggered if I'm going to let him.'

'Tell grandpa here to get his own fucking box. I got it first.' I'd thought the younger guy was quite attractive, with his curly dark hair and brooding, brown eyes, until he'd opened his mouth.

'Well, I hate to inform you,' I said, moving around between them, 'that it belongs to neither of you, and I'm going to have to ask you both to put it down.' At that the young guy flicked his eyes in my direction, then returned them back to the task at hand.

'Fuck off and get your own box.'

'Nice manners,' I said, trying to keep my blood pressure down. 'Let me introduce myself. I'm Detective Constable Shephard. What you are doing is theft, and if you continue, I'm going to have to arrest you. So put the box down.'

'That's what I've been trying to tell the little shit. It's not his property and he can't take it, but he won't bloody listen, none of them will.' Moustache Guy, with a look of immense relief, let go of the box, sending the younger chap staggering back a few steps. He still wouldn't put the thing down, though. He looked around, checked out the various people busy on the beach, then looked back at me, giving me the old up and down, before pointedly turning to walk off.

'Hey,' I yelled, 'didn't you hear me? You keep walking and I'll have to arrest you.'

'Try it,' he said with a voice that was more threat than invitation.

'Oh, bloody hell,' I said as I ran alongside him and grabbed at the carton. 'Put it down right now.' I wasn't used to having my authority flouted and it wasn't doing anything for my mood. I might have been a fraction of his size, but I wasn't about to be walked away from by anyone.

'Fuck off,' he said as he jerked the carton away from my grasp.

'Let it go.' Now it was me gritting my teeth, as I reached and got a grip on it again. Once again he flicked it to the side, pulling me off balance, forcing me to let go to avoid a dive into the sand.

11

'Okay, you're starting to piss me off,' I said, my dander rising. 'I warned you, I'll arrest you if you don't stop what you are doing.' I made one more grab for the carton. 'Now let go of the box right fucking now.'

Before I could register what was happening, he did let go, and as I dealt with the unexpected weight of the carton he swung around and punched me, right in the side of the face, hard. White-hot stars and searing pain exploded in my head, and the next thing I felt was cold wet sand as my cheek hit the beach. My water-filtered and swirling vision took in the sight of Moustache Guy tackling my assailant, and getting in a few hits, before the red curtain descended and the lights went out.

2

'How are you feeling?' The words sounded muffled to start with, then cleared in that weird, whistley kind of way, like when your ears pop after swimming. 'Whoa, don't sit up so fast, here you go.' I felt hands reach around my back as an almighty head-spin took hold. I put my head between my knees.

'Ugh, what happened?' I asked. The movement of my jaw sent sharp jolts of electricity through the already substantial burning pain on the right side of my face.

'Some idiot threw a punch at you. You've been out cold for a bit. Here, maybe we should lie you back down.'

God, yes, it all came back to me: the unexpected weight of the carton pulling me forwards, then wham. Didn't see that one coming. I put my hand up to him to indicate, no, I didn't want to lie down again. Now I was sitting upright, I intended to stay upright.

'Did someone nail the bastard?' I tried to speak without moving my mouth. I could taste the sharp tang of iron and the smell of blood filled my nostrils.

'Ah, yes.' Finally my voice-recognition software kicked in. The voice in question belonged to John Farquhar, the Port Chalmers constable. Judging by its close proximity, he was the one propping me up. 'He got well and truly nailed;

13

too nailed in fact. We're waiting for an ambulance.'

I tried to recall those last moments from my horizontal viewpoint. 'By the older guy with the mo?'

'Stronger than he looks. Mind you, by the look of you, the other chap deserved everything he got.'

'Is it that bad?'

'Let's just say I hope you're not lined up for any beauty pageants this week.'

I did a little gentle testing to check out the damage. I swung my jaw from side to side, and although it hurt, it did move, which was encouraging. A run of my tongue over my teeth told me they were all still there, although, to my horror, a couple had a bit of a wiggle. The inside of my cheek was a bit mashed; the source of the blood, I imagined. I wiped the sand on my hand off onto my trousers, and then gingerly lifted it up to check out the face.

'Hey, watch where you touch, Sam. You've got a bit of a split there. Here's a tissue for you.'

I reached up with the tissue and, yup, as suspected, the swelling was pretty much proportional to the pain. There was an egg, complete with lashes, where my right eye should be. When I touched my cheekbone a flash of searing white fire shot through my head, and I sucked my breath in with a hiss. My eyebrow felt sticky, and when I looked at my fingers they were coated in blood. Jesus. I only hoped nothing was broken. I folded the tissue into a wad and tried to apply pressure to my brow — enough to stop the bleeding but not so much that I wanted to pass out with the pain. With my good eye I looked up and noted I had a bit of an audience. I wondered if anyone else had come to my assistance, or if it had been left to Moustache Guy to defend my honour? Judging by the prone recovery-position state of the young guy, Mo Man might have been a little overzealous in his administrations.

'What's your name?'

I pulled my focus back to the legs squatting beside me. Dumb question. 'You know my name, John.'

'Humour me. I need to check you're functioning properly. What's your name?' He sounded like a schoolteacher.

'Samantha Shephard, Detective Constable Samantha Shephard. Do you want my serial number too?'

I heard a little snort. 'And what's the date today?'

I had to grapple for that one. I wasn't good with dates at the best of times, let alone when someone had smacked the crap out of me. I had to work backwards. I knew this Friday was Dad's birthday, but through my foggy head the maths still took a while. 'Ah, it's Sunday, Sunday the thirtieth of August, I think.'

'Can you lift both your arms up above your head?'

I didn't feel like I could do anything other than hug my knees right now. Bloody stupid question, I thought, until it dawned on me he was checking brain function, not whether I'd

15

done my shoulder in.

'I copped a wallop, not a stroke,' I said, but obliged.

'Good, now smile for me.' That was pushing it, but I managed a pained grimace that might pass.

'We'll put you in the ambulance too, when it gets here. You were out cold for a few minutes, so they'll want to check you over and make sure you haven't got concussion.' I could pretty much guarantee I did. 'That cut's going to need stitches, and I imagine an X-ray will be in order too, make sure he didn't break anything.'

Terrific.

The throbbing in my head had developed a gut-churning accompaniment that shifted from being insistent to urgent, and with a groan I leaned away from John and added to the detritus on the beach.

This day just kept getting better.

3

Under normal circumstances I wouldn't be too pleased about being in such close proximity to someone who'd just beaten the crap out of me, but today was turning out to be far from normal. The young guy was strapped securely into the gurney in the back of the ambulance and looked a damn sight worse for wear than me, which was saying something. Lying there, pale and hurt, he seemed so innocuous and vulnerable, the ferocity of his attack now felt unlikely and unreal, despite the very real and painful evidence I bore. What the hell had he been thinking? To hit anyone like that, let alone a police officer, let alone a woman? Didn't his parents teach him anything?

I was the kind of girl who was reluctant to take any kind of medication, reserving paracetamol for the stiffest of headaches, but with the hammering and underlying ache going on in my head and face right now, I was willing to adjust my standards. Bring on the dancing drugs, and now would be good, please. The swirling stomach persisted and, despite the earlier emptying out, I still felt nauseated, and clutched at a plastic pot, just in case. Not that I was going to get pain relief any time soon. The ambulance was crewed by the grand sum of one, and he was driving. It was just me and Mr McFists in the back. No kind paramedic to make 'there, there, ever so there, there' noises and dole out the good stuff. No one other than me to make sure the beat-up guy was doing all right and not about to make trouble. Not that I thought he would, given he was still unconscious and strapped in. Great to see our emergency services so well staffed and resourced.

I looked out of the ambulance window at the wall of shipping containers stacked behind the chain-link fence alongside the road from Carey's Bay, and then saw the bums and giraffe-like necks of the huge blue-and-white cranes at Port Chalmers loom up, filling the sky. Two more police cars whizzed past on the opposite side of the road, heading out, a bit belatedly, to deal with the mess at Aramoana. I never thought I'd ever see a scene like that in New Zealand. That was the sort of thing that went on in places like East Timor, or even in the United States in moments of desperation and despair after hurricanes, not in little old Dunedin. It just went to show that beneath the thin veneer of civilisation, we were all capable of violence and crime. Even this guy.

At the time I remember he had appeared handsome, clean cut, well groomed and harmless, yet he'd turned feral in an instant and attacked me over nothing — a box of random goods. It showed how all our social conditioning and manners could fly out the window in the face of greed and opportunism. Common sense certainly went south, because this chap clearly didn't think about the long-term consequences of assaulting an officer. Not just being beaten up himself — who could have foreseen that? — but a criminal conviction, and maybe even a jail term. That would put an end to a vast number of job prospects, and even opportunities for travel. In this day and age, with many countries twitchy about terrorism, even a minor conviction could put paid to any sightseeing trips abroad. Bet he didn't think about that.

Taking a sideways glance at him my internal alarm mechanisms rang, and I examined him more closely. Something wasn't right. I leaned over and angled my head to get a better look at him with my good eye. An oxygen mask covered his bloodied face, making it difficult to see anything. What was bugging me? I looked him over once again, and then realised: shit, his chest wasn't rising. I got to my feet, reaching out to brace myself against the side of the ambulance as we went around a bend, then reached out, fingers searching for the carotid pulse in his neck. Nothing. Fuck.

'He's stopped breathing,' I yelled to the ambulance driver.

Training immediately kicked in, and I flipped the bed back to the horizontal, released the top strap on the gurney and pulled back the blanket covering him.

My eyes searched the cabin for the AED, but I couldn't see it anywhere obvious.

'Where's the defib?' I yelled.

'Some bastard stole it while we were down on the beach. Start CPR.'

Fuckity fuck.

My fingers felt down his sternum, until I

found the right place, clasped my hands, and tried to balance as I felt the ambulance swerving and slowing to a halt.

I pressed down vertically.

Press and release.

Fast and hard.

Press and release.

Having to tiptoe to do it.

Press and release.

Feeling the give in his ribcage.

Press and release.

Praying for his life.

Press and release.

4

'Gidday.' Paul's voice sounded strange through the infrequently used neural pathway via my left ear. The right one, normally used, was out of commission and would be for a while. It felt damn weird holding the phone on this side. Paul Frost was a detective in Gore, and despite my previous mantra of not screwing the crew, was the current object of my affections. It was quite a convenient arrangement. He lived there, I lived here, we had fun in the weekends. Nothing too taxing. Although, I had to admit, today Paul and Gore seemed all too far away.

'Hi.' My voice gave a tell-tale crackle.

'Are you okay? What's wrong?' I gave him full marks for picking up on the cues. He was good like that.

'I'm sitting in A&E.'

There was a moment's silence.

'What's happened, are you hurt?'

'Kind of.'

'What do you mean, kind of? Were you in an accident?'

'Sort of.' The sound of his concerned voice eroded my fortitude. I took a big shuddery breath. 'Someone had a go at me.'

'How bad is it?'

'Black eye, five stitches, big bruise, no fracture, hopefully vision's okay — too swollen to tell. Loose teeth. Concussion. Bloody sore.' Short

21

sentences managed to stave off a girly break-down.

'Jesus. Did they get the guy?'

'Yeah. Shared ambulance. He's not good. He . . . ' My mind flashed back to the image of standing over him, desperately pumping, the blast of pain through my face as I pressed my mouth over his to breathe life back in. 'I . . . I had to jump-start him.'

'What do you mean?'

'Stopped breathing, had to resuscitate him.'

'You saved the life of the guy who beat you up?'

'Yes.'

'Sam.'

That one word expressed his concern, sorrow and amazement. The tears flowed hot and stinging down my face.

'Who dealt with him? Not the police, surely?'

You could only imagine the furore if it had been one of us. Even in defence of another officer we'd be pilloried by the media as heavy-handed.

'No. Public. Someone came to my aid.'

'They must have got a bit carried away, then.'

'Guess so. Don't know, didn't see. I was out of it.'

'Was this all to do with that ship I saw on the news?'

'Yeah. People went a bit nuts.'

There was another short pause.

'God, I can't even come up tonight. I'm completely tied up with work. Listen, I'll make a few calls, but I don't fancy my chances, we're overrun here. I'm sorry, Sam.'

My heart sank. Normally I'd vote against being rescued by an overprotective male and instead plump for standing on my own feet. But after the day I'd had, heck, sometimes all a girl needed was a knight in shining armour.

5

I was feeling a little more together after a hefty dose of something containing a Class B controlled drug and a chat to a friendly voice, even if the voice wasn't going to be able to make it here in person. Perhaps that was just as well because I doubted I was looking my most attractive.

By the time Smithy turned up, the pain relief was kicking in, the lovely lady from Victim Support had calmed me down somewhat, and I was a little more objective about the events of the morning. Detective Malcolm Smith was my kind of mentor; he was supposed to keep an eye on me while I was still a puppy-detective, although he seemed to like the 'give 'em space and let 'em learn by their mistakes' approach to supervision. This normally suited me just fine, although I certainly could have done with his guardian angel presence this morning. Smithy had a face like a dropped pie, a beautiful set of cauliflower ears and a don't-mess-with-me demeanour. All set in a six-foot-plus frame, it made for a menacing package. Perfect for a detective, or a front-row forward dishing it out in the rugby scrum.

I was getting used to people's reactions when they caught a look at the face. Smithy didn't disappoint.

'Jesus effing Christ, Sam. What does the other guy look like?'

The drugs must have been working, because I managed a laugh. 'Far worse than me, that's for sure.'

'Just goes to show, you shouldn't pick on the little guy, or gal.' He gave me a look that hung halfway between sympathy and something I think might have been admiration. 'I heard about what you did for him. For the record, I'd like to have you around if I have a heart attack someday, because you seem to have a knack for bringing people back from the dead.'

I smiled, appreciating the vote of confidence. 'Duly noted. I can't promise anything though. It might be a more effective life-insurance policy for you to lay off the beer and the chips.'

'What? I've spent years cultivating this splendid motor,' he said, jiggling his belly with both hands. 'Why have a six-pack when you can have a keg? I'm not about to give it all up now.'

I noted the now-familiar awkwardness of those who talked to me — do I look her in the left eye, or do I look her in the right eye and appear to be rude and staring? So far most were non-committal and flicked between the two, so of course my eyes followed theirs, and the constant sway gave me a feeling somewhat like motion sickness. I tried to look down at the floor, but that hurt the muscles in my eyes so I settled for a spot just below Smithy's Adam's apple.

'So, what's the story then?' I asked.

'The beachcombers seem to be under control now.' That was a nice euphemism for what I saw going on. 'Was it just me, or did everyone seem to go a bit crazy?'

'It wasn't just you. It was like a Hollywood disaster movie, with the scavengers moving in, except the people I saw weren't extras hamming it up for the camera. They were deadly serious.' As I spoke my hand drifted to my face. I didn't wince this time; those drugs were damn good.

'What about the woman who found that human skull?' Smithy said. 'Everyone seems to feel sorry for her — you know, poor old lady gets a big shock. But I'm thinking, what was a supposedly nice old granny doing out stealing other people's property on a beach? What were any of them doing? It was like stick them out there, isolated with all that temptation and suddenly all morals go out the window.'

'Can't answer that one for you, I'm afraid,' I said. I was starting to feel a touch spacey. 'It's a bit of a worry though.'

'Yeah, very *Lord of the Flies*.'

I looked back up at Smithy, surprised. 'I didn't know you read . . . Golding.' I'd had to fumble around in my brain and memories of fifth-form English for that name.

'I'm full of surprises, but don't tell anyone. I have an image to maintain.' He certainly did a good job of maintaining it, with his rough-cast exterior. But now he was showing himself to be a thinking man's meathead, Richie McCaw on platform shoes.

'By the way, the guy who did over the guy who bashed you.'

'Moustache Guy?'

'Yes, Moustache Guy; he's been charged with assault. There were so many arrests out there because of all the looting, the court had to do a special sitting to process everyone. He wasn't remanded in custody though.'

'Assault? That hardly seems fair. He was just protecting me.' If he hadn't come to my rescue, would anyone else have stepped in? I wondered. My normally unshakable faith in human nature had been a bit rattled this morning.

'It went a little bit beyond protection, Sam. In fact, thanks to you, he's very lucky he's not facing a manslaughter charge, or worse.'

'Yeah, but still, it's no wonder people are reluctant to go to anyone's aid nowadays. Not when the chances are you'll end up in hospital, or in court, and the other bugger will get off scot-free, and probably get awarded damages.'

'I wouldn't call being unconscious in ICU scot-free, but I see your point. Don't you worry, Sam. I'll be having a little chat with your assailant when he's up to it. Did he know you were police?'

'Yes, I told him, and that I was going to arrest him if he didn't stop what he was doing and put the box down, but it didn't seem to make any difference.'

'Not very smart then. Judges get a bit perturbed about things like assaulting an officer. He's extended his sentence by a fair amount, I imagine.'

'So what about the skull? That sounds really freaky.'

'The area's cordoned off, the SOCOs are there and ESR is on the way from Christchurch. The victim clearly wasn't killed on the beach this

27

morning, so it must have happened elsewhere. So we have a murder enquiry, a maritime enquiry, several dangerous driving charges, a few assault cases and a shitload of looting charges to keep us busy.' He rubbed his hands together with glee.

I found it a bit difficult to muster up that level of enthusiasm, but one thing was clear: Dunedin's reputation as Grand Conservative Central had just been shot to hell.

6

I'd been having a delightful conversation with the teeniest, tiniest little spider who was making the most amazing web between the pipe thingies coming out of the wall, bringing oxygen and whatever other stuff they pumped into people. Her name was Crystal and she had been busy explaining why Einstein could not possibly have believed all that stuff about mass and matter, and that she'd told him this, again and again, but he wouldn't listen, and now look what had happened, and we were all stuck with this cumbersome theory of his. She also thought he should have done something about his hair. I was just about to point out to her that, in fact, we humans were quite taken with the man and his ideas, when my flatmate and favourite friend, Maggie, walked into the room.

'Maggie, great to see you, come meet Crystal, you'll like her. She's great. She was just telling me — '

'Good God, Sam, look at your face. That's gotta hurt.'

I put my hand up to my face to make sure it was still there, and then laughed. 'I know. You'd think that, wouldn't you? But they gave me this drug, I don't know what it was, but I must get the name of it because I think it's rather good, even if I had to have a jab in the bum, and you know I don't normally like needles, but this

29

wasn't so bad, and the male nurse was kind of cute, and I'd quite like some more actually, because I feel kind of nice, but it doesn't hurt anymore, well it does, kind of, but not really, you know?'

'Do you think they may have given you a little bit too much?'

I looked more closely at Maggie's hair. She'd clearly forgotten to brush it after she washed it this morning because the titiwai glow-worms were still trying to make their strings of beautiful little diamonds to trap the flies. They sparkled and glittered, and their luminosity threw such a pretty light on Maggie's face. They must have been annoying her though, because she lifted up her hand to swipe them away.

'Wow,' I said, as she swept her arm and a multicoloured rainbow trailed the movement. 'How did you do that? Can I try?' I waved my arm in front of my face, but it didn't quite work properly, so I tried again, and again, and then on the fourth and most enthusiastic try it worked a treat, but I nearly fell out of the bed. I gave a squeal of delight, straightened myself back up and practised a few more times, just to make sure I'd got it right.

'They called me to come and take you home, but I'm thinking that's not such a good idea right now.'

At that moment Crystal butted in and said, 'Don't look, but she's put her eyes in back to front.'

So, of course I looked, and they were, all of them, and it was so funny that I burst into fits of

30

giggles, which floated out across the air and popped like little bubbles against the walls.

7

'Oh, God, someone shoot me.' The clamps squeezing my guts gripped even tighter, another wave of saliva flooded my mouth and I retched once more into the toilet. When I was done turning my innards inside out I sat back on my heels and accepted the warm facecloth that was placed in my hand. I held it over my face while trying to breathe away the explosive pain in my head. It wasn't working.

'Not enjoying the happy drugs quite so much now, huh?' Maggie said, with a charming combination of mirth and concern.

'Ugh.' I pulled off some toilet paper to wipe my eyes and then blew my nose. It hurt. The happy drugs had well and truly lost their charm. I felt like a dead duck in a thunderstorm.

With some assistance from Maggs, I got to my feet and shuffled over to the washbasin, where I made the unfortunate mistake of looking in the mirror. I immediately wished I hadn't. On any normal day I quite liked what I saw: large, warm brown eyes under high eyebrows, straight nose, full mouth and smooth, olivey skin, all framed by longish dark-blonde hair with a slight wave. I'd have liked curls. I didn't consider myself to be beautiful — more, pretty. That was on a normal day. There wasn't anything normal about this.

My eyebrow looked like a row of five little blue spiders were going for a constitutional along its cracked, red ridge. The bruising had developed into beautiful shades of crimson, purple and black. Their depth of colour and contrast with my general pallor was quite striking. The bruising I could handle. Unfortunately, the swelling was beginning to subside, which meant my right eye had opened up to a slit. And while I could see out of it, which was a huge relief, the sight of it alarmed me. A blood vessel had broken, which made me resemble some bruised, red-eyed alien/human hybrid. I made an executive decision to avoid mirrors for a week or two.

'Ew,' I said to Maggie. 'You didn't tell me about that.'

'I couldn't quite find the words,' she said. 'It could be worse, it could have been both eyes; and you should be happy your nose is where it belongs.' She was right. At least I'd taken the blow more to the side of my face. And my sense of vanity felt slightly buoyed by that thought. The cut was right on top of my eyebrow, so any scar would eventually disappear and there'd be no permanent reminders of the assault. I'd just have to live with the artistic bruising, red-eye special, ringing ear and 6.8-on-the-Richter-scale headache for a bit longer.

'I need some paracetamol,' I said, and shuffled for the kitchen.

'That won't do anything. Shouldn't you take something stronger?'

'After that stuff they gave me, no way. It was fun for a while, but man, what a downer.' I'd been a horribly conservative teenager and had never smoked cigarettes and never tried drugs; way too much of a control freak for that. A token drag on a marijuana joint when I was eighteen didn't count, especially when the resultant coughing fit took all the fun out of it. And after this experience, I didn't think any high, no matter how 'whoa, dude', would be worth this kind of crap. This experience had made it crystal clear to me that my body and anything potentially hallucinogenic didn't mix. Trust me to be one of the 0.5 per cent who may experience hallucinatory side effects according to the package insert. Marvellous.

'For the record, you were really entertaining when you were high, but not so much fun anymore. You're a bit messy now. Interesting reaction though. I'm sure that doesn't happen often or else they wouldn't dare administer it to people.'

'Yeah, well, aren't I the lucky one? I can't actually remember much of the evening. Was I bad?'

'I wouldn't say bad, more like amusing. I really loved the way you got back to nature, communing with the animals, particularly the bugs. Very *Charlotte's Web*.'

'Promise you won't tell anyone?'

'I don't know. What's it worth?'

My brain wasn't working well enough to think of a currency with enough appeal, so I lay myself at her mercy. 'Name your price.'

Maggie's eyebrows shot up. 'You must be feeling bad. Lucky for you I'm not the sort to take advantage of the infirm, so a packet of

Toffee Pops and we'll call it square.'

'Done.' And we shook hands on the deal.

Maggie was my flatmate/confidante/psychologist/ social secretary/voice of reason/long-suffering friend. She had put aside all regard for her own personal safety and continued to live with me despite the inadvertent danger I seemed to be good at putting us in. We had flatted together back in our Mataura days, as well as elsewhere in Dunedin, with interesting results. Perhaps she felt her life lacked an element of excitement or danger, and associating with me, more often than not, provided it. Her loyalty defied all logic.

Besides supplying me with stability, amazing coffee and fair-trade chocolate, she also gave wardrobe advice, which I desperately needed. She did effortless chic; I did thoughtless conservative. Her way looked better. I hoped one day a little bit of her innate style would rub off on me, but it hadn't so far. Mind you, it helped that she was tall and shapely and had that gorgeous milk-chocolate-coloured hair and the skin of someone whose mum was *tangata whenua*. She oozed a grace and elegance that I sadly lacked.

For now, it was some ungodly hour of the morning and Maggie, way beyond the call of duty, was playing nurse to my beat-up, head-clutching, vomiting patient. With great dedication she'd been waking me up at hourly intervals, as instructed by the hospital, to shine a vicious little light in my eyes to ensure I hadn't had some kind of a vascular blow-out. I was sure I'd thank her for it at some stage. This time, though, she'd woken up to the dulcet tones of my violent retching and come a-running. Like I said, way beyond the call of duty.

I was glad she was here, and glad I was at home instead of sharing a hospital room with lots of sick people. I had a norovirus outbreak, the resultant ward shut-down and not enough hospital beds to thank for that. I was also glad that Paul had called earlier to say work had thrown a wobbly at his attempts to get time off, and he couldn't make it tonight. I couldn't picture any guy coping with this punch-drunk, hungover, retching, red-eyed, poor impersonation of a human being.

8

It felt decidedly odd to be on the other side of the police mechanism. I was feeling restless, het up and about ready to explode at home, so I came down to the station to make my statement. The paracetamol had barely dented the head-ache, but seeing as I hadn't thrown up for at least five hours, I decided I was up for it. Judging by the amount of whiplash-inducing double-takes and sympathetic looks from my colleagues, the face wasn't good. I wouldn't have known, I hadn't looked that morning. The hair probably wasn't much better. Mind you, if it had been particularly awful, I'm sure Maggie would have said. She drove me down to the station. Even I realised I shouldn't be in control of a car when I was still having trouble maintaining control of my legs.

Smithy was going to do the honours. Yesterday's hospital visit had been to take a few pictures and assess how I was, which was a bit too woozy to remember much. Today I was more lucid and we had to get down to business.

'You know, Sam, I could have come up to your flat to do this,' he said as I settled into the chair and wrapped my hands around a warm mug of coffee — today I was desperate enough to settle for instant crap.

'I know, but I needed to get out of the house.'

'It can't feel as bad as it looks then.'

'Oh, don't you worry, it feels plenty bad.' Short of one or two memorable hangovers, I couldn't recall having ever felt worse. Mind you, judging by the interesting shape of Smithy's nose and his few battle scars, I'd say he knew exactly how I was feeling.

'Then why the masochism? Are you trying to go for the sympathy vote?'

I didn't know what to say to that. I didn't think I was so desperate to be accepted here that I'd play the sympathy card. But, while my closest colleagues liked me well enough, there were those who still questioned my fast-tracking into the CIB. Surely my subconscious hadn't dragged me here because of that.

'Shall we get on with it then?' I tacked away from that subject.

I did my best to recall the chain of events at Aramoana the previous morning. It took a bit of an effort to remember the details, but I certainly remembered the mood. Common decency had given way to looting and assault and battery. After the battery bit, it was all a little hazy.

One thing I did remember was the cordoned-off area that contained the skull and, as I'd been in a bit of an information blackout, I was more interested in finding out what was going on with the enquiry than revisiting an assault that was a bit too fresh in my mind. But Smithy had other ideas and insisted on making me repeat my story, my actions and the words I'd spoken to Mr McFisticuffs; he wanted to ensure that I'd clearly identified myself as an officer and warned him of his pending arrest.

The guy now had a name, Felix Ford. I positively identified him from a selection of photos of similarly aged and similar-looking guys. There was no hesitation, that face was burned into my memory. Likewise, I identified the man who had come to my rescue, a Mr Iain Gibbs. He was easy to pick out, courtesy of the walrus moustache.

Smithy then took me down to the photographer for a few more pictures of my glorious face to go with the ones he'd taken yesterday at the hospital. I declined his kind offer to look at the snaps on the cameras digital display.

'So, how is this guy, Felix, now?' I asked. I'd finished giving my statement and knew Smithy couldn't fob me off any longer. I was torn between fury at Felix Ford and concern for his well-being. Not an easy tussle. Despite all that, I felt somehow responsible for him, which, given the circumstances, seemed stupid. Still, I couldn't ignore my feelings; I wondered if this was a hangover everyone who had saved a life felt. 'So is he awake and talking?'

Smithy shook his head. 'Still in a drug-induced coma until the swelling in his brain goes down. His parents came in and identified him for us earlier this morning.'

'Oh.' That didn't sound very promising. 'What's his prognosis?'

'They'll have to wait until he's conscious before they can assess if there's any permanent damage. If it all looks good for him, he'll have plenty of long-term recovery time in a nice, comfy prison. Assaulting an officer and resisting arrest doesn't tend to sit well with the courts, or any of us for that matter. So you don't need to worry, he'll be dealt with appropriately.'

I couldn't help but think he'd been dealt with already. But then, if he'd done this to one of my colleagues, I'd want the book thrown at him too. Sometimes I was a bit too soft for my own good. I'd been working hard at building up a thick skin, despite a few of my colleagues trying to pick away at it, but I was beginning to face the fact that on the scale of humanity, I was down the nurturer end of the spectrum. Sometimes that was a good thing; at other times it was a curse.

'What about the murder investigation? What's happening with the skull on the beach?'

'Come, see for yourself,' he said with a grin. Smithy didn't often grin, and it was a disturbing sight, especially in the context of what I'd just asked him.

We'd taken the statement in the staff canteen, so this would be my first venture into our CIB squad room.

A wolf whistle greeted me from behind Reihana's desk. 'Looking pretty this morning.' I noted he had his usual Johnny-Cash-wannabe uniform on. His sentiment was echoed by similar comments from around the room.

'Looking good, Sam.'

'Damn fine.'

I did a slow twirl and then framed my face with my hands, as if posing for the camera. 'Thank you, thank you very much, thank you for your concern.'

This was odd. The mood was altogether too jovial considering there was a murder investigation going on. My eyes flitted to the whiteboards, expecting to see a list of names assigned to facets of the investigation, but there wasn't one. Where was the hubbub; where was the tension?

'So, what's going on?' I said, my voice wary.

'Come over here; pop quiz for you.' Smithy pulled a folder off his desk, and after a flick-through pulled out six photos. He placed them side by side on the desk. 'There you go. Get this right and I'll shout you a drink on Friday night.'

The photos were of a skull, with measurement markers, taken from the front, back, in profile, from above, and from below.

'This is the skull they found at Aramoana?'

'Yes, one and the same. Tell me what you see.'

'Is this a trick question?'

'Kind of, but there's a beer in it.' A couple of the others had gathered around to watch. I had the strange feeling quite a bit rode on my response. The vision from my right eye was still pretty blurry so I had to squint and blink a bit to take in the details. The blinking didn't help the pain levels at all. I took a few moments to examine them.

'Well, for a start, it's a very clean skull, quite white,' I leaned closer, 'and very smooth.' Not that I had great experience with skulls. Most victims of crime I saw were of the flesh-covered, and mostly still alive and kicking, variety. I'd seen plenty of shiny, bald scalps, in varying states of repair, but a shiny skull was a novelty. 'That

41

would suggest it's not new or fresh, I guess.' I saw them eyeball each other, twitches of smiles in the corners of their mouths. This was a game, and I didn't know what the rules were, but I suspected it ran along the lines of 'trip up Sam'. I wasn't in the mood for public humiliation today so I checked for the obvious. 'There's no apparent injury, and all the teeth look intact. The jaw's missing.' Still the conspiratorial looks. Okay, what assumptions was I making? Was it bone? I checked for tell-tale moulding marks or seams, but apart from the cranial sutures which should be there, nothing. 'It looks like it's real bone, not a facsimile.' I saw heads cock at that comment — I must have been closer to the mark. My eyes skipped over the smaller anatomical features and came to a skidding halt when I looked at the photo taken from the underneath perspective. I picked it up for a closer look, closing my right eye and peering at it with the left. That wasn't natural. 'It's got a serial number.' It was minute and pale brown, but it was definitely there, handwritten by the looks of it, right by the hole the spinal cord would have passed through. What kind of a skull would have a serial number? Then I clicked. 'You're kidding me, this is a specimen skull; a medical specimen? I thought most medical specimens had a flip-top lid and hinges or a hook out the top for hanging, but this is entire. So that's why there's no murder investigation going on?'

'Bingo! I owe you a beer. Quick too, you got it faster than everyone else here.' I felt ridiculously pleased with that comment. So it was a test.

Thank God I didn't make a git of myself then.

'Yeah, congratulations,' a new voice said, except the tone was minus the good humour. The throbbing in my temple picked up the tempo. 'You're a regular little detective, aren't you?'

The smile on Smithy's face melted, and the others made their way back to their desks. Detective Inspector Johns, aka my boss and chief party-pooper, had made his presence felt. I hadn't heard him enter the room. Normally my radar could pick him up from fifty metres. It must have still been off-line from the bashing. I hadn't had my customary few seconds to prepare and don my mental armour, so the barb hit home.

'That was careless, letting yourself get assaulted.' No *hello, how are you?* 'You shouldn't have put yourself in that position.' He had green eyes, kind of feline — verging on reptilian; they carried no warmth, in either colour or emotion. Combined with his short black hair, pale skin, and the dark-grey suit with monochromatic tie he always wore, everything about him said cold-blooded. 'When will you be back at work?' It was delivered in more of a get-your-arse-back-here way than a you're-hurt-so-take-as-much-time-as-you-want fashion.

'I'm not sure,' I mumbled, looking at the floor in front of his feet.

'Tomorrow,' he said. It wasn't a request.

9

'Ouch,' I said, gently pulling away. 'Sorry, but even that hurts.'

'You are in a bad way if I can't even kiss it better,' Paul said, his hand carefully cupping my jaw, on the good side. 'You won't feel offended if I don't gaze adoringly into your bloodshot eyes though, will you?'

'I can forgive you, just this once. I'd hate to give you screaming nightmares, and considering I refuse to look at myself, I won't punish you with that horror.'

'That's mighty decent of you. I'll have to stare at your tits instead,' he said, and planted a kiss on my forehead, while giving my right breast a fondle. Who said men couldn't multitask?

I wrapped my arms around his middle and leaned my head against his chest. The reassuring *lub-dub* of his heart and warmth of his arms enveloping me allowed me to breathe out and relax some of the tension in my body. It made me realise just how tired I felt and how, as much as I hated to admit it, I needed that sense of security only he seemed to be able to offer. A big fat tear rolled its way down my cheek, and was promptly followed by another. I didn't bother wiping them away.

'Hey, Shep, you're making my jersey soggy.'

I gave a short laugh. 'It's the price you pay for coming to pick up the pieces.'

'Small price; I can cope with that. But I am sorry I couldn't get here earlier for you. You know what it's like in this job — sometimes you can't get away.'

Boy, did I understand. 'That's okay,' I said: 'You wouldn't have liked the chundering version anyway, believe me. But I hear what you're saying about the job. Hell, here I was thinking I was going to have a restful weekend out at the beach looking after someone's pooch, and next thing I know I'm being clobbered in the name of duty.' I felt his hands rubbing big, slow circles on my back. I closed my eyes and relaxed further. 'Hazard of the job, I guess.'

'Well you do seem to have a knack for attracting crackpots. I'd go have a quiet word to this one, but he's probably already got the message.' Paul was the king of understatement.

Everything about Paul felt good: he felt strong, warm, loving and he even smelt good. God knows he looked damn fine, like a more mature and handsome version of Ben Affleck, but with a wicked twinkle in his eye. The depth of his voice felt solid and reliable, and I was glad he was here. Even though it was only a couple of hours down the road, Gore had seemed a long way away in the last day. For the moment, he'd bridged the gap.

'I'm so glad you're here,' I mumbled into his jersey.

He squeezed me tighter.

'This does bring up something that's been weighing on my mind,' he said. His hands paused on my back. 'I was going to tell you when

I saw you this weekend, but now seems an appropriate time.'

'Let me guess, you're horribly bored with being a detective and are chucking it all in for a career as an artist?' I'd seen his attempts at doodling; they weren't what you'd call accomplished.

'Not quite, but it does involve a change of scenery.'

My instincts pricked up, and my innards started to develop a vague sense of impending doom.

He took a deep breath. 'The thing is, I've applied for a transfer to Dunedin; they've been advertising a vacancy in the CIB here, so I've gone for the job. I don't want to be so far away from you all the time. I hate us only being able to get together on the weekends. So if I get this, we'll be able to spend more time together.'

I sucked in my breath and felt a cold wave flow up my face, closely followed by a hot one. A transfer? Here? I loosened my grip from his waist and stepped back, unable to hide the confused look on my face.

'What?' he asked. 'What's wrong?'

'What's wrong? A transfer? Don't you think that's kind of big, kind of sudden? Moving over here? Shouldn't you have asked me about this first?'

A frown crept across his forehead. 'I thought I'd surprise you, I thought you'd be pleased.'

'Pleased? Well, hang on; it's a big step to take from casual shagging at the weekend, to upping sticks and moving cities to be closer. This is something we should have talked about first. You don't just go and decide you're going to move in without asking me.'

'Hey, I didn't say anything about moving in, so you don't need to panic.' I wasn't panicking. The constriction in my throat and hammering in my chest wasn't panic, it was surprise. I stood right back from him and crossed my arms over my chest.

'This is a big step,' I said, fumbling for the words. 'I thought we were just, you know, having fun. What you're talking about, this is serious.'

Paul put his hands on his hips, a guarded expression descending over his face. 'I thought we were a bit more than just fun, Sam.'

'Well, we are, but we're not . . . not, you know . . . '

'No, I don't know. What are we, then?' I could see the hurt look in his eyes, and I felt a pang of guilt, which was promptly replaced by annoyance. Damn it, why should I feel guilty when he was the one who'd dropped this bombshell on me. And his timing was lousy. No, I wasn't going to wear it.

'You could have asked me first. Don't I get a say in this? Or do my feelings not count?' My voice sounded defensive and angry.

'Of course they do. But I honestly thought you'd be pleased.' A hint of doubt had crept into his voice.

'Well, I . . . I don't know what I am. One minute you're here to cheer me up, and the next you're basically announcing you're moving in. What am I supposed to think?'

'Man,' he said, forcing his breath out with the word. 'This isn't playing out like I thought it would.' His gaze bore into me, those crystalline-blue eyes so intense I had to look aside. 'Okay, Sam, let me state this categorically, because I can see you're standing there like a possum trapped in headlights. I'm sorry, I didn't mean to upset you. Me moving to Dunedin, it isn't a marriage proposal, or moving in together, or an expectation that I want much more from you, or us. It's something I want to do for my career — I'm not dumb enough to just drop everything for a woman, no matter how charming she is.' He gave a fatalistic smile. 'But I do want to see more of you.' His voice softened. 'I love you, you know that, poor sod that I am. I love you, can't help myself.'

There was a vulnerability to his admission that melted me for a moment. I heaved out a sigh. The world felt very heavy today.

'I'm not asking you for more. I'm just wanting the opportunity to see if there could be more.' He stood before me, shield down, heart exposed.

It was now my call. Shit. My head and my heart were pounding. I lifted my hand up and wiped at my face, wincing at the sharp pain.

'Look Paul, I'm sorry,' I said, looking at his feet. 'This isn't a good time. I just can't promise anything right now.'

10

'Stop looking at me like I did something wrong.'

Maggie stared.

'What?' I said.

She gave me a look that could have melted steel.

'Oh, for God's sake, what was I supposed to have done?'

One eyebrow went up.

'He caught me at a bad time, that's all. I'd just been assaulted, for heaven's sake, and concussed, and my head was away with the fairies because of those damn drugs. Anyway, it's not like I dumped him or anything.'

The other eyebrow joined the first.

'Well, it was his own damn fault. What did he expect me to say?'

She folded her arms across her chest.

'I wasn't about to jump into his arms and say, 'Wonderful, let's move in, hell, marry me tomorrow, let's elope.' Of course I needed some time to think about it all. That was way too big a surprise to spring on a girl. What was I supposed to do?'

I watched as Maggie's hands slipped down to her hips, and she gave me the look once more.

'No, I'm not going to apologise to him.'

11

Here I was, two days after being KO'ed, looking very much the worse for wear and feeling even worse than I looked. I was back on the job and I felt like one of those Neanderthal rugby players who basically had to be carried off the field, all the while arguing that they'd be okay, just strap some tape around it and let them keep playing, when their foot was facing in the wrong direction. It wasn't entirely out of choice though. DI Johns had made it very clear he wanted me back doing my duty to Queen and country, and if there was one lesson I had managed to learn in my time here with him, it was to pick your battles. So, despite all common sense telling me to stay at home, I was here, toughing it out in an attempt to placate an arsehole boss.

There was one big advantage to dragging my sorry butt into work — it took my mind off the bombshell Paul had dropped the previous night. I suspected I may have overreacted. To be honest, my recall was a bit hazy, but the man had appalling timing. What sort of idiot would spring that on a girl in my condition? He deserved what he got, which must have been a bit. I think I shot with both barrels, because he turned around and drove all the way back to Gore. When was the paracetamol going to kick in? I rubbed at my temple, but that only caused a jolt of pain that made matters worse.

It was good to be sitting down. I still felt a bit unsteady on my feet. The sensation wasn't helped by the vicious, blustery winds that buffeted the city. The slight sway of the building and the funnelling noise added a vertiginous effect to it all — hooray. Wouldn't it be great to be seasick at work?

Not a hell of a lot was happening around here. There was no murder enquiry to get stuck into. There were a couple of serious assault cases — mine, and the assault against Felix Ford. Smithy was heading up those. For some reason they saw any involvement from me as a conflict of interest, so that left me stranded in the team dealing with the aftermath of the looting.

The skull may not have reached the beach by nefarious means, but an owner still had to be found. People, especially the press, got a bit twitchy about unidentified human remains, no matter how clean and catalogued. No one had stepped forward to claim it so far, which surprised me given the amount of media coverage this whole debacle had received. It had made CNN and the BBC, with the inevitable comparison to Britain's own Branscombe Beach loot-fest a few years back. Perhaps the skull was part of a container of personal effects, and the owners were en route to their new home here, oblivious to all the excitement. I was sure they'd be thrilled when they found out their precious belongings had been hauled out of their supposedly secure container, riffled through for the good stuff and the leftovers discarded across a beach. Welcome to Dunedin, *haere mai*, enjoy your stay.

The looted property could be anywhere by now. A fair amount had been intercepted by police on the road out of Aramoana, confiscated from the car boots of dumb-nuts, but plenty would have been spirited away before the road was closed and checkpoints set up. Who knows how much was now sitting in the cribs and residences of the local, supposedly law-abiding citizens? There was nothing we could do about that. No judge would issue a search warrant for a domestic dwelling on the basis that it happened to be close to the scene of a large-scale crime.

My navel-contemplating was interrupted by a sharp voice from the doorway.

'Shephard, I'd like to see you in my office, now, if you please.' It was DI Johns. Shit, my radar had failed again.

My heart rate skipped up a few beats, even though his tone was relatively neutral. I wondered what Dickhead wanted today. I stood up and pushed my chair back with my legs. The moment I started moving towards the door I realised something was off. The ringing in my ear picked up in intensity, a swarm of grey bees clouded the edge of my vision and I felt helpless to resist as my body tilted to the right, causing me to veer off course until my steps couldn't keep up with the lean and I fell sideways, like some drunk comic-book character, or a kid trying to walk straight after a big stint on a playground roundabout. Despite my slow-motion attempt to break the fall, I ended up sprawled on my side in some strange horizontal dance, my face greeting the carpet.

My low-angle, sideways perspective saw an alarmed, then angry, look on the DI's face. Through the buzzing I heard him say, 'What the fuck are you doing back at work if you're that bad?'

I thought, *Your fault, arsehole,* before throwing up on the carpet.

12

A week of enforced holiday hadn't done me any favours; well, not mentally anyway. I didn't do rest and relaxation well. My idea of rest and relaxation involved long runs to blow away the cobwebs and stretch the legs, or bike rides — since I'd discovered the world of mountain bikes, the muddier and hillier the better — or going for a good gallop on a horse, or even wielding a racket of some sort and whacking the crap out of a little ball, anything but being still. I didn't do still. But the doctor had said 'rest', and meant it.

There were only so many books you could read, crosswords and Sudokus you could complete, and websites you could visit before cabin fever set in. Especially as Maggie had been out every day at university and I had got to enjoy all of those splendid activities alone. I believe it was day three that it got really bad. So bad, in fact, I'd opted for the last resort of last resorts, and, due to the doctor giving me the hard word about getting behind the wheel, got the bus home to the Olds on the farm.

Dad had welcomed me with a warm embrace and sympathy. Mum had greeted me with a lecture. No surprises there. But I could put up with barbs and pings from she-who-must-be-obeyed, at least for a while. The opportunity to escape outdoors and do quiet jobs with Dad was worth the trade-off. It also meant I got to be home for his birthday, and despite all my grumbles about my mother, she put on the best roast lamb and veggie dinner on the planet, and no one, but no one, could beat her gravy. Then the traditional birthday dessert was the icing on the cake, or I should say, the cream on the Pavlova — with passionfruit, not those stupid bright-green slices of kiwifruit.

It had been great to get out there with Dad and potter around, as he put it. There was something about ambling around the lush green pastures, dodging the odd steaming cow pat, inhaling the rich scent of earthy humus with a hint of sileage, that instantly relaxed my tensions, both physical and mental. My brother Steve and Saint Sheryl, his perfect wife, had recently taken over the early-morning grind of the milking and the day-to-day running of the place. They lived in a brand-spanking-new farmhouse on the property while Mum and Dad stayed in the original homestead. I liked the old house better, with all its memories. It was slightly dated in a charming kind of a way, just like my parents. It was the perfect arrangement for them; I could never imagine them suffering the indignity of moving into a little unit in town upon retirement like so many of their friends had. I think my dad would just curl up and die if that ever happened. As it was, I could see that he was slowing down and wasn't the same strong and strapping man of the land he used to be. It pained me to think he wasn't getting any younger and that he wasn't my Superman dad anymore. He'd certainly struggle to leap tall buildings, and the way he'd thinned meant the superhero suit would look a bit baggy nowadays.

I'd come away from my stint at home feeling physically better and a damn sight easier to look at, now the bruising had diminished to a pretty purple with jaundice-yellow highlights; but I was slightly on edge courtesy of the constant eggshell-walking required around my mother. Also, the realisation they had retired and were slowing down left me with a vague sense of sadness.

Being at home had also meant I'd conveniently sidestepped the Paul Frost issue. We'd been in touch in the polite and stilted way used by people who'd hurt each other, avoiding any deep and meaningful dialogue but trying to keep some semblance of civility. He'd been the grown-up and made the first contact. That annoyed me in a way, because I had intended to be the first, but he beat me to it.

A few days after the phone call Paul had popped down to the farm for a day trip, and I'd be lying if I didn't admit I had been pleased and relieved to see him. The admission came with a certain amount of anxiety, though, but that was allayed by the Shephard-family smothering machine. Paul being Paul, he'd completely charmed them. Mum fell all over herself, playing the part of the gracious hostess, and Paul and Dad had that infuriating boy-bond thing and disappeared off to the shed for an hour to do man stuff. Naturally, Mum took the opportunity to interrogate me, but my years of training in mother-diversion techniques meant I was able to give her satisfying answers without actually divulging any information.

Courtesy of the ever-present folks, Paul and I didn't actually get any time alone. The avoidance tactics weren't going to last though, as I had to return to the real world eventually and Paul would be heading to Dunedin the following weekend. I only had a little time to figure out what the hell I wanted.

13

My allocated recuperation time was over, and I could finally get back to doing what I did best. The occasion called for a front-door entry rather than slinking in the back way; besides, I liked looking at the massive work of art that greeted everyone who walked through the main entrance foyer of Dunedin Central Police Station. I thought it would look good in our flat. My security card made a very satisfying *thwick* as I slid it through the reader and the door released. I trotted up the stairs to the CIB floor, gave a cheery 'hi' to Laurie at reception and strode down the corridor.

'So, did you miss me?' I said to all as I swept, with flair, into the squad room. When in doubt, make a grand entrance, especially as I had made a rather grand exit last week.

'Oh, look what the cat dragged in,' Smithy said as he leaned back against his chair and stretched. 'Decided to come back and join us, did you?'

'Pretty shade of yellow there, Shep; nice.' That was Reihana. 'It's the in colour this season, I hear.'

I gave him a token *hardy-ha* look.

'Cool, I don't have to make the coffee anymore.' That would be Otto.

It was good to be back.

'The rubbish bin's just over there, if you need to throw up again. Try to get your aim right; it took the cleaner ages to get the last lot off the carpet.' Smithy waved his arm to where they'd strategically placed the bin — right next to my desk.

'Thanks, Smithy. Thank you so very much. Damn good to know you care.'

'What are friends for?'

I walked over to my desk, and when I pulled out my chair, there was a motorbike helmet sitting on it with a bright-yellow Post-it note stuck to it.

I plucked it off and read it aloud: ' 'In case of emergency beach excursions'. Oh, ha ha, guys, I suppose you think you're funny.' Judging by the snorts and chortles around the room, they certainly did.

I returned the helmet to the only bloke who was mad enough to ride a motorbike to work in an icy Dunedin winter, then plonked myself down at my desk, tapped my fingers on its veneer surface, and looked about expectantly.

'So, where do I start? What's happening? What's the go?' I asked Smithy.

'Anyone would think you were glad to be here. Could you please try to be a little less enthusiastic? You're showing us up.'

'I've spent the better part of a week under the same roof as my mother, so, believe me, I am glad to be here. But I'm sure it will wear off, given time.'

Smithy gave a small shudder, which looked ridiculous on a large man, but then he'd met my mother.

'You could start by telling me how Mr Fists is?'

'I take it you mean Felix Ford, the guy who organised your holiday?'

'Yes.'

'He's out of hospital, doing okay, healing up, bones mending. He seems to have all of his faculties — well, the few he had to start with for someone thick enough to assault an officer — and he will get to use them very soon as I believe he's due in court today,' Smithy said. 'I can find out what time, if you want to attend.'

Did I want to see him again? Look him in the eye? Yes, actually, I did. Although the thought of it caused a faint squirmy sensation in my stomach, I felt a compulsion to keep him under watch.

'That would be good if you could. What about the other man, Moustache Guy?' My defender. I couldn't bring myself to say Felix Ford's assailant. He was rescuing me for God's sake.

'Iain Gibbs? He's already had a hearing and pleaded not guilty to assault. His lawyer's taking the angle that because he was defending an officer down, he shouldn't be charged.'

'Do you think it will work?' I asked. Smithy shrugged. In a way, despite him going a bit overboard, I hoped it did. Hell, if he did get convicted, it would be another reason for Joe Public not to step up and help out if someone was in trouble. Why would you consider going to the rescue if, as well as the obvious personal risk, it carried the chance of prosecution rather than thanks? Iain Gibbs had gone too far, but, that aside, I'd always be grateful to him.

'Is there anything else exciting happening?' A week away seemed like a lifetime. My mother had that effect.

'Not what I'd call exciting, no. We've tracked down the owner of the skull. Turns out he's a big-time collector and an anthropology buff from Britain, who's shifting house here. God knows why they'd want to emigrate to Dunedin, and after all this they're probably asking the same question. It was among his household items and quite legit.'

'So we called out the SOCOs and forensics guys for nothing?'

'No, not for nothing. We'd hate for them to get lazy, so it's good practice, keeps them on their toes. And they wanted to get a look at that ship before it was refloated and towed away. I don't think any of us will forget that sight in a hurry — or the three-ring circus that followed. I have to say I felt a bit sorry for the old lady who found poor Yorick though. I think she wet herself.' For a big guy with a don't-shit-with-me demeanour Smithy could be a bit of a bleeding heart.

'Well I wouldn't be feeling too sorry for Granny. She was out nicking stuff, just like the rest of them.'

'True.'

'So what about the skull owner? What's his name?' I asked.

'Trubridge. Peter Trubridge.'

'Well I bet Mr Trubridge wasn't too pleased when he found out his belongings were strewn over the beach, being pilfered by all and sundry.'

'No, apparently not. Someone local let him know what had happened, I gather. Interrupted his nice little tropical island stopover.' Yeah, I'd be getting one of those in too if I was moving to a Dunedin winter. 'He's quite the collector, this Trubridge. Everything from art, to books, to artefacts — you know, ancient weapons, tools, fossils and bones, that kind of thing. He's very keen for us to retrieve it all. So is his insurance company as it is all quite valuable. Not a happy family; the man's kids lost half their toys and books.' That explained the Lego I'd seen trodden into the sand.

'Bummer.'

'Bummer's right. So in answer to your earlier question about what we've been up to: not a hell of a lot. Mostly trying to track down stolen goods for the insurance companies. The majority of the containers on the ship were goods in transit. A few of those came ashore, along with a couple filled with commercial goods destined for Dunedin and just the one container with the household contents.' It sounded like a bit of a scavenger hunt. Gosh, how jolly exciting. Didn't sound like a CIB job to me.

'So why are we doing this and not those downstairs?'

'We started it because of the skull discovery and it kind of ties in with the assaults; half of downstairs is out with the flu, and we've got nothing better to do.'

That was fair enough. 'So where do you want me?'

I could see from the look on his face he was about to make a smart-arse comment, but before he could let fly he hesitated and looked towards the door. I turned my head to follow his gaze. DI Johns stood in the doorway. My body gave its obligatory allergic response.

'Good to see you back, Shephard.' Polite or sarcastic? I couldn't quite tell which from the voice, though I could guess.

'Thank you, sir.'

'If you're looking for something useful to do, I've got a job that's just come in.'

DI Johns took sadistic pleasure in giving me the most menial or demeaning task he could find. He was a little more subtle about it these days: after a few complaints — not from me — his superiors had reminded him to play fair. But it was still his favourite sport.

'What's that?' I asked, girding myself for the inevitable crap.

'I need a detective on the scene for a body recovery.'

I looked up, startled. He was offering me something decent — a body, not chasing taggers or litter patrol. Even Smithy looked surprised.

'I can do that,' I said quickly, before he could change his mind.

'Good. The boat leaves from Port Chalmers in forty minutes. It's a marine recovery so you'll go out with the dive squad, and I guess you'll need your wet-weather gear. Report to Sergeant Blakie.' He gave his usual shark-like grin, then turned and headed down the hallway. I turned, looked out the window and took in the horizontal driving rain.

Shit.

14

I wasn't the only one along for this foul ride. As well as the police dive squad, who had been flown down from Wellington, and me, tricked into it by DI Dickhead Johns, we had a university student on board. She looked like a young Marilyn Monroe, but without the pout or the peroxide and, as far as I could judge, she was handling the trip far better than I was. Seasickness had never been a problem for me before now. I'd been on dozens of open-sea trips across the notorious Foveaux Strait between Bluff, at the southernmost end of the South Island, and Stewart Island. My Uncle Baz lived in Oban, so the resort town — as the locals called it — was a frequent holiday destination, summer or winter. My seediness today had to be a remnant of the whack to my head. My ear still had a telltale buzz and I was only ninety-seven per cent steady on my feet. Under normal circumstances, this pathetic one-metre excuse for a swell wouldn't be a problem. At least I hadn't fed the fish, yet.

'So what you're studying is kind of like the maggots and flies to a corpse principle, except on a submerged body?'

'Yeah, that's the one.'

'Nice. It must be a real conversation stopper.'

She smiled. She was extraordinarily pretty for a nerdy type. 'It's not the kind of thing you bring up for general consumption. I learned a long time ago to sanitise it somewhat when chatting at parties, unless I'm surrounded by like-minded people.'

'That would be people fascinated by death and decay, flies and maggots and rotting bodies, that kind of thing?'

'Yes, sick puppies like me who don't mind talking about decomposing pigs' heads over a nice roast pork dinner.'

That would definitely be a vegan-free zone. 'Excellent, count me in for next time,' I said. 'So give me the layman's version: decomp for dummies.'

'Well, you can get a timeline and an approximate time of death by studying the life cycles of the invertebrates that inhabit a corpse on land. We're looking at the same idea, but of course we can't do that with flies and beetles underwater, they ain't there, so we're studying the colonisation of the body by bacteria. Like the bugs, they have a definite succession order in which they arrive at a corpse. We're trying to establish a reliable timeline that can be used forensically to give a time of submergence and therefore maybe death.'

'That wasn't quite for dummies,' I said, 'but I get the idea. That's pretty cool and would be damn useful for people in my business.' If they could get it accurate and reliable enough to stand up to scrutiny in the courtroom, it would be bloody brilliant.

Tamsin was a doctorate microbiology student at the University of Otago whose skills had been recognised by the forensics people. She was personable and chatty, which took my mind off the fact we were huddled in the cockpit of a small boat on choppy seas, in a shit of a wet southerly off the coast of Dunedin, in the middle of winter. However, it didn't successfully distract me from the fact we'd be dealing with a cadaver in pretty bad condition sometime soon. A foot had been pulled up by a fisherman, who'd had the sense to buoy and GPS the spot. So here we were, looking for the rest of the foot's owner. The foot had looked well nibbled.

'Well, dealing with a real body is going to be a bit different to swabbing pigs' heads,' I said.

'Yeah, I know. I'm not really looking forward to that aspect of it. My prof made me attend a post-mortem so I'd get to experience a body in less-than-perfect condition before I had to swab one, but I'm still not too sure about it. I suppose you've seen lots of dead bodies before?'

Not lots, but they were all one too many. 'A few,' I said. 'But this is my first up-close-and-personal with a sea recovery.' I was impressed with the dive squad and the determined way they looked happy in their work, even though it must be revolting at times. 'I haven't been to a post-mortem yet, so you're one up on me there. Oh, and I've never had to submerge and swab pigs' heads before, so you beat me again.'

'You're quite fascinated by the whole pig's head thing aren't you?' she said with a laugh.

'I've just got this mental image of the strange looks you must get fronting up to the butcher, asking for 'half a dozen pigs' heads, thanks'. No offence, you just look a little bit too, shall we say, delicate for that kind of thing.'

At this she laughed all the more. 'Well, now that you mention it, being 'delicate', as you so nicely put it, helped, because one of the guys at the butchery department at the supermarket took a bit of a shine to me, so has been ever so co-operative. We've had pigs' heads on tap.'

'Nice.' I was about to ask her how the local fishermen appreciated having dead pig bits submerged in the harbour, but then things started happening. It was action time.

I'd seen and smelt some pretty disgusting things at home on the farm: carcasses in various stages of bloat and decay; entrails; effluent by the mile; but this beat all. The knowledge that this macerated, swollen, clearly scavenged-on piece of flesh was once a human being didn't help at all in terms of reference points and landmarks. The fact that it was still partially encased in a wetsuit gave the only obvious clue as to its origin.

'Oh, dear,' was all Tamsin muttered before she visibly steadied herself and set to work with the swabs.

Oh, dear, I kept repeating in my head as the body started to react to the air, and the putrid gases, previously dispersed into the water, were now airborne and found the back of my nose. The utter, utter stench was worse than anything I could have ever imagined possible, and I had to turn away and brace myself for a few moments before I could get on with my job.

68

15

Looking at this wreck of a body, I had the feeling dental records would be the only quick means of identification. No one would recognise anything from what was left of the face. In this age of CSI programmes, people seemed to expect DNA identification within half an hour. But the reality was that it was slow, took months even, and was expensive. Sometimes old technology did the best job. And at least teeth didn't tend to get eaten. The extremities poking out of the wetsuit were well scavenged. The remaining foot had almost disarticulated, and the divers had encased it in a plastic bag to stop the water movement from the recovery finishing off the job. Ditto the hands. There was a large rip in the wetsuit along the back of the right leg and buttock, which had unfortunately allowed access to predators. Worst of all was the separately recovered, sodden, matted wad of orangish fibres that had once been hair but which were no longer attached to the head.

The sight of this mess left me feeling sickened on many, many levels. This was once a human being, a living, breathing, animated person. Someone must have loved this person — mum, dad, family and friends — and had hopefully reported them missing. There hadn't been any new missing persons that I'd been briefed on, although I'd only just put my foot back through the office door when I'd been whisked off here. A lot could have happened in the week I was away.

You had to hope someone's life made enough impact that people noticed when they were gone. Otherwise, it would be a very sad existence, like those poor people discovered years after they'd died, shrivelled up and mummified, and still seated in their armchair staring eyelessly at a blank TV screen, while their ignorant neighbours said inane things like: 'They always were a bit quiet' or 'Now you mention it, there was a funny smell for a little while'; and their surviving children said, 'We never really kept in touch, but how much do we get in the will?'

My mind had a nasty habit of projecting forwards to people's funerals, including my own, visualising the flower-draped casket centred reverently in the church. I wondered how many people would come out to mourn this poor person. Would it be dozens or would it be hundreds? Would there be any? That thought made this situation feel all the more forlorn. I hadn't mastered the art of professional detachment. Part of me thought the day I did would be the day it was time to quit.

Judging by the level of decomposition, they must have been down there a while, although I was hardly experienced on the subject and looks could be deceptive. In the real world no one could take one glance at a rotting body and say they've been dead for four days, three hours and thirteen minutes, give or take a second, as they did on the telly. And they most certainly didn't pass judgement in full hair and make-up, with a plunging neckline, chunky jewellery and six-inch stiletto heels. We were all sporting non-shedding zip-up hooded jumpsuits and booties with matching face masks. They weren't particularly glamorous, waterproof or warm. They didn't protect against the stench either.

I felt huge admiration for Tamsin as she went about the job of swabbing. It can't have been pleasant.

She paused over one of the hands. 'You might be able to get a fingerprint from that,' she said, gesturing to a shred of plastic-looking stuff in the bottom of a sample bag. 'The skin's slipped off, and it looks like it could be from the fingertip.' If she was right and it was usable, it would be a huge boost to our chances of identifying the body.

'Fantastic,' I said, and leaned over for a look. 'They'll be able to do that creepy human glove thing.' I was glad it wasn't my job to insert a finger into the sloughed off skin of a dead person, although it was a fascinating concept in a ghoulish kind of a way.

My body must have been adjusting to the pitch and roll of the boat, as I was starting to feel a little better, despite the putrid smell. I risked a closer look at what was left of the face. The remaining tissue had the strangest appearance, mottled white and almost soap-like, especially the cheeks. 'Do submerged corpses always look like that — so waxy?' I asked.

'Not always,' Tamsin said, as she carefully labelled her last swab and put it in the chilly bin.

71

'They can sometimes saponify, where the body fats literally turn into a soaplike substance, but that takes quite a while — months — so I doubt it has happened here. Sometimes just the fact that all the skin has slipped off and they've been decomposing underwater makes them look like that.'

I watched as she recorded the time, air and water temperatures, and the 100 per cent humidity, and made other observations of the light and situation. The body had been photographed, had visible details recorded and now, finally, could be closed up in its body bag. The divers had taken video footage of the whole process, above and below water, capturing every piece of useful information possible in a constantly mobile and changing environment. At last we were done.

Despite not being the religious sort, I felt compelled to offer up a choked 'God bless, rest in peace' as the zipper slid across the ravaged face.

I hoped I would never have to see anything like that ever again.

16

The first thing I did once I'd fulfilled my official duties as officer in charge of the body was text Maggie. After the deep-seated chill this morning's effort had injected into my bones, I felt the need for bright light, strong coffee, good food and friendly company. A late, late lunch was better than no lunch. Despite the borderline obsessive skin scrubbing and frantic hair washing, I was sure I could still catch a whiff of dead-man stench.

'If I'd known you were going to talk about grotesque stuff like that when I'm trying to eat, I wouldn't have agreed to meet,' Maggie said, her face screwed up with distaste.

'Sorry,' I said around a mouthful of lamb salad. I swallowed it down, appreciating the salty tang of feta. The visual image the cheese conjured up was not so great, though. 'It's just that it was indescribably awful.'

'I don't know, you were doing a pretty good job of trying to describe it. And you don't smell so good.' We were in one of our favourite haunts, The Good Oil. The tables were quite close together, and Maggie's comment made me feel self-conscious — concerned the people on either side of us would be wondering who had the personal hygiene problem. I took some surreptitious sniffs, which unfortunately confirmed her allegations. Shit, I'd have to have another shower when I got home. All I'd wanted was to go somewhere cosy, and with damn good coffee, to try and brighten my day. Apart from the pong paranoia, it was working so far. The raspberry and coconut cake helped too. With cream, not yoghurt. Yoghurt was for wimps.

. 'So, to change the subject from the uncomfortably yucky, to the plain uncomfortable,' Maggie said, as she waved her fork at me. 'What's going on with you and Paul?'

'Do we have to talk about that now?' I asked, partly because I didn't want to talk about it, but mostly because I had no idea how I felt. My feelings seemed to lurch from one extreme to the other. How could I express what I couldn't fathom? 'Couldn't we just make inane small talk? My, what lovely weather we're having today.'

She smiled at my diversionary tactics. 'Yeah, if you're a duck. No, come on. Last I heard before you headed to your folks', you'd panicked because he wanted to get a job over here and you left him hanging. Where are you two at now?'

'I didn't panic, thank you very much.'

'You practically ripped his throat out, stomped on him and left him bleeding to death on the floor.'

'You make me sound like a heartless cow. Thanks.' I downed the last of my flat white. 'Well, it was his fault. He shouldn't have sprung it on me like that. You have to admit, it was a rather large decision for him to make — unilaterally, I might add; not only did he neglect to talk with me about it first, he had really, really bad timing. I was not at my best.'

'He should have known not to corner a wounded animal, huh?'

'Something like that.'

I'd only arrived back in Dunedin from the olds' the previous night, and Maggs had been out at the movies with her latest stud muffin, Rudy. She'd found herself a bona fide aristocrat from France, one of the poor-but-noble variety. After the last few loser boyfriends she'd had, this seemed like a good'un and, I had to admit, hot. In fact the French accent tipped him into the realm of seriously hot. Due to the fact she'd still had a guest this morning and had been slightly preoccupied, we hadn't had the chance for a decent catch-up.

'Paul came down to the farm to see me, so of course, the olds were all over him like a rash. We didn't actually get a second to ourselves. It felt like being a chaperoned sixteen-year-old all over again, with them following us around, gushing.'

My parents had a tendency to fall in love with my boyfriends. This was great, until the inevitable split, and then, invariably, they sided with the guy. Dad would be all long-faced and sad because he'd lost a mate, and Mum would usually interrogate me at great length as to what dreadful thing I'd done to lose or drive the man away this time. It was just another pressure to bear in mind when entering into relationships. It certainly wasn't helping the situation with Paul.

'But you'd have talked with him since then.'

'Well, not really.'

She gave me one of those looks. 'How the hell do you think you're going to sort it out if you won't even talk to him? How old are you?'

'Yeah, yeah, yeah. Whatever. It's not the sort of thing you can get all deep and meaningful about over the phone, is it? He's coming up this weekend. I'll deal with it then, when we're face to face.'

'Well make sure you do. And don't stuff it up. He's a great guy.'

17

'Shephard!' DI Johns hollered around the corner of the squad room door.

As usual, I jumped. So, I noted, did Smithy. 'Sir?'

'You haven't finished your job from this morning yet.'

'But I've signed the body over to the morgue, everything's in order.'

His perfect teeth glinted in the fluorescent light. 'The post-mortem starts in an hour. Be there.'

I could feel the blood draining from my face.

18

'I'll talk you through it. If you start to feel a bit woozy or think you're going to be sick, just walk away and take some deep breaths. Crouch down. No one's going to laugh at you; we've all been there.'

I was grateful that Alistair was the pathologist doing the honours at this post-mortem. He'd been an itinerant part of our family for years. Back in our school days he was in my older brother's class at Southland Boys High. His parents were of the well-endowed-with-brains-but-not-so-endowed-with-time-or-empathy category and, consequently, when the school booted the boarders out for the holidays, he came home with us, to bask in that special kind of love and attention only my mother could give.

It was a relief that an old friend could guide me through my first post-mortem. Alistair had very kindly offered to take care of that other first time, down in the hay shed, when I'd turned sixteen. I'd politely declined him then. He continued to offer his services in that department to this day. He was considerate like that.

'I'm sure I'll be fine,' I said to him. I didn't sound that convincing.

Stephanie, the morgue technician, was already decked out in her blue disposable jumpsuit. It was a stark contrast to this morning's skirt, designer tights, knee-length heeled boots, v-necked purple knit top and something classy and expensive-looking around her neck. She wasn't what you'd expect for someone who worked with dead people all day. She took me to the girls' room and waited while I got myself into the sterile suit. I glanced in the mirror and marvelled at the ability of my skin to look translucent. With the remnants of yellow around my eye, and in my eye, it was a particularly fetching effect.

'I'll warn you now,' she said. 'The marine ones are always really bad, and the smell can kind of stick to you.'

The stench and I had already been formally introduced.

'It might take a few showers and hair washes to get rid of it, and I hope those are old undies you've got on, you'll be tempted to throw them out afterwards.' I didn't actually possess any flash undies, so that wasn't an issue, and judging by how much the smell had clung to me before, these ones were definitely destined for the wheelie bin.

'We don't normally get on to post-mortems this quickly, but in the case of marine decomposition like this, it's best to get it over and done with as soon as possible so we can seal the remains.'

'If I'd known I was going to be doing this, I would have skipped lunch,' I said as we headed towards the door.

'It's better with food in your system. Otherwise you end up faint from hunger, not just faint from nerves. Anyway, I'd prefer to throw up with some substance than to retch on nothing.'

'Thanks for that.'

It was odd, but seeing the body up on the stainless-steel table, surrounded by the various tools and cutting implements in the glaring, concreted, impersonal environment of the morgue, made it seem less human than it had on the boat. The butterflies that had been careening around in my stomach since the dreaded news of attending a post-mortem had begun to settle as fascination with the process took over. Even the stench seemed somehow less overwhelming in this place. To distract myself from the nerves and horror of it all I was taking copious notes. Hopefully the paper wouldn't prove to be too odour absorbent. I watched and marvelled at the calm efficiency with which Alistair and Stephanie worked. I listened to Alistair's familiar lazy drawl as he delivered a running commentary of his observations.

'The individual is a male.' I could now definitively think 'he', rather than the neutral 'they', although we'd suspected all along it must be a guy as he had been wearing a man's wetsuit.

'There is marked animal predation of the body to areas of exposed flesh not covered by the wetsuit, and where the tear was along the right buttock and thigh.' He continued to describe the physical state and injuries with a calm, even voice. The sound had a settling effect on me, counteracting the rather negative effects of the visual and olfactory stimuli.

Tamsin would have been pleased to know she

was right — that it was a piece of slipped fingertip skin, as she'd thought. I'd buy her a beer for that call. It was carefully bagged to go to the environmental science and research experts in Christchurch for fingerprinting.

Initial observations done, it was time to remove what remained of the wetsuit. Stephanie used heavy-duty scissors to cut away and then gently lift off the neoprene. The swirling sensation in my stomach became a bit more insistent. This was where he started to look more human again, and I knew it would soon be time to open him up — the bit I really wasn't looking forward to. With a sideways glance I looked at the marbled and mottled skin of his bloated abdomen and chest. The wetsuit didn't seem to have protected him that much from the sea life.

'Sam?' Alistair said, after a few moments' observation. 'Did you say that this was thought to be a diving accident?'

'Yes, looks that way. Why?'

'You might want to rethink that. Those are contusions, a lot of them. This man's been assaulted.'

19

Our squad room was packed to the gunwales. As well as its usual CIB inhabitants, there were people from the uniform branch taking up every available space and surface. It was one of the strange things about being in the CIB: I didn't know what to call my other colleagues now. To call them 'ordinary police' seemed too condescending, just 'police' seemed like I was being exclusive, and 'uniform branch' was too formal. As I wasn't into being exclusive or condescending, formal usually won by default.

I was up the front, waiting to give my report, while DI Johns filled everyone in on the discovery of the body. To avoid looking at the boss I studied some of the faces before me, before becoming so unnerved by the number of them staring back I took to studying the carpet instead.

'Detective Constable Shephard will now give you a summary of the preliminary post-mortem findings.'

We swapped positions, and I politely said 'thank you', secretly enjoying the fact that he had to hand over to me. Judging by the nasty vibe he was giving off and his clipped consonants, it did not sit well. When you considered that the only reason I was here was because his sick idea of a joke had backfired and left me as a pivotal part of the murder investigation, it wasn't a surprise he was a bit tetchy. And there wasn't a damn thing he could do about it. His Royal Bastardness wouldn't be able to find a way to demote me to the shitty jobs now. I suppressed a grin.

'Good morning, everyone. The victim is a young male. Age is estimated to be early twenties. As the DI said, his body was found at sea after a fisherman dragged up a human foot.' What anyone was doing fishing early on that grotty day made no sense to me. And it wasn't like the man even had to make a living from it; this guy had been purely recreational. 'The body was quite decomposed and had marked predation by sea life.' A number of faces grimaced with that piece of information. Humans liked their place at the top of the food chain; we didn't like the thought of being something else's dinner. I didn't tell them the dive-squad guys had initially thought the body was draped in seaweed, then realised the seething mass wasn't kelp but eels. 'It was initially thought to be death by drowning as a result of a diving accident, but the post-mortem has indicated the victim was assaulted: he had numerous contusions to his upper body. He had also suffered a broken nose, fractured skull and broken ribs. The provisional cause of death is blunt-force trauma to the head.' I talked further about the injuries to the body and the evidence of assault.

'Indications are the victim was killed on land before being dumped at sea. There were signs of livor mortis along his left side, on his arm, thigh and calf, indicating he had been on his side

— we can speculate he was curled up in a foetal position, perhaps being transported in the back of a vehicle. The pathologist said that drowned and submerged victims usually show signs of livor in their hands, feet and face, as bodies naturally orient themselves into a prone position in water, and gravity pools the blood into the lower extremities.'

There was one last detail that had come through that morning from the trusty lab technicians at ESR, and it made this case even more curious. 'Indications are the victim was already dead when put into the wetsuit, as there were no traces of urine present.' Divers didn't bother going through the hassle of getting out of a wetsuit to pee, and just relieved themselves in the suit. I supposed it warmed them up nicely too. The victim's wetsuit was pee-free. Of course, being submerged in water for a long period may have reduced traces of urine, or he may have been in there only a short time and not needed to relieve himself, but when looked at in the context of the injuries he sustained, there was the very real possibility of his being stuffed in after death.

This meant that someone had gone to an awful lot of trouble to make it look like a diving accident. It was hard enough for a warm, live and willing body to squeeze into a wetsuit — it was almost considered an extra event in a triathlon. But my mind boggled at how they could possibly have managed to force a corpse into one. You'd have to do it before rigor mortis set in, which only allowed a small window of opportunity — just a few hours, if my memory served me right. I'd check that later. Perhaps the perpetrator thought the sea would take care of the evidence, and if the body did happen to pop up, people would think it was just another diving accident. God knows they happened often enough. They clearly had no idea about decomposition though, otherwise they'd have known the wetsuit would slow the whole process down and reduce the chances of the sea hiding the evidence of their crime.

The wetsuit had been a mistake.

20

A search of our files had come up with four young men in our victim's age group who had been reported missing from the Otago area within the last two months. Two of those had gang affiliations and were part of an active investigation into a large drug ring. They were peddling the blight that was methamphetamine, AKA ice, P or crystal meth. Nothing fucked up lives quite like it. A glance at their photos made me discount both of them as our victim. Both were Māori and heavily tattooed. Their tattooists must have provided photos of their work, as the men's files contained full torso shots as well as the snapshots given by family and police photos from prior arrests. Some of the tattoos were quite beautiful — the professional ones, not the pin and ink badges of prisonhood. It wasn't something I could do, permanently marking my body like that. I couldn't even bring myself to get a tasteful little dolphin or butterfly hidden on a hip or butt cheek. And most certainly not one of those god-awful tramp stamps some young women liked to show off, poking out between a crop top and hipster jeans, and accompanied by a whale-tail G-string. Maggie had a small, stylised flower on her right shoulder blade, and had called me a wuss when I declined to get something at the same time. It suited her. Somehow it would just look silly on me. Even the temporary ones looked dorky on me.

There had been no sign of tattooing on the body at the morgue. Assault? Yes. Tattooing? No.

The third man coughed up by NLA, the police computer system, was more than ten centimetres shorter than our man, which, taking into account any margin of error, effectively ruled him out.

The fourth missing person on the list, Jack White, was the only one who had characteristics in common with our victim — he was the same approximate height and build. His dental records would be compared with what was left of the victim's mouth later today. He'd been reported missing three weeks ago and was last seen leaving his former partner's home in South Dunedin in his car, which hadn't been found either. He'd had an altercation with her new boyfriend, which had come to blows, but both the woman and her boyfriend declared he was alive when he drove away — a prerequisite for driving I would have thought — but was also angry and threatening to come back. She had then gone to the trouble of getting a protection order taken out against him.

Perhaps her boyfriend or her family had taken matters into their own hands? It had happened before and was certain to happen again. But that was idle speculation. We were now just waiting: waiting for the dental comparison between Jack White and our victim, which wouldn't take long; waiting for ESR to work their grisly magic and come up with a fingerprint, which would take a bit longer; and then the hopeful wait for a comparison in the Automated Fingerprint

Identification System database, or AFIS as we lovingly referred to it. In the real world pretty computer displays didn't miraculously come up with a match within 3.1 seconds, complete with handy photo, address, last known whereabouts and favourite takeaway restaurant, like they did on television.

The result I was really curious to hear about was from Tamsin, the doctoral student — her evaluation on how long the body had been in the water. Alistair had been very quick to point out that his time-of-death estimate hinged on gauging the body's decomposition — a notoriously inexact science. He'd given a preliminary assessment of between one week and a month, which gave a little too much leeway for our liking and would have seriously disappointed anyone who was a CSI junkie and expecting a plus or minus three seconds estimate. When I'd phoned Tamsin, she'd been preparing the bacterial samples for DNA identification. But again, these things took time — she estimated a week for a snapshot, and two or three weeks for a full analysis. No instant result, no flashing screens, no fantasyland.

21

'Do you want the good news or the bad news?' Smithy asked as I walked back into the squad room after my lunch break. My hormones had told me that the healthy ham and salad sandwich I'd brought from home wasn't going to cut it today and I'd have to supplement it with a big, fat custard square from the bakery and a double-shot takeaway flat white from The Fix. Who was I to argue with my hormones?

'Get the bad news out of the way first.'

'The dental comparison came back and the victim is definitely not Jack White.'

'Bum. Would have been neat and tidy if it was.' At least with a definitive identification we could have had a lot more to work on than a worse-for-wear body and some scuba gear. It would also have solved the mystery of what had become of Jack White. I was sure his family would prefer to know what had happened to their son and brother, even if the news was the worst. It had to be better than spending the rest of their lives waiting for him to walk in the back door and plonk down at the dining-room table waiting for dinner like nothing had happened. In a way it was a good thing for his ex-girlfriend and her new boyfriend, as it meant there wasn't going to be the might of a murder investigation knocking on their front door anytime soon. Well, not yet, anyway.

'What's the good news, then,' I asked.

'The boffins at ESR just called. They managed to get a good-quality print off that piece of skin. They'll pop it through AFIS as soon as they can and call us back if there are any hits.'

'You're kidding? God, they're amazing. Throw them some chocolates, will you? And some beer. And give a beer to the police diver who managed to bag the skin, too, because I saw what was left of those hands, and believe me, there wasn't anything much to fingerprint — you need fingers for that. Urrgggh.' I couldn't help but shudder.

'Too much information,' Smithy said.

'Sorry, didn't think you were the squeamish type. So, we've got a print, all we need to do now is hope the victim had been in a spot of trouble at some stage and is in our system.' Fingerprints were all well and good, but you had to have something to compare them with, otherwise they were nothing more than miniature *Te Papa* logos — without the grandeur of being plastered all over the side of the National Museum.

'Fingers crossed,' Smithy said. I winced at his choice of words.

It still amazed me they could get a fingerprint from slipped skin. Even the word slipped was kind of creepy in that context. But the technique wasn't new, and it had helped immensely with the identification of victims after the Boxing Day tsunami back in 2004. That must have been one hell of a huge and horrible task. This fingerprint was quick work on ESR's part. Maybe the novelty factor bumped it up the to-do queue.

'What else did they have to say?' I asked him.

90

'The wetsuit was a mass-produced brand, available from basically any dive, surf or sports shop, and it was a model from six years ago. Likewise, the cylinder, regulator and BCD were of a common type.'

'BCD?' You could tell I'd never been scuba diving.

'Buoyancy Control Device, a bit more high-tech than the old weight belt. The cylinder was empty — surprise.'

'Guess you don't need oxygen if you're already dead.'

'Not usually, no. The gear looked reasonably worn, as I said; wasn't new and there was grime around the regulator that suggests it hadn't been used for a while. They did find some fibres caught in the zipper so have their experts looking at those.'

I thought about the paraphernalia associated with diving.

'How much would it cost to kit yourself out in scuba gear, by the time you get the tank, regulator, wetsuit, BCD, accessories, etcetera?'

'It's been a long time since I dived,' Smithy said. A long time since he'd squeezed his bulk into a wetsuit too, I imagined. 'And it wasn't cheap then. But I'd guess, with inflation, I dunno, around four or five grand new. We could make a phone call and find out easily enough. Why do you ask?'

'That's quite a lot of money to toss into the sea to cover up a murder,' I said.

'Yeah, but what's a bit of gear when you've got a lot to lose?'

'True. I still don't get why they'd bother though. Surely they'd have been better off tossing him in clothed, or even naked. The sea and the fish would have taken care of the evidence quicker.'

'The body was quite a way offshore. Someone found fully clothed would look a mite suspicious out there, and someone found butt naked would set alarm bells off everywhere. Maybe they were trying to be clever.'

'Maybe. Or maybe they panicked and thought, shit, how do we make this look like an accident, and the whole wetsuit thing seemed like a good idea at the time. It was an error of judgement on their part because not only did it slow down the decay, but it must also have involved the use of a vehicle and a boat to transport him out to sea, so there are more things we can look for. Did you say ESR found fibres? They could be from the perpetrator or they could be from the boot of a car or the cabin of a boat. All grist for the investigative mill.'

'Last time I looked there were a shitload of boats moored around the inner harbour and at Port Chalmers, let alone all the ones parked on trailers in backyards everywhere from Brighton to Warrington.'

'It was just a thought,' I said, smiling at the look on his face. 'I'm not suggesting you personally go out and check each one — we've got the uniform branch for that.'

Smithy inhaled audibly. 'Don't ever let them hear you say that, young lady. They have clever ways of bringing young, upstart trainee detectives back down to earth.' I knew there were a number of them who'd love to see me come to grief. Thanks to some unknown benefactor, I'd been fast-tracked into the detective training programme ahead of a number who'd been applying for years. Memories could be long around here.

'You don't need to remind me, I get it from above and below, remember?' Between DI Johns and the eternally miffed, I felt I walked a tightrope. 'Anyway, I do think that whoever did this had access to scuba gear to throw away. Most scuba divers need a boat at some point, whether it's their own, or a mate's. Someone involved is a scuba diver, whether they're the murderer or helped dispose of the evidence.'

'Not necessarily. I'll check if there have been any reports of stolen gear, or boats recently. If they're capable of murder, they're quite capable of theft.'

At least that gave us something useful to do until the result of the fingerprint analysis came in.

22

My cellphone rang while I was doing half a
dozen things at once, so I didn't pause to check
who it was before I picked up.

'Gidday.'

Bugger, that lapse backfired. It was Paul. It
was too late to pretend I was otherwise occupied.

'Gidday, yourself,' I said. The now-familiar
knot formed in the pit of my stomach. I hoped
this would be short because the room was full of
colleagues and I didn't feel like having them
listening in on my domestic crisis.

'How's the head?'

'It's getting there. It would be great if I could
shake off the lingering headache though.' Was
there a point to this call, other than chit-chat?
'You don't normally call me at work. You must
be bored.'

'Pretty much. Gore's not what you'd call
riveting.'

'Hey, I'm a bit busy right now . . . '

'Yeah, I heard, a murder case, and that you'd
finagled your way into being officer in charge of
the body.'

'News travels fast, and it wasn't exactly
planning on my part.'

'So it wasn't you sucking up to your favourite
boss?'

I laughed at that comment. Paul knew my
workplace woes only too well.

'So are you okay? I hear you had to be at the post-mortem.' His voice was full of concern, and I realised with a lurch that he was the kind of guy who would have realised being OCB was a big thing, that a person's first post-mortem could be bloody hard and traumatic, and that there would be tasks ahead that would be just as difficult. He was the kind of guy who would pick up the phone, despite the tension and uncertainty of our relationship, to make sure I was coping.

I felt a constriction in my throat and the photograph in front of me started to swim. 'I'm doing fine, thanks,' I said as I turned aside, hoping my colleagues wouldn't catch the slight crackle in my voice. 'But I'm really busy right now. So we'll talk at the weekend, okay?'

23

'Go buy a Lotto ticket, it's our lucky day. We've got a result from that print!' Smithy had just got off the phone from what, by his standards, had been a very animated conversation. Even more disconcerting, he came over and gave me a fist bump.

'Bloody brilliant,' I said, giving my knuckles a rub. 'What are the odds of that?' A print from a sloughed-off, scungy-looking bit of skin pulled up from the bottom of the Pacific Ocean. I always had great respect for the people at ESR, but this was tipping that respect towards hero worship. 'So who and how?' I asked.

'The print was a match for the right index finger of a Richard James Stewart, also known as Clifford, aged twenty-two. And no, no idea why,' Smithy said in response to my raised eyebrows at the god-awful name Clifford. 'Last known residence, Castle Street, Dunedin.' That was smack in the middle of the University of Otago student area. 'He had a previous conviction for possession of marijuana for supply, and for the sale of stolen goods, and according to his driver's licence is an organ donor, but I don't think anyone is going to be wanting them in a hurry.' I could vouch for the last comment.

'And this has been confirmed with dental records?'

'Chasing them down as we speak.'

'So has he been reported missing?'

'No, doesn't look like it.'

'But he could have been dead for weeks. God, that's a bit sad if nobody noticed. Did he have flatmates? And what about family? Surely someone would realise he hadn't been around?'

'You'd think. Best we go pay a visit to his last known address.'

★   ★   ★

From the outside, the Castle Street flat was a tip. It looked like somewhere the media would offer as an example of a typical Dunedin student hovel. The kind of housing that made parents all over the country apoplectic, and reputable landlords cringe. There was a decrepit grunge-brown couch sitting on the porch, springs shoving up through the ancient horse-hair stuffing. A number of beer crates looked like they served as portable seating and drinks tables. There were enough empty stubbies and cigarette butts around to show it was a well-used facility. It also had tiered seating — someone had put an equally well-maintained armchair on the veranda above the porch. There wasn't so much a lawn as a dirt pit. I didn't think they'd have to worry about mud inside though, because you could use the stepping-stone path of discarded junk mail to keep your shoes clean. The curtains in the villa's bay windows were pulled closed, although one looked like it was clinging to the rail by two fingernails. The exterior had a modernist transport theme, with a line-up of supermarket trolleys straddling the ridgeline of the roof.

'Well, this is cosy,' Smithy said, surveying the front of the property.

'Just think, Smithy. One day your kids could be living in splendid student squalor like this.'

He snorted his derision. 'Not bloody likely. The five-year-old manages to keep his stuff tidier than this. Pigs.'

Smithy didn't go in for academic types, and he had an allergy to student shenanigans. It was probably just as well for the more energetic of the student population that the CIB, and in particular, Smithy, didn't get their hands on them unless they were in serious trouble. Normally it was the uniform branch who got to deal with the drunks, out-of-control parties, occasional couch-burnings and ill-conceived supposedly fun social events. We all still held our breath around the annual Hyde Street Party. Many of us had memories of the unruly mess that was the Undy 500 — an invasion of University of Canterbury engineering students in barely roadworthy vehicles containing large quantities of alcohol for ballast. The resultant booze-fuelled riots had led to considerable damage to property as well as the University's reputation, and the event had been banned. But the odd naive Canterbury student still tried for an underground version. *We can keep it under control, sir. It's the fault of the Dunedin students, or people who aren't even students, sir. It will be better this time.* Yeah, right. Dunedin as a whole embraced the fact it was a university city. It added vibrancy and diversity to the conservative Scottish Presbyterian settler base. If it didn't have the students Dunedin would probably be seen as Grand Boredom Central by the rest of the country, so love them or hate them, we needed the students. There were only the occasional idiots who made us all rue the fact.

'Ladies first,' Smithy said, and indicated it was going to be my pleasure to do the honours here.

He called the shots and I wasn't about to argue. I felt a little twist in my stomach. I hated being the bearer of bad news. 'Gee, thanks,' I said, and stepped around the bottles to knock on the front door.

Nothing.

I waited a few more moments and then knocked again, louder. I heard a thump, and then footsteps moving slowly towards the door. An apparition opened it. I'd have guessed he was in his early twenties, squinty-eyed at the sudden influx of light. He was wearing a grubby white T-shirt with the word 'Vague' across the chest in *Vogue*-style lettering, and striped pyjama pants that hung off his bony hips, big rips in the knees. I believe it was the first time I'd ever seen someone with a blonde dreadlocked-mullet hairdo.

'What?' he said, like it was an immense effort to get the word out of his mouth.

'Good morning.' It was morning, just. It was 11.45 a.m., and he'd clearly missed the best of it. 'I'm Detective Constable Shephard, this is Detective Smith. We were wanting to know if this was the residence of Richard Stewart, or

Clifford, as I believe he was known?' Shit, I said 'was', not 'is', and twice, but Mr Vague here didn't pick up on it.

'Yeah, but he's not here at the moment.'

'When was he here last?'

The young man looked like this was way too hard for his brain to compute. I wondered what interesting substance was still lurking in his system from the night before. One of his eyelids had a distinct droop.

'Ah, a week ago, maybe two.'

'Did he say he was going anywhere?'

'He'd talked about going home for a bit, to his parents', so he must be there.'

In other words, he had no idea where he was, and he clearly had no idea his flatmate was dead. Mates were supposed to look out for mates — some sort of friend this one turned out to be. But not every flatting situation was ideal, I had to remind myself. Maggie and I were the exception rather than the rule.

'But he normally does live here?'

'Yeah.' A suspicious edge crept into his voice. 'Why, what's he done?'

'Look, we really need to ask some questions about him. Can we please come in?'

A look of abject panic flew across his face, and I guessed there might have been a few, shall we say, implements of illegal substance abuse floating around the house. I took a few moments to enjoy his discomfort, but decided, in the interests of getting to the bottom of the murder investigation, we'd forgo the little stuff. We could always send someone back with a warrant later.

We'd be calling in a team to go through the flat, regardless.

I looked him in the eye and said, 'You've got one minute.'

He understood the message, loud and clear, and darted down the hallway, leaving us standing on the porch.

'Is that what you'd have done?' I asked Smithy.

'That was minor-infringement guilt on his face, not major-crime.'

'Glad we're on the same wavelength.'

Whatever the cause of Mr Vague's consternation, it must have been small because he appeared back in the hallway well within his allotted time, and had also managed to pull on an oversized and seriously tatty sweatshirt. Judging by the crumples, he'd slept on it. Judging by the food stains, he'd eaten off it too.

By the time we reached the kitchen and dining room, I was not at all surprised to see what looked like a week's worth of dishes festering among the week's worth of food scraps. And that's just what was on the bench. The air was more than a little ripe. When he indicated the seats at the table, I felt a little reluctant, but the surface was more or less clear. It was slightly damp, which meant part of his forty seconds involved wiping as well as hiding. Nice effort, but unfortunately I'd caught sight of the dishcloth, and it wasn't pretty. I avoided actually touching the table. Even Smithy looked a little cautious, and I knew his standards weren't all that high. I'd seen him eat things that had fallen on the floor before. I wouldn't let my dog eat something off this floor.

'What's your name?'

'Jase. Jason Anderson.'

'And what's your date of birth, Jason?'

'Eighth of the eighth, nineteen eighty-eight.' He didn't look as lucky as his birth date would suggest. 'So what's Clifford done this time?' he said.

I was curious as to the 'this time' reference, as if the police showing up was a regular occurrence. I decided to ask about that later. For now, it was time to break some bad news. I was never sure how to start, but decided that, in this situation, he probably had enough of something mind-altering running around in his system to buffer any shock — assuming he would be shocked and didn't have something to do with the death. I could see from Smithy's face it was time to get to business and knew he'd be watching Jason's reactions closely.

'I'm sorry to be the bearer of bad news, but we believe Clifford is dead.' It took a few seconds for Jason's brain to register this news, the moment of realisation obvious by the sudden draining of colour from his face and the watering-up of his eyes. His mouth hung open and he didn't, or couldn't, say a thing.

'We've confirmed his identity with a finger-print, but still have to check his dental records.'

Finally words came out, with a hoarse whisper. 'Do I have to identify him for you?'

My mind flashed to the bloated, gnawed remains, and I had to work hard to suppress the shudder. 'No, that won't be necessary. What we do need, though, is for you to tell us everything you know of Clifford's activities in the weeks up to the last time you saw him.'

'Do his parents know? He was their only child. Shit.' Maybe he wasn't quite as uncaring as his first impression portrayed.

'No, not yet. We'll be contacting them once we've confirmed the identification.' That was something I wasn't looking forward to. As OCB, it was my responsibility to inform the next of kin. It had to be one of the hardest parts of the job, and it was probably the reason I was informing young Jason here. Smithy would have realised what was in my immediate future and was giving me a practice run.

'What happened? Did he have an accident?' I was supposed to be asking the questions, not Jason, but for the moment his reaction had disarmed me. I couldn't have been ballsing it up too much though, as Smithy hadn't interjected.

'No, it would appear that he was murdered.'

I didn't think it was physically possible for someone to get any more pallid. 'Murdered?' he said, head now shaking with disbelief.

'Yes, murdered. So we are going to need to know everything you can tell us about Clifford and his activities, and also we need to know about any other flatmates you have. We'll need to have a search through his room and the rest of your flat for anything that could help us with our enquiries.' I didn't know how far we would get with the questioning of Mr Still-bombed-out-of-his-skull here. He might need another few hours

103

to detox, probably down at the station. But we'd get the SOCOs in straight away and we'd ensure Jason wasn't left alone in the house with any potential evidence, and the opportunity to hide, accidentally damage or contaminate it.

'Yes, yes, of course,' he said. There was none of the furtive guilt and panic displayed before. He too seemed to realise there were bigger fish to fry.

24

'So, what do you think of him?' I asked Smithy as we walked back to the car.

'Harmless.'

'You think?'

'Yeah. I've seen more spine in a jellyfish, and probably more brain cells. All bluff and bluster, that one.' Not that he displayed enough life to manage bluff and bluster. Jason made an amoeba look complicated.

'His reaction certainly looked pretty genuine, even if it was padded by something illegal.' I thought about the state of the flat and their chosen lifestyle. 'The drugs aspect could be something to look at. He was definitely using something, and our victim does have that drug conviction lurking in his past. Although I can't picture Jason there as a drug lord and criminal mastermind. And, judging by the state of that flat, none of the inhabitants were living in the lap of luxury, provided by a roaring drug trade.' Even the television was elderly, and was artfully situated on top of another, old console-type model, its screen smashed, with brick still in situ. 'There's always the possibility Clifford Stewart was small fry and did something to piss someone off that required his disposal. Mind you, dumb nut there seemed completely oblivious to his flatmate's disappearance, let alone any potential risk to his own safety. He didn't seem the least bit concerned that there could be any connection between drugs and Clifford's demise, or that maybe, because he lived at the same address and clearly was using something himself, he could get caught up in this. But then, maybe we're completely off the scent there.' I was doing a bit of a monologue and turned to look at my partner. 'Are you okay? You're very quiet today.'

'Yeah.'

'It's just that you haven't said much.' Not that he was exactly garrulous usually.

'Not feeling talkative.'

That was the absolutely wrong thing to say to me. I asked the natural next question. 'Why, what's happened?'

'Nothing's happened.'

'But you just said you're not feeling talkative, which means something's wrong.'

'No, it doesn't.'

'Did I do something wrong back there? Did I make a mistake? If I did, you have to tell me.' I thought I'd done all right. Maybe I shouldn't have given Jason that head start, but Smithy said it was fine at the time. Was he just being nice to my face, but was annoyed underneath?

'It wasn't you.'

'Then who was it?'

He gave me a long-suffering look that said he realised I'd badger him until he told me. With a defeated sigh, he announced his news. 'I'm going to be a daddy again.' He didn't sound that enthused by the idea.

'Well, congratulations. When did you find out? Veronica must be thrilled.'

'That was my coffee-break surprise. I think she's as shell-shocked as I am.'

Oh. 'Not planned, I take it?'

'Hell, no.' Smithy had come to love and family late in life, and Veronica was in her early forties, so I could understand how it might be a bit of a shock for all concerned. Their youngest had just started school, so I could see that going back to the baby days might not be that appealing.

'I'd appreciate it if you didn't tell anyone,' he said.

'Of course I won't. And despite your obvious misgivings, I think it's lovely news.' I didn't add the other thought clanging around in my head — *rather you than me.*

'Yeah, right,' he said. 'So excuse me if I'm a bit distracted, but feel free to banter away, knock yourself out. I'm listening.'

Smithy's bombshell had interrupted my train of thought, and it took me a few moments to pick up the thread.

'What I was getting at is that I didn't think Jason had the look of someone who had killed or harmed anyone, or of someone anxious that they might be next on the receiving end. He couldn't even offer any suggestions in the enemies or motive department.'

There was silence from Smithy.

'I don't think his brain was that functional. He might be of more use when he's not bombed out of his skull.'

'True.'

25

Come the afternoon, Jason seemed to have recovered some of his memory. We'd been back to the flat earlier to see how the SOCOs were getting on. They brought us up to speed on a few of their discoveries so we would be armed with information for our second attempt at an interview with him. The SOCOs had also made a few disparaging asides about contracting something nasty from the cesspit squalor. While there I'd noticed several details about the flat that had escaped me in the sensory overload of my earlier visit, including the charming poster displaying every novelty condom known to man, and the one with the rather buxom young lady almost wearing a wet T-shirt.

Now we were in the clean and, by comparison, sweet-smelling environment of a second-floor interview room, trying to get sense out of Clifford Stewart's flatmate.

'Jason,' I said, sharp. 'We need to know everything we can about Clifford so we can find who did this to him. Help us here.'

His head jolted up so quickly he almost gave himself whiplash. If every weekend resulted in such a neurone-killing bender, he'd be down to the IQ of a flea in no time.

'Yeah, of course,' he said, blinking slowly, as if his lids were Velcroed to his eyeballs. The eyelid I'd noted for its droop earlier had lifted slightly, so I took that as a sign of partial recovery.

'His friends. I need to know the names of all his friends.'

'Oh, yeah. Well, we have a few of the same mates. Scotty, ah, Jonesy, Bulldog, Smithy.' My Smithy's left eyebrow twitched. 'The touch rugby guys.' What was it with guys and the need to Jonesyfy their names? You didn't find girls chucking an affectionate 'ey' sound on each other's surnames. No one would dare call me Shephardy.

'Real names would be helpful.'

He squinted his eyes as if he was thinking really hard. I swear I could smell plastic burning.

'Scott Palmer, Nick Jones — er . . . Nicholas Jones. Bulldog is Caleb Walsh. Josh — I mean Joshua Smith, Evan Williamson. God, who are the others?'

'While we're on the topic of nicknames, any idea where Richard got the nickname Clifford?'

Jase looked a little uncomfortable but still smiled as he told me: 'Because he's big and red and a bit of a dog.' He may have thought the kids' TV show reference was funny, but the image that immediately jumped into my mind was of the sodden matted mass of red hair the divers dragged up that wasn't attached to the body. I shuddered and moved on to the next question.

'Any friends not in your usual social circle?'

'There are a couple of guys: Spaz, who he's at uni with. And Frog.'

I gave him a look.

'I don't know their real names, okay? Spaz,

everyone knows Spaz because he's, you know, a spaz.'

I gave him one of my extra-special looks.

'Geez, everyone calls him that,' he said, palms up like, *whoa, lady*. 'He walks kind of weird and lurchy, and twitches and stuff, and talks funny, but he's supposed to be a proper genius. He's got a beard, dark hair. He's a student.'

'Which department?'

'Where?'

'At the university. What department is' — I struggled to bring myself to say it — 'Spaz in?' Could you charge someone with self-inflicted brain-damage?

'I dunno. Computers?'

I gave up on that line of questioning before I was forced to grab his neck and shake him.

'And Frog?'

'He works at that second-hand place on George Street. You know? Where you can flog things off for money. Cash for Goods, I think it's called.'

We referred to that place as Cash for Crap. It often came up on our radar, as the owner was pretty good at spotting and reporting anyone trying to offload stolen goods.

'What about his girlfriend?' I suspected Clifford didn't have one, as what woman would let her man disappear for a couple of weeks like that without contact in some shape or form? Mind you, I also suspected that none of the guys in the flat would have had a girlfriend; what self-respecting woman would set foot in that dump?

'Nah, he hadn't had a woman for a while. Last one buggered off overseas, and that was the end of that.'

'No casual flings?'

'If he did, he didn't bring them home.'

Surprise.

'And where's your other flatmate? When's Leo due home?'

'Dunno. Haven't seen him for a few days. Probably shacked up at his missus' place.'

Okay, maybe my theory was slightly off. Someone had managed to attract a woman, but it wasn't far from the mark if he was at her place.

'Have you got his cellphone number?'

'Yeah.' He sat there looking vague.

'Then can we please have it?' I said it very slowly, firstly to make sure it sank in, and secondly because, if I didn't, I was likely to reach over and slap him one.

I smiled sweetly and sat on my hands. He got his cellphone out of his pocket and poked away at it until he came to the right number. He rattled off the digits.

'It's pretty clear that you dabble in some illegal substances.'

The young man looked shocked to hear the sound of Smithy's subterranean baritone. Bless him, he saved Nasty Sam from having to make an appearance.

'Was Clifford into narcotics?' Trick question — we both knew of his previous conviction.

You could see the tussle of emotions on Jason's face. If he was capable of that many thoughts at once, I'd pick he was weighing up dobbing in his mate versus protecting his own butt. Smithy's voice had beautifully conveyed both query and threat. When he responded, Jason took the mumble approach.

'Yes, he did a bit.'

'Sorry, couldn't quite hear that?'

'Yes, he enjoyed the odd joint.'

'And was this for his own use, or was he a bit more ambitious than that?'

There was a distinct hesitation.

'Look, son.' Smithy had pulled out the son card. 'We're not bloody stupid — we can tell you're hedging. He was growing for supply, wasn't he? Where was his plot and where did he store his harvest?'

The SOCOs hadn't found anything in Clifford's room, but no one with half a brain would risk being caught out in this flat, which may as well have had a neon-lit, six-metre-high 'raid me' billboard erected on its roof. This would explain why they found what looked like some hash, half a dozen ecstasy tablets with a dove stamped into them and a semi-live, barely-hanging-in-there marijuana plant in Jason's room, but nothing in Clifford's. They also found a couple of big, orange roadworks signs, some traffic cones and a Castle Street road sign.

Jason had a look of utter misery on his face. 'I don't know. He never told me — he kept it secret. But his folks had a crib down in The Catlins. The times I went there I didn't see anything, but maybe he hid something out that way? Dunno.' Clifford must have had some sense. I wouldn't have trusted this oaf with the whereabouts of a potential high either. The profits would have gone up in smoke.

'When were you down there last?' I asked.

'Where?'

Lord, give me strength. 'The Catlins.'

'Oh, not since summer. Too friggin' cold in that place. Nah, if we all went to the beach for a weekend, we went to another mate's crib out at Aramoana.'

'And when did you last do that?'

'We had a big party out there a couple of weekends ago, you know, when that ship got stuck. That was so cool, man.'

When he saw the look on my face he shut up and decided not to look so enthused about it.

Jason seemed genuinely clueless and harmless enough, but he could also be dumb enough to do something stupid. You could never discount basic stupidity as a motive for murder.

26

My head felt like an overstuffed cushion, and its perpetual low-grade ache had escalated into something more substantial. It had been a full-on day anyway, but I'd then had to finish it off with the unenviable task of informing Clifford Stewart's parents that their beloved and only son had been beaten to death, his body dumped into the sea. In a strange way it went better than expected — well, it seemed so at the time. I delivered my well-rehearsed news, and it seemed to stun them into silence. There wasn't the wailing and hysterical rawness of grief that can be incredibly hard to witness. On the other hand, their muffled sobs and sober intensity left me with a deep-seated sense of distress.

Of course, they'd wanted to see the body, to touch and say farewell to their son. I hated having to tell them that, no, that wasn't possible, and to try to intimate to them with kindness and without going into detail that he wasn't in good condition. It brought back memories of my Nana's death: of dressing up in my Sunday best as a little girl and going to the funeral home, fearful and unsure, my hands firmly gripped in Mum's and Dad's. She looked so tiny and out of place in the satin-lined coffin, her face, normally so animated, still and without expression. Dad lifted me up so I could kiss her goodbye. I reached out to touch her and felt with my own hands that she was hard, cold and indeed very much dead. There was no doubting it then, no room for a child's imagination to concoct wild ideas and dreadful images. It demystified her death, and from that moment the nightmares stopped. There would be no such relief for Clifford's parents. For them, the nightmare had just begun.

Oh, the relief of a scorching-hot shower, washing away the chill and weight of the day. After what felt like hours stuck in cesspit squalor, and then being the bearer of bad news, despite the headache I'd felt the need for an after-work burn-off and the meditative effects of pounding one foot in front of the other. My doctor had told me to lay off exercise for a while, but I decided the mental-health benefits of a run outweighed any possible physical risks. My chosen route avoided the botanic garden — there were memories there I didn't need to revisit right now — and instead the allure of the Green Belt had beckoned. Our native forests were mostly evergreen, so even in its winter guise, its dense, darker-hued solitude and stillness soothed my mind and warmed my mood. And with it snaking across the city, reaching halfway up the hillsides, you were rewarded with tantalising peeks of the harbour and out to sea. Maggie and I lived in a semi-detached bungalow up in Roseberry Street, which meant that in order to get home each night I had to pass through the Green Belt. Its trees and lush-green foliage seemed to provide a mental, as well as the obvious physical, demarcation between the hassles of work and the haven of home.

'I will never complain about you skiving off washing the dishes ever again,' I said as I shoved aside last night's pots to make room for my cup of tea. After my interludes at the Castle Street flat it had been tempting to get clean before my run, but I was glad I managed to resist the urge to shower until after my exertions. Still, it was a temptation to decontaminate my work clothes, or at least sprinkle them with flea powder. I had decided Maggie's and my housekeeping prowess wasn't as bad as we originally thought.

'That's rich coming from someone who seems to be allergic to vacuuming.'

'Well the damned thing sucks, or doesn't, which is the main problem.'

'You could try emptying it.'

'Oh, is that what the little red indicator thingy is for?'

Domesticity was never going to be one of my strong points. I was perfectly capable, just reluctant. As far as I was concerned life was too short, and no one ever died from a lack of housework, although I suspected disaster might only be an infestation away in Castle Street.

'What are you up to tonight?' I asked. My headspace had improved, and I was in a get-out-of-the-house mood. Although, if I was honest, I was in a stay-away-from-the-phone mood. I'd decided on the perfect solution to avoid being hassled by landlines or the cellular variety. 'We should go see a movie.'

'Can't, sorry,' Maggie said. 'Mr Hunk's taking

me to a faculty function — one of those boring things where you drink too much wine, don't get enough food to absorb it all, then have to try and hold intelligent conversations with people who make Einstein look like a dunce and know a damn sight more about everything than you do.'

'Yippee. Why go then?'

'Did I mention the wine was free?'

'Sounds fun. Need a chaperone?'

'No.' Maggie let out a laugh. 'So,' she said emphatically. 'When's Paul coming over next?'

Damn, was I that transparent?

'This weekend, I think,' I said, and pretended to get busy tidying up the bench. My diversionary tactics didn't work.

'You think? You're not sure?' I could tell from her sceptical tone she wasn't going to let it go.

'This weekend, definitely.'

There was a pause, and I was pretty confident what the next question was going to be.

'Have you talked to him since you got back?'

Yup, as anticipated. I turned around, to see Maggs standing there, head tilted, sporting her *well-I'm-waiting* look.

'He rang today to see how I was, but there was too much happening at work to talk for long,' I said, which was the truth. The office wasn't exactly private either, and Smithy had never warmed to Paul and gave me frosty looks whenever I was on the phone to him, so I avoided it as much as possible.

'I really hope you're going to sort it all out this weekend. You can't go on being so non-committal about him, it's not fair. Not fair on him and not good for you.' It wasn't like she was saying anything I didn't already know, but it wasn't as simple as just sorting it out. If only.

'We'll talk about it this weekend, face to face and when we've got time. Until then I've got way too much going on at work to waste energy worrying about it.' A defensive edge had crept into my voice. I dropped my eyes to avoid her laser-beam glare.

'All I can say is, don't cock this one up, Sam. Life seldom throws you a guy like him. Don't do anything stupid.'

27

Marlene Stewart wore a sharp black trouser suit, with a black turtleneck jersey underneath the jacket, and a black silk scarf knotted around her throat. The only hint of colour in her ensemble was the navy-blue calfskin gloves lying perfectly, one atop the other, on the table beside her pale, clutched hands. Her makeup was flawless, the striking red of her lipstick contrasting with the pallor of her skin. She wore eyeliner and shadow, but not mascara. The perfect arch of her eyebrows framed a face fighting for control and etched with pain. Richard Stewart Senior stood behind her, flagpole rigid, but with one hand on his wife's shoulder. Richard Junior's nickname of Clifford could have applied to his father too. He was big and redheaded, with the damaged skin of someone fair who had spent a lifetime in the sun.

'Thank you for coming in today. We appreciate how difficult this must be for you both.'

They had declined the offer to be interviewed at their house; I could understand them not wanting the police or anyone associated with the criminal business of their son's death defiling the precious sanctity of their home.

'Why don't you take a seat, Mr Stewart.' I indicated the chair opposite and noted the shared look of despair between the two as he sat and they reached out for each other's hands.

'We need to ask you some questions about your son. I apologise in advance if any of them may seem difficult or inconsiderate, but we need as much information as we can get in order to bring Richard's killer to justice.'

Smithy had asked me to conduct the interview. He thought a feminine touch would be better, given the circumstances. Just because my system was oestrogen-heavy, though, didn't mean I was any better equipped to handle these emotionally charged occasions.

'If we could start by asking when you last had contact with Richard?'

It was Richard Senior who answered the question, his voice firm, if slightly nasal. 'We were talking about it last night, after you left, and it was definitely on Sunday the thirtieth of August; that was the weekend that ship got stuck at Aramoana.'

The ship grounding was going to be one of those pivotal events in history around here, one of those moments when everyone could remember where they were and what they were doing; like I could remember where I was when Lady Di was killed: a kid, in the milking shed with Dad, listening to reports on the radio. Or, for those a little older, where they were when man first landed on the moon.

'Did you see him, or was this a phone call?'

'Phone call. He was at home for dinner with us on the Friday night, but we didn't see him for the rest of that weekend because he had something on with his friends. He didn't say what exactly. Marlene would have talked with him on the phone on Sunday evening around eight-thirty, wouldn't it have been? Just before *Bones* started on the TV?'

I looked at Marlene for clarification and she nodded before looking away.

'Did he regularly come home for a meal?'

I'd addressed the question to Marlene, but Richard Senior replied. 'He did most weeks; at least that way we knew he got one decent feed. I don't think they ate well at his flat.' It would seem they had decided Richard Senior was the designated speaker. 'We didn't like his flat. It was very . . . Well, it was foul, and down there with all the students — but he seemed to think it was all right. He wasn't about to move, although we thought he could have done better.'

I got that; as a parent, I'd have been disappointed too.

'Was he a student?'

'Not exactly. He had a job as an electrician, at Cartright's, but he was doing a few business papers at the university part time to expand his skills. At least that was something positive.'

'Did he talk much about his flatmates?'

'No, not really. One of them, Leo, we already knew, as they went to school together. He was a nice enough boy. But the other one was a dead loss. To be honest, we didn't often bring it up with him — or the other areas of his life we didn't agree with — it just ended in arguments and upset everyone, so we tried to keep the peace. He didn't tell us much about anything and we stopped asking.'

I felt a pang of pity for this man, for both of

121

them. He was acknowledging his son wasn't exactly squeaky clean, and I was grateful he was gracious enough to provide me with an opening for what could otherwise have been an awkward line of questioning. It couldn't have been easy for them.

'So you were aware of his past convictions for drug supply and stolen goods?'

He took a large breath. 'Yes, and it broke our hearts. You know, we're a good family. We gave him everything he could need as a child, did our best for him, but he got in with the wrong crowd as a teenager and he went a bit off the rails. Not hugely, I mean — he wasn't doing any major crime or anything like that and, thank God, he didn't seem to have a big problem with using drugs himself. He was a good boy, deep down, a really good boy.'

Marlene's shoulders were starting to shake and I saw Richard Senior lean over and give her a little nudge of reassurance.

'Do you think he was still involved in the drug business?'

'Like I said, we couldn't talk about anything like that with him, but yes, I do believe he was still involved.' His resolve was beginning to crumble and the change in his voice was reflected in the increased crumpling of Marlene's face. 'And we're really worried that all this, everything that has happened to him, is because of it.'

It was clear I had two people here who dearly loved their son, but could not reconcile themselves with what he did. It would seem they regretted their lack of communication with him, but what else could they have done? He was a grown man who made his own choices. Still, I guessed that was something they'd mull over for a very long time. I was trying to be as objective as possible and not fuel their assumptions; that way any information they gave would be unbiased and not tailored to fit our preconceived ideas. I chose my words carefully.

'We have to consider that Richard's death may have been as a result of his involvement with drugs, especially considering his previous conviction; but we also have to be open-minded and look at all possibilities in this investigation.'

A moment of quiet descended upon the room — quiet suffused with anguish.

'They made it look like an accident, dumping him? What kind of people would do a thing like that?' Richard Senior asked.

'Yes, they did,' I said. 'I know it is hard to imagine that there are people capable of committing such acts.'

His next question came out hoarse, almost a whisper. 'And he's so bad we can't see him, not at all?'

Jesus. The mental image of Clifford came into my head, and I found my eyes misting up despite my efforts to stay strong, stay professional.

'I'm sorry,' I said. My voice wavered. 'Please, you don't want to remember him like that.'

The last shreds of control deserted Marlene's face, and large tears rolled down her cheeks. She reached out and grasped at my hand, the shock of physical contact almost as much as the shock of hearing her grief-laden voice.

'You find who did this to my boy,' she said, her eyes locked with mine. 'You promise me you'll find them.'

I felt the warmth and trickle of moisture down the side of my face.

'I will,' I said. 'I will.'

28

I slid into a chair at Nova, thanked the waitress who placed a glass of water in front of me, and checked out the menu. After this morning I needed a breather and a complete change of scene, not to mention some real sustenance. I'd have killed for a wine. I'd been a good pixie and made my lunch most days this week, so I'd sidled today's into the rubbish bin on the way out the office door. I quite enjoyed dining alone, even if you did get odd looks from the other punters. At least it was lunchtime, so the looks didn't carry the sympathetic edge they often did for those flying solo at dinner. What was so odd about a girl dining alone? Mind you, if I kept up my cowardly ways, I'd be dining alone permanently. I'd taken the pathetic way out last night and pretended I was at the movies, seeing as I couldn't do the real thing. I turned my cellphone off and didn't answer the landline when it rang. Sometimes a girl just couldn't face confrontation, even if it came cached in gentle words and a melty voice.

There was something decidedly odd about the chap dining at the table opposite me. He was quite an attractive guy to look at: dark hair, full beard, mid-twenties, though it was hard to tell with all the face fuzz — that was one trend I wished would go away. He was tidily dressed, but there was nothing regular about his eating style.

His movements were jerky and pronounced — they reminded me of when kids take a big lurching swing at things and miss. It took him three goes to get his mouth into position to drink his coffee from the straw balanced in the cup, then, when he finally did, he knocked the straw and it fell out onto the table. I watched the painstaking process of swinging his hand to pick it up and then getting the straw back in the cup. The coffee would have gone cold in the time it took. I looked at what he was eating and realised there was no way in hell he was going to be able to cut up the bacon by himself, although the eggs were doable. I looked around to see if any of the waiting staff were keeping an eye on him, but they were busy running around after the recent influx of lunch guests. The people at the next table had positioned themselves with their backs to him, probably so they didn't have to watch, because it was slow and laborious, and borderline excruciating. By this time he'd managed a slurp of the coffee and was directing his attentions at the bacon.

He had a couple of goes at it, failed, and then, with his jerking movements, looked up, trying to catch the eye of the waitress. None were in the vicinity. His eyes then fell on me. He had startling, pale-blue eyes that were sharp, penetrating and eagle-like. You could almost see the cogs whirring around at high speed — the brain was clearly in much better working order than the body.

The moment he looked at me, one word popped into my head: 'Spaz'. It had to be. I

126

made an executive decision, got up and walked over to him.

'Hi, I'm Sam.' I pointed to his lunch. 'Do you want me to cut that for you?' I hoped he wouldn't be offended at my offer. Was it politically correct to offer assistance nowadays or were we supposed to politely ignore those clearly in need of help, in case we hurt their feelings? I opted for the possibility of a large social faux pas and took the 'help out' option.

He looked up at me with a jerk. He had to move his jaw to the point of dislocation to come out with the words 'Yes, please'.

I set to cutting up the bacon and arranging things on his plate so they were in bite-sized piles. I'd had to perform similar operations for my niece and nephew, and one of the farm workers when he'd busted his arm and had one of those stickie-outie casts. How could I approach the question of whether or not he was a colleague of the victim? I couldn't come straight out and ask, *Hey, is your name Spaz?* That was the kind of thing that could silence a room and result in being thrown out by the management. I took the safe option.

'What's your name?' I asked.

'Cedric,' he said, eventually. At least I think it was Cedric.

My God, not only did he have cerebral palsy or something equally challenging, but his parents had saddled him with a name like that. No wonder everyone called him Spaz.

'Cedric, are you by chance at university?'

He nodded. 'Why?'

'I'm actually a detective, Sam Shephard,' I gave myself a promotion to avoid having to explain the 'detective constable' bit, 'and someone gave us a description of someone like you' — shit, that sounded condescending — 'as part of one of our enquiries, but they called them Spaz.' I said the name as quietly as possible but still imagined everyone in the restaurant turning around to look.

'You're a bit short for a detective.'

'Pardon?' I looked at him and saw the sparkle in his eye and realised he was taking the piss. I recognised the reference with a clunk from my misspent deep-space-obsessed youth, and couldn't help but laugh. Personally Han Solo was my man, I always went for the rakish ones.

'You've been watching too much *Star Wars*, and no, I'm not here to rescue you.'

'But you have,' he said and nodded towards his plate. The movement just about threw him off balance. He then lifted his hands up and thrust them at me, wrists together. 'Am I under arrest?'

Talk about 'don't judge a book by its cover'. Here I was feeling sorry for the guy, and as it turned out he was a bloody comedian, and strangely charming at that.

The waitress finally turned up and looked at me with suspicion. 'Is there a problem?' she asked. Suddenly I felt guilty, which was nuts. I could see Cedric's amusement at my discomfort. Was it politically incorrect to clip a disabled guy around the ear?

'Ah, no, I was wanting to order something to

eat.' The waitress looked at him, and he gestured to the other seat, which I took.

'I'll have the eggs too, please, but with salmon. And a flat white, thanks.' With reluctance I decided to forgo the wine. It didn't go well with eggs. I felt quite relieved when the waitress went away.

Cedric was looking pleased with himself. 'A lunch date with a detective.'

'Don't push it, sunshine.'

He smiled in his crooked manner.

'So are you the man known as Spaz?'

'Why?'

I could see I could spend a lot of time playing games here, so I launched in — well, partially. I didn't really want to break the news that his friend was dead over a plate of bacon and eggs in a cafe.

'We're concerned about the safety of a man named Richard Stewart, also known as Clifford, and are enquiring about his movements.'

'You're a bit late; he's dead.'

It was my turn to gawp. 'Well, yes, he is. But how did you know?'

'Smithy, this morning.'

Smithy didn't tell me he'd tracked Cedric down. Surely he would have mentioned if he did. Then again, he was rather distracted at the moment.

'Detective Malcolm Smith?'

'No, Josh.'

Of course, Jase had mentioned a Smithy in the line-up of Jonesys and Scottys. News travelled fast. I looked more closely at him to gauge what he was feeling. He was trying to smile, but his eyes were on the brink of overflow.

'I'm sorry.' I had to resist the urge to reach out and hold his hand. 'Did Josh tell you of the circumstances?'

'Yes.'

I thought about Clifford's circle of friends and the patterns that were emerging, and took a punt. 'How did you know him? Was he a friend, or were you a client?'

He looked quite startled, an expression that was very exaggerated on his face. 'You're direct.'

'Would you prefer me to be more circumspect?'

'Direct's good.' He took a pause to have a go at his lunch and consider his reply. While he did so I looked through the glass wall into the art gallery and pretended to have a great interest in the nearby stand of greeting cards.

'Friend and client. You won't arrest me here? Make a big scene?' He'd regained his composure and cheek.

'No, you're quite safe. It would probably cause a riot. Anyway, I haven't had my lunch yet and I'm hungry, so you're off the hook. For now anyway.'

My meal and my coffee arrived, and I thanked the waitress. She still eyed me with suspicion. I guessed Cedric was a regular here, and yes, the staff did look out for him.

'What did he supply you with?'

'Pot.'

I'd have thought he had enough challenges in life without throwing illicit plant life into the mix. He must have read my mind; either that, or my poker face struck again.

'It helps with the spasms,' he said.

I turned to my meal. At least now I could concentrate on eating, instead of trying to ignore my urge to feed Cedric.

'Is that why he was killed?' he asked.

'We don't know at this stage, but we have to look into every aspect of his life.' He must have upset someone pretty bad to have that done to him. 'Was he, shall we say, self-employed, or did he have a boss?'

'Own boss. Small time, I think.'

Perhaps he'd stood on someone else's toes or ventured onto their territory. People who were into petty crime — not that drug-dealing was petty, it was way up there in my book of base occupations — often dabbled in more than one felony. What other sources of income did he have? I wondered.

'He was a grower, then. Do you know where his plot was? Was he outdoors, indoors or hydroponic?' If he was an electrician, he'd have had the skills to set up a nice little indoor system. It made sense in Dunedin's climate.

Cedric shook his head. He didn't know.

'Did he have any other sideline enterprises, or dabble in something harder?'

'I don't know, Captain Kirk. He didn't tell me.'

So I had stumbled upon a *Star Wars/Star Trek* geek. My mind automatically censored the geek reference, then I laughed at my own stupidity. Cedric had, in this brief meeting, already shattered a few of my misconceptions, and I found him totally disarming. I wondered if he had this effect on everyone who met him, particularly the girls. I had to overcome my urges to mother-hen him.

'Thank you, Mr Spock. So when did you last do business with him?'

'Eleven days ago.'

Most people weren't that exact and certainly not that quick. But then, according to Jase the Ace, Spaz here was supposedly some kind of genius, so exact was probably standard.

'Was that the last time you saw him?'

'Yes.'

'And where was this?'

'Aramoana.'

Aramoana again. 'At a party perchance? The weekend of the ship grounding?'

He nodded.

'Did Clifford do quite a bit of business among his friends?'

'Yes.'

Easy customer base, I guessed.

'It's likely he's been dead for a while.' I saw Cedric's face crumple a bit at that and reminded myself this was a friend I was talking about. 'But no one reported him missing. Had he mentioned he was going away anywhere?'

'Said he might go to the crib in The Catlins for a week. Otherwise I would have been worried.'

'So you stocked up?'

'Yeah.'

'Did he often do that — take off for a bit?'

'Yes.'

We both turned our attention to our lunches. Chances were that Clifford's plot was down that way and that he had headed off to do a spot of garden maintenance. A hydroponic or indoor setup would blur and extend the borders of the natural growing season.

'Did he ever say he was being hassled by anyone — other dealers or clients — or did he seem worried about his safety?'

'No. Happy guy all around.' Yeah, probably high most of the time.

While it was refreshing being able to be this direct with someone, it also seemed rather sad. And yes, although it was my sworn duty to report certain drug-related aspects of this conversation to my colleagues, there was no way in hell I'd be able to do that to Cedric . . . no, Spaz, he suited Spaz. Some selective filtration would be in order. Anyway, this was just a little chat with a new acquaintance over lunch. I wasn't on the clock, as it were.

29

When Smithy and I walked into Cash for Crap, the first thing that hit me was the sheer volume of junk; the second was the dank smell. No matter how new or how clean, there was the unmistakable scent of second-hand tat, that nose-twitching mustiness that triggered an immediate urge to sneeze. The owner of this establishment did his best to present the stock like it was brand-new, but the illusion failed in a tired and forlorn kind of way. It didn't put off the punters though; I could count five individuals and a young couple perusing the aisles. We headed towards the counter, and even from a distance it was clear this was our lucky day.

'Oh my God. Check him out — that has to be Frog,' I said to Smithy.

He took one look at the specimen behind the counter and snorted. The young man was wearing a black Metallica T-shirt that did nothing to hide his major attack of the skinnies, nor did his posture — shoulders hunched, head jutting forwards like it was too much effort to hold it upright. The shirt colour-coordinated nicely with his jet-black hair, and they both contrasted in a stark, almost three-dimensional way, with his incredibly white skin. He had a major case of a Dunedin suntan. The first word that popped into your head when you saw his protruding, bugged-out green eyes was 'frog'.

The eyes reminded me of my great-aunt Dolores, who had a thyroid problem and a set of optics to match.

'Your turn or mine?' I asked Smithy. Rhetorical question, really — his mood hadn't improved any.

'Knock yourself out.'

I gave him a sideways look. We walked up to the counter, and I could tell by the sudden change in demeanour that Kermit had picked us as cops.

'Hi, I'm Detective Constable Shephard and this is Detective Smith. And you are?'

'Joe, I mean Josiah.' He said it like a person who seldom used the full version. 'Do you need to speak to the boss? He's out of town at the moment.'

'Do you have a surname, Josiah?' He had a very biblical Christian name for someone who dressed like that.

He mumbled something inaudible.

'Sorry, I didn't hear that.'

'Winterbottom,' he said and looked down at the floor. No wonder the poor kid went by Frog. Smithy had to walk away and take a look at a toaster.

'Do you happen to go by the nickname Frog?'

And I thought he looked uncomfortable before. Now his chest caved in on itself even further. With the skill of the socially awkward he had managed to avoid all eye contact thus far.

'Er, sometimes.' At least he had the sense not to lie.

'We need to ask you some questions about

Richard Stewart, also known as Clifford.' I made the assumption that he, like all of Clifford's associates, had caught up with the fact he'd been killed. It was the correct assumption judging by the sudden rush of colour to his face, repeated swallowing and moisture to his eyes. 'You are aware of what has happened to him?'

The head nodded.

'When was the last time you saw Clifford?'

'I dunno. I suppose a couple of weeks ago.'

'I need you to be a little more specific, please. Can you recall when and where you saw him last?'

'There was this party out at Aramoana a few weekends back. That would be the last time, and he was fine then.'

'This was the weekend of the ship accident?'

'Yeah.'

Familiar territory yet again. 'So it would be the Sunday morning when you spoke to him?'

Frog was probably out treasure hunting like the rest of them, looking for some loot to flog off here — make some pocket money to pay for his next pair of pointy-toe black boots or bottle of hair dye.

'No, I had work on Sunday, so left the party early. You can check. I brought four others back here to Dunedin with me.'

'Define early.'

'Two in the morning, I guess.'

I didn't point out that was technically Sunday morning. I didn't want to put him further off speaking, as he wasn't exactly running free at the mouth.

'And there had been no signs of aggro or trouble at the party up until the time you left?'

'No, it was sweet. There weren't any troublemakers.'

I wasn't sure whether to believe anything from a guy who made no eye contact throughout the conversation. But then, I was getting the impression young Josiah here had difficulty making eye contact with anyone, let alone a woman — let alone a woman detective.

'You were friends with Clifford. How often were you in contact with him?'

'I dunno, couple of times a week?'

'Were you concerned that you hadn't heard from him the week following the party?'

'No. He'd mentioned he might head off for a week, so I assumed he must have gone away.'

So far, same story. I wondered if he had something else in common with the others we had interviewed. 'So, Josiah, were you a friend and a customer?'

He started and accidentally looked me in the eye before regaining his composure. 'What do you mean?'

'We know he supplied dope for his mates. Were you one of his customers too?'

He sighed and slumped some more. 'No, don't touch the stuff.'

I'd swear he was almost embarrassed to admit it. If he drove a carload of mates back to Dunedin at two in the morning, then it was likely he wasn't much of a drinker either, or else he was the sensible, responsible type. That kind of thing was probably not too good for his image.

'But others in your group did?'

He hesitated. 'I don't know.' Square and loyal.

'He's not what I expected from one of those elmos,' Smithy said as we left Cash for Crap and breathed in some welcome fresh air.

'I believe the term is 'emo', Smithy. You're showing your age. Although, despite the carefully cultivated appearance, he seems more prudish than most.'

'Never trust appearances.'

I didn't need to be told. I was slowly learning to overcome my innate need to trust everyone and to question my unwavering faith in humanity, but I was still at the beginning of my journey to fully fledged cynic. Smithy had a black belt.

'I don't. If I did, I wouldn't be standing within cooee of you.'

30

'Okay, so has anyone else noticed that the flatmate, Leo, who's apparently shacked up at his girlfriend's, is proving difficult to contact? He doesn't seem to have been around for a while. Perhaps we'd better check if 'a while' has been four or five days or if it extends to weeks.'

We were having a team meeting in the squad room. It was a far more relaxed affair than usual, because Dickhead Johns was off at some compliance conference, so we all had a day off wanker-watch.

We'd been placing informal bets on who dunnit and why they dunnit. So far, eighty per cent voted that he'd been knocked off by some disgruntled customer or competitor. I'd chucked in the flatmate query just to be awkward. We were waiting on Detective Billy Thorne from the drug squad to come and brief us on current events. They'd been having a quiet word here and there to see if there were any interesting rumours circulating. Despite it being in their best interests to be secretive, there were always those in the criminal world who were inclined to brag. There were also those who weren't averse to selectively leaking a little information; a deterrent to any players muscling in on their territory. Nothing like the graphic description of a vicious beating to keep the troops in line.

'Yes, we had noticed, but people don't always

come to light immediately. I thought we'd established he was with his girlfriend and were working on that?' Smithy said.

'It's still all hearsay. Stone-head flatmate Jason said he was, and also a couple of the touch-rugby team guys. But no one has definitively located him yet. And Clifford's name has been released into the media, so if the flatmate was oblivious to what's been going on before, he should have heard word by now. Everyone else in their group seems to.' Mind you, some people weren't physically grafted to their cellphones. We'd managed to get my mum out of the Stone Age and buy her a cellphone, but it didn't mean she remembered to charge it or turn it on. Maybe Leo Walker was of that ilk. Also, some people lived in a current-events vacuum. I was a bit too fond of newspapers for that. My day wasn't right until I'd had two cups of tea and my dose of the *Otago Daily Times*.

'Do we have the girlfriend's name and address yet?' Reihana asked.

' 'Trina' is all we know, or 'The Screamer' as one of them told us. They all seem to be on first-name or nickname-only basis, even though they've known each other for years. Considering that these are the same guys who didn't notice their mate had been missing for over a week, I think we need to get serious about tracking this guy down. We have a cellphone number, which I've left messages on, but there's been no response. I think it's time to get a warrant and check his activity with the phone company.'

'Perhaps you'd better pay another visit to our

friend Jase, while you're at it, and find out when exactly he last saw his flatmate, and where he might possibly be,' Smithy said.

'Ew, I don't want to go back to that flat. I might catch something.' I accompanied the comment with the appropriate hand actions.

'Hey, you brought it up.'

He had me there. Sometimes it didn't pay to volunteer too much.

Billy Thorne had been doing drug-squad duty for five years. If anyone could catch a whiff of a rumour it was him. He didn't fit the profile of someone who spent the day dealing with the seedy underbelly of the city. He was a bit too clean-shaven and shiny. He'd never manage undercover work; he didn't have the serious smoker crags and crinkles you'd need for that lark. But for all the sparkly appearance, he had a knack.

'Sorry I'm late. Had to go see a man about a job.' He'd also seen The Fix, judging by the large takeaway coffee he had in his hand. I noticed I wasn't the only one in the room coveting it.

'You're all right, Billy,' Smithy said, as he took a sip from his mug of god-awful instant with enough sugar to curl his hair. He still held the record for the most sugars per cup — three. Olympian effort. 'So, what do you know?'

'Not a hell of a lot to help you, I'm afraid. Your victim seems to have been strictly small-time pot. Small enough not to stand on any toes from serious enterprise. Some were aware of him, mostly because he was dumb enough to get caught, but he was tolerated, and no one had seen fit to pay him a visit.'

'Did anyone know where he was growing?'

'No, or else they'd have ripped him off before now. No honour among thieves.'

'So you don't know if he'd have had an indoor or outdoor set-up?'

'In Dunedin you'd have to think indoor to guarantee success. Anyone well resourced would go indoor. God knows it's easy enough now with the specialty hydroponic stores around. I understand our man was an electrician, so he would have had the skills to set up a good operation. When we got him on his conviction a few years back it was indoor. Nothing sophisticated then. A dozen plants in a converted sunroom in his flat. Flatmates kept mum, probably encouraged by a free supply. You can be pretty sure his parents never came to visit.'

'We've been to his flat. It's got 'police-raid target' written all over it,' I said.

'And we have raided it periodically, especially when he was subject to parole conditions. Nothing found. The victim had more sense. I'm not sure about the flatmates, though.' Yes, ole droopy eye had proven how impaired his judgement was. 'The growing season has finished, but we'll keep hunting.'

'He hadn't ventured into something harder?' Smithy said.

'No chemistry experiments from what I've heard. If he had, I imagine he would have had a visit from our more organised elements. They tend to guard their business jealously.'

'They could be lying to you,' I said. 'The way

142

he'd been assaulted and his body disposed of suggests someone wanted something — information, drugs — or was sending a message. Also it suggests that the perpetrator had resources and access to a boat. Most people wouldn't throw away dive gear like that. So you can't be sure this isn't drug-related.'

'Never say never in this game. They could well be lying to protect themselves, and we'll carry on the investigation from our side assuming that they are. Don't trust them as far as you could kick them. But for the moment it would appear this guy was a little fish.'

An unfortunate choice of words given the circumstances.

31

Jason, or someone, had made an effort. There had been a few cosmetic changes to the flat since I was here last and since the SOCOs had finished their work. Firstly, the charming roof ornamentation had gone: the public attention must have prompted the local supermarket to come and claim back their shopping trolleys — there would have been a few thousand dollars-worth of hardware up there. It might have prompted the landlord to have a word too, as the litter had been picked up from the front yard and the beer bottle and crate collection dealt with. It almost looked habitable. I hoped the makeover extended to inside the flat as well, but I didn't hold my breath.

When the door finally opened, Jase didn't look too thrilled to see me. I noted he was wearing the same T-shirt as last time. I hoped it had been laundered since then.

'Now what?' he asked. He had mastered the victimised look.

'A few more questions — about your flatmate Leo this time.'

'Isn't this, like, harassment or something?' he asked. He almost seemed hopeful.

I gave him my charming-with-added-menace smile. 'No, if this was harassment, I'd have come at two o'clock in the morning. And I would like to think you'd do anything you could to help us find the killer of your flatmate, unless of course you had something to hide. Do you have something to hide, Jason?'

'Humph,' he said, or something to that effect. 'I suppose you want to come in, then.'

I didn't really, but it was bloody cold and I didn't feel like having this conversation on the porch. In a toss-up between getting hypothermia and septicaemia, I thought the odds were slightly lower for the latter. I could always take some antibiotics later.

He held open the door and I walked past him and into the student tip. The moment the door clicked shut behind me and the last vestiges of natural light deserted the hallway, I felt a wave of heat wash over my face and my heart rate kicked up several notches, pounding beneath my ribs. I could feel the tension of the air pressure on my skin, the smell of mouldy mustiness and unwashed male assailed my nostrils. My chest constricted and I had to open my mouth to gulp in air with rapid sucks. What the hell was wrong with me? Was I having a heart attack? No, surely I was too young for that. But something was definitely wrong. God, was I going to have to call an ambulance? Then realisation struck as suddenly as the palpitations. This was my first time out solo on the job since the assault. My body was telling me I felt nervous about this, and now that my brain had made the connection it only got worse. I forced myself to take each step down the hallway towards the kitchen. It was like every nerve ending in my body was waiting for the whack over the head or the knife between the shoulder blades, and was screaming out, *Run, Sam, run.* Why the hell did I let him walk behind me? Why oh why had I not done the basics: assessed the risk properly and worn the hated stab-proof vest? I was here alone for heaven's sake. I had to force myself to inhale and exhale steadily. *Don't be so bloody stupid, Shep. It's just Jase. He couldn't hurt a fly.* But what if he could? At least Smithy knew where I was. And Jase hadn't shown any tendency towards violence before. In fact, he could barely muster anything. What was I being so babyish and damn panicky about?

The moment we made it down to the kitchen and open space I spun around to face him. He stopped short, startled at my sudden movement, and then stepped back a pace, caution creasing his face. He was more scared than I was. Stupid.

'Er, take a seat,' he said, and wafted his arm in the direction of the table.

'Thanks,' I said, and managed to sit down, all the while facing him.

While I extracted my notebook from my bag, I took the precaution of slipping my pepper spray into my pocket. It helped to quell my nerves a fraction. My notebook felt like it stuck a bit against the table surface. Nice. My hand was shaking, and I gripped the pen tighter. It didn't alleviate the problem at all, so I hoped my memory would hold up, because I doubted I would be able to jot anything down without looking like a complete twat.

'We still haven't been able to locate your

flatmate, Leo. Have you heard from him at all since we were here last?'

'No. I thought he was still at his bit's?'

I gave him a glare. 'I take it you mean his girlfriend, Trina.'

'Oh, yeah.' He looked a little abashed. I still marvelled that someone would have a dreadlocked-mullet hairdo, but the more I encountered Jason, the more it seemed to suit his character.

'When I was previously here, I asked you when you'd last seen Leo. You said it was four or five days ago. I'd actually like you to be more specific than that.' I looked into his eyes, took in his general demeanour and guessed he was in a reasonable state of lucidity. The eye droop wasn't too bad compared with last time, so he might even be capable of thought. Rational thought might be pushing it, though. I realised this cleaning-up act of his was partly due to the police confiscating all his drug doings the other day. That and a little court appearance he'd have to make sometime soon. I smiled at the notion. Jase noticed and it seemed to make him more wary. How marvellous that I could make a big lug of a thing nervous.

'What day last week are we talking about here?'

'I dunno. Thursday, Friday, I can't be sure.'

'Come on Jason, you'll have to do better than that.' This wasn't the time to be vague. 'I want specifics. Day, time.'

He sat down and did what I guessed was thinking, before he came up with a reply. 'I think

147

it was Monday, 'cos I'd just come back from a lecture.'

I had to hide my astonishment that Jase managed to go to any lectures. Study looked like it would be a stretch for him, other than the odd bit of practical horticulture. Also, Monday was quite a bit different from his initial Thursday or Friday.

'Did he talk to you? What did he say?' He started doing that squirmy, non-eye contact thing again. 'Well, Jase?'

'I didn't actually see him, as such.'

'What do you mean?'

'Well, I know he'd been here 'cos he'd collected his mail and some of his stuff, so I thought he must have got some things and gone back to his . . . ' he checked himself before I got the chance to give him a look ' . . . to Trina's.'

'Okay, so you didn't actually see him then. When exactly did you see him last? And I mean clap eyes on and talk to him.'

'A while ago, I guess. I can't be certain, but I suppose I wouldn't have seen him since the party at the end of semester.'

'How long ago, Jason?' He noticed the use of his full name, and I watched as his Adam's apple bobbed up and down uncontrollably.

'I guess, two weeks ago?' He said it like a question I was supposed to know the answer to. I did know one thing. Two weeks ago was a familiar date. So was the party.

'This wouldn't happen to be the party out at Aramoana, would it?'

'Yeah. It was great.'

'Okay, now I'm asking this question in all seriousness, and I'd like you to think very carefully about the answer, because you haven't seen your flatmate Leo for about two weeks, and your other flatmate Clifford has been dead, for, gosh, about two weeks, so you can see what I'm getting at here. Would Leo have had any reason to want to harm Clifford?'

Jase looked like he was in information overload. Too much to compute. He took on a kind of frozen-screen look. When he was finally reanimated he uttered two shocked words.

'Fuck, no.'

32

'Okay, I think we've got a serious suspect, guys,' I announced as I swept into the squad room. It sounded very grand, but a girl always had to make an entrance. It backfired a bit though, because there was only one person in the room and he looked decidedly underwhelmed.

'So are you going to stand there looking pleased with yourself, or are you going to enlighten me?' Reihana asked.

'Where is everyone?'

'They'd be out working, following leads, detecting — you know: that thing we're paid to do?' What was it with CIB and sarcasm?

'Did something come up?'

'No, just the old-fashioned legwork thing. Heard of it?'

At least coming from Reihana, I knew it was a good-natured ribbing. With some of the others I was never quite sure. There were those who still resented my presence in the CIB, especially some downstairs. Apparently I'd queue-jumped and, if you believed some of the rumours, screwed my way here, both of which were considered worse than being a child molester. I still copped plenty of jibes and barbs, and unfortunately my hide hadn't thickened any since I'd been here.

I gave Reihana the response he was expecting. 'Yeah, yeah, heard of it, even do it sometimes,

150

but only if desperate.' But then I was distracted from my train of thought by a box on his desk. 'What's with the chocolate?' I moved over to have a nosey.

'Fundraiser for the kids' school, you don't get out of the room alive unless you buy at least two bars.' Reihana flogged off a continuous stream of fundraisers for his kids' schools: raffle tickets, Instant Kiwi boards and that great Southern staple — the cheese roll, AKA Southern Sushi. That's what you got having so many of the things — kids that is, not fundraisers — and he had five of them.

'Chuck us two Dairy Milk and two Caramello. No, make that three Caramello; may as well make it ten bucks.'

'Knew you'd be a sucker,' he said, looking pleased. 'So what was it you were so desperate to tell me?'

'Oh yes, that. Leo Walker, Clifford's flatmate, has been AWOL for a bit longer than we'd been led to believe.'

'How long's a bit?'

'Try two weeks since he was seen last, at the infamous party at Aramoana. Jason, the flatmate, thinks he called into the house on the following Monday to pick up a few things, but didn't actually see him then. Apparently Jase got a bit confused about the meaning of the word 'see'. So it would appear Leo has snuck in to get some gear together and scarpered.'

'That all sounds a bit more than coincidence to me.'

'My thoughts exactly. So I'm thinking we need

151

to have a little chat with all concerned about what exactly happened at that party, and it's time to pull out all the stops on locating Leo. I know Otto was trying to track down him and his girlfriend, without much success, but there's a bit more impetus now. We should have got serious about this earlier.'

'You'll be wanting the boss's job next.'

Comments like that triggered my self-preservation mode, and I couldn't help but look over my shoulder to see if DI Johns was in the room. He seemed to have this knack for walking in on conversations at exactly the wrong time. Reihana noticed my look, and let out a chuckle.

'Relax, Shep. He's still out of town, remember?'

'Sorry, habit.' Ingrained by dire experience. 'Where's Smithy?' I asked and pulled my cellphone out, ready to give him a call to let him know Jase's revelation.

'He said something about a doctor's appointment.'

Doctor's appointment? That could mean one of several things. He was sick, which wasn't likely — Smithy had the constitution of an ox and had never taken a sick day in the time I'd been here. Or it could mean he wasn't taking chances on any more surprise additions to his family and was sussing out the ole snipperooni. Or he and Veronica were perhaps serious about not wanting to be parents again. It was a Friday, and those particular appointments always took place on a Friday, as was evidenced by the usual three or four anti-abortion protesters outside the hospital entrance this morning, none of whom actually possessed a uterus. The news had thrown him into a pretty strange mood, and his mind was definitely elsewhere. I hoped he was okay. Whatever the reason, this could wait. I put the phone back in my pocket.

'I'll get on to acquiring a warrant to access Leo Walker's cellphone records. They're sure to have his girlfriend's number. Perhaps she can shed more light on things, because so far no one else can tell me where he's been or even where he works, or if he works. What is it with these guys? They're supposed to be great mates and all, but none of them seems to know what the other is doing, or anything about each other's lives. And as for the situation in that flat — wouldn't normal people want to know if their flatmates were going to turn up for dinner? It doesn't seem to matter to this lot. They can disappear off the planet for weeks, and none of the others even bat an eyelid. Great mates. And doesn't anyone in this generation have a proper job?' I was starting to sound scarily like my mother.

'Different world, Sam,' Reihana said. 'But I'm with you on the exasperation. It brings to mind the whole 'with friends like these, who needs enemies' concept.'

33

Finally, someone who had a clue. Once I'd faxed through the warrant, the cellphone company had quickly coughed up Leo Walker's phone records. The most frequently used number led straight to Ms Trina Sanderson, who was now seated before me in a station interview room. It was one of the pleasures of having DI Johns out of the picture — I could get on and do what needed to be done without having to adjust to his whim and permission. Smithy was still preoccupied and everyone else was following other leads, so I took the initiative.

She was smartly attired in her ANZ bank uniform, her brunette hair swept up in a French roll, face lightly made up, and looking nothing like how I had imagined Trina the Screamer might look. I was sure she'd be mortified if she knew what they called her. When I'd phoned her, Trina had offered to come down to the station straight away. She struck me as one of those people who would bend over backwards to help anyone. It made me wonder how she'd managed to get herself tangled up with anyone from that tip of a flat.

'So you last saw him on Monday the thirty-first of August. And you're certain it was that date?'

'Yes, he stayed over on the Sunday night because he was going off on one of his work trips

154

on the Monday morning, a long one, and we wouldn't get the chance to see each other for a while. I leave for work at eight-fifteen, so that would have been the time when I saw him last.'

'And his work trip was for the Department of Conservation?'

'Yes. He and another guy are tracking and surveying kiwi numbers in some remote part of Fiordland. It was going to be a two-week trip at least. I didn't think it sounded much fun for them, it's so cold at this time of year, but he always really enjoyed getting out in the bush and away from it all. He didn't seem to think it was risky at all and laughed when I mentioned the possibility of getting lost or hypothermia.'

'When we asked his flatmate about it, he didn't mention Leo was away with work.'

'You mean Jase? Jase doesn't know which foot to stick his shoes on half the time. He's utterly useless and the worst slob I have ever met. Leo probably didn't bother to tell him, and if he did, Jase wouldn't remember. Have you met him? If you had, you'd know what I mean. I don't think I've ever been there when he's been entirely with it. And have you seen their flat? It's the biggest dump ever. It is the gold-standard in student dumps.' Trina was clearly not a one-word-answer kind of a girl.

'So if the flat was that bad, why did Leo live there?'

'Because of Clifford.' I noticed the familiar welling-up that occurred when any of these people talked about him. The impression I got was that he was loved and highly regarded by his mates. 'Clifford invited Leo in last year. I don't know how Clifford knew Jase, so I couldn't tell you why he was invited into the flat, but Leo had known Clifford since school and they were great mates. And the rent was dirt cheap.' Dirt being the operative word. I wondered if the squalor improved when the other guys were about and if it was only Jase who let everything descend into complete piggery.

'Was Leo at the party Clifford attended at Aramoana on that Saturday, the twenty-ninth of August? Were you there?'

'Leo went to the party, but I gave it a miss. He invited me, but I had a girlfriend's birthday bash to go to at Eltrusco, and I wasn't about to miss that. Nothing against his friends, but a girl's night out was more appealing. He told me about it though. Said it was a great night, good bunch of people, good music. No one got too plastered and made a nuisance of themselves. And then there was the boat thing in the morning, he said that was really freaky.'

'So he stayed the night out there.'

'Yes. He'd never drink and drive, so he crashed on a couch. I think there were others coming back into town, but he was going to hang out there with the guys and make a night of it, seeing as I was off doing something else. We hooked back up together in the afternoon.'

'And he seemed all right on Sunday? He didn't behave strangely or seem a bit off?'

'No, he wasn't acting odd or anything. I think he was a bit tired after the party. I doubt they got much sleep.' They weren't the only ones. The events of the morning didn't seem to do anything for people's moods either.

'If he was there on Sunday morning, did he mention people taking any goods from the containers on the beach and if people from the party had participated?'

Her face reddened and she looked down at the table as she gave her hesitant reply. 'Well, yes. To be honest, he said they took a bit, and I told him that kind of thing was theft and really bad, but he said it was like salvage rights and finders keepers, and they didn't do anything wrong. We had a bit of a row about it actually.'

'What did he say he did with the items?'

'Nothing. After the row he wouldn't talk about it anymore, and I didn't push it. It would have just caused another argument.'

Seeing as we were already on to uncomfortable subjects, I tossed another at her. 'Would Leo have had any reason to harm Clifford?'

Her eyes widened and it took a few moments for her to get the words out. 'No, never. They were best mates, like I said, they'd known each other since high school. You can't possibly think he had anything to do with Clifford's murder, can you?'

I wouldn't have asked if I didn't entertain the idea. 'Well, he did happen to disappear from the scene around the time Clifford was last seen alive, and no one has been able to contact him since. It's been all over the media, so surely, if he was the great mate you say he was, he'd have come home when he heard. Let's be honest here, it is very suspicious that he hasn't.'

'That's because he's stuck out in the middle of the bush, in the middle of nowhere. There's almost no communication out there. He's out of range for everything, radio, television, cellphones. He can't know, or else he would have come back straight away, I know he would. He'll be devastated when he does find out. No, he'd never harm Clifford, no way. He'd never harm anyone.' Her face and voice implored me to believe her.

It was feasible. Fiordland certainly qualified as the back of beyond. There were parts of it that hadn't even been explored. In fact, some excitable people were convinced if you looked hard enough in the remotest pockets of ancient forest you could find wild moose out there, or even the supposedly extinct moa.

'We'll have to talk to DOC and get them to locate him. As you can imagine, we do need to ask him some important questions.' I also hoped DOC would be able to tell us when Leo clocked in on the Monday so we could figure out his timetable and if it included enough time to knock someone off and discard the evidence out at sea.

A large chunk of Trina's hair had been dislodged from its clasp; she'd repeatedly pushed at her forehead as her composure began to disintegrate. I felt truly sorry for her. She seemed a lovely girl and genuinely loyal to her man. Still, I had to ask the next question.

'We know Clifford was a dope dealer. Was Leo one of his customers?'

She sighed and slouched back into the chair.

'Another thing we disagreed on. He thought it was okay to have the occasional social smoke. I told him it was wrong, and illegal, and that he should stop it. We didn't really talk about it because it would only lead to an argument, so I tried to ignore it. He would never smoke when I was around because he knew how I felt about it.'

'So he wasn't a heavy user?'

'No, and not into anything else, before you ask. Just beer and the odd joint.'

Leo was sounding less and less like a prospect, but you couldn't go on the word of one or two pals and a girlfriend. I tried to couch the next line of questioning gently.

'Out of curiosity, is Leo into scuba diving at all?'

'Scuba diving? No, he's never done it — wouldn't do it. He hates being on or even in the water. He gets horribly seasick.'

'So he wouldn't have a boat or access to a boat?'

'I think he'd rather have his teeth pulled than get on a boat.'

34

Jesus, some people didn't understand the concept of urgent or serious. I'd just spent a frustrating hour chasing up someone, anyone, with clout and a spine, at the Department of Conservation. When I rang the various DOC offices and explained that we needed Leo Walker to be contacted and fished out of the bush as soon as possible, I got: 'Is that really necessary?'; 'They're hard to get hold of'; and my personal favourite: 'I haven't got the authority to order that, but you could try ringing . . . '

To my credit, I remained calm. I didn't yell at anyone or threaten to ram their phones down their throats, but there was a new gouge mark on the surface of my desk and I'd had to throw back a couple of paracetamol. Smithy had returned from whatever appointment he'd had earlier — he wouldn't elaborate — and after I'd reported my conversation with Trina Sanderson, he'd taken perverse pleasure in delegating this job to me. He must have had experience with DOC before.

We never had this kind of trouble mobilising them for the idiots who got themselves accidentally lost in the bush — they were always fantastic then; so why all the hassle for an employee and someone they were supposed to be in regular contact with?

It didn't help matters that every time I was

knocked back by someone, or had my time wasted, the vision of Marlene Stewart wafted before my eyes, as she grasped my hand, pleading with me to find her son's killer. Somehow that moment had made this into a personal crusade, like I needed that kind of emotional baggage thrown on top of everything else going on in my life.

I was about to ring what would hopefully be the last number on my phone trail when my cellphone bleeped and nearly sent me through the roof. My central nervous system was stranded in caveman mode and not hard-wired for a modern, bleeping world.

The name on the screen didn't help any. Paul. I'd been working very hard to forget the fact he was coming over and there was bound to be some discomfort involved. I opened the message.

See you tonight at 7. Pxx

Christ, it was the last thing I felt like. I'm sure I would be more rational and objective about it if I didn't feel so damn awful. But with the emotional turmoil going on in my brain about Paul, droning on like one of those constant background computer hums you're aware of but trying to ignore, coupled with the demands of a murder investigation, sidestepping the boss, and my post-bashing permanent low-grade head-ache, I was feeling tired and rather brittle. Here he was being friendly and considerate and my first reaction had been to want to sob. With a roomful of men present, though, I stifled it with a kind of strangled hiccup noise and excused myself to the bathroom.

35

'You know, you've carefully avoided talking about my shift to Dunedin all evening.'

My heart clenched at the words, and I looked straight ahead at the headlights of the oncoming traffic. We'd managed to have a pleasant evening out at Plato. We'd talked about the murder case and the weather and the rugby, anything to avoid the actual issue at hand. Wine had helped. Now he'd decided to broach the subject.

'What's there to say? You've already made your decision.'

The windscreen wipers and splattering of rain gave the lights a hypnotic strobe effect. The sodium streetlights overhead reflected off the road, making it look like a molten sea of orange.

'I'd like to know what you're thinking.'

I didn't know what I was thinking, so how could I possibly tell him? My thoughts weren't ordered into coherent strands. They knotted and twisted and drifted, ungraspable. I was afraid that if I opened my mouth and let the words spill out that it would spew out all wrong, and that very bad things would happen. I kept my mouth shut.

'You know, things don't have to change between us. Just because I might be moving over here doesn't mean that we have to move in together or I have to live in your back pocket. I'm the kind of guy who needs my space too.'

Didn't he realise things had already changed? That his decision had altered everything?

I bit my lip and looked out the side window.

'Won't you at least say something, Sam? I've never known you to be short on words before.'

I couldn't win. I didn't want to hurt him, but I could tell by the careful levity of his voice that I already had. I took a big breath.

'Paul, I . . . I just wish you'd talked about this with me before you made a big decision like that. I was happy with the way things were. You move over here, and even though you say you won't, suddenly you'll have all these expectations, and I don't know if I'm ready for that.'

It was his turn to pause.

'And when would you be ready, Sam? Now? Someday? Never?'

Oh, Jesus. That was what I was afraid of. This was turning into one of those moments. One of those what-you-say-now-will-affect-the-rest-of-your-life moments. I could feel his eyes flicking over to me, could sense the tension in his body and his hands grasp the steering wheel more firmly. My mind was swirling at such a pace, I had to rest my head against the window, the cold glass burning a patch on my temple.

'That's not a very fair question right now.'

'And when would it be fair? You know, Sam, this isn't just about you. My life can't go on hold because you're shy of any kind of commitment. You know how I feel about you, and I'd happily spend the rest of my life with you, God help me.'

Fuck, fuckity, fuck. My heart was booming in my chest. Not here, not now.

163

'And before you panic, no, I'm not proposing, I'm just stating a simple fact. But, another simple fact is that I need to feel sure of where my life is going. I'm not getting any younger. I've made a decision that is going to assure my career. I need to know where I stand with you.'

Trapped in a car and backed into a corner. Not a good position to be in. Maggie's words were echoing in my head: *Don't cock this one up, Sam.* I knew she was right. Paul was a good man, and hot, fun and loving — everything I ever wanted. But a huge part of me was coiled tight, ready to explode.

The cellphone going off gave me such a fright I hit my head against the window. I fumbled for it, for once thanking God for the damn thing's intrusion, relieved at the chance of a reprieve,

I managed to get the phone out of my bag without making eye contact with Paul, and bumbled a few buttons before hitting the right one.

'Shephard.'

'Why didn't you tell me Dad had cancer?' The voice yelling down the phone was so distorted by anger it was unrecognisable.

'Sorry?' It must have been a wrong number, and someone was clearly very upset.

'You knew, Sam, but you didn't tell me. How could you not tell me?'

My name. The neurons started making connections and it started to dawn on me who it might be.

'Stephen?' I asked. 'Is that you?'

164

'Of course it's me. How long have you fucking known?'

My mind was struggling to cope with this sudden change of direction from arguing with Paul, to having my brother screaming expletives down the phone. He must have been drunk. I'd never heard him like this before, and my already squirmy innards and thumping heart upped their tempo as his words started to filter through. I lifted my other hand up to massage the pounding that had started in my temple.

'Known what? Hang on, what are you talking about?'

'You knew Dad had cancer. Why the hell didn't you tell me?'

I felt the chill slap across my face. My eyes locked onto Paul's.

'Dad's got cancer?' I said, my voice small, remote.

My reaction must have registered through his rage, because the voice that responded was a little less accusatory. 'You didn't know?'

'No,' I replied, this time with a croak as my throat constricted. I felt the damp warmth as unexpected tears spilled down my cheek.

'Mum said she'd told you.' The accusation had returned.

'I think I would have remembered if she'd told me something like that, Stephen,' I said, my voice hoarsened by the effort of swallowing back sobs.

'Well, why would she say that if she hadn't told you?'

'I don't know why, she was probably upset,

but she was wrong.'

'Are you saying she was lying?' His voice was on the rise. Jesus, this was going from bad to worse. I felt Paul's hand rest on my leg, give it a gentle squeeze.

'No, I'm not saying she was lying. She must have just got confused, because she hasn't told me anything. What . . . ' I stuttered over the words. ' . . . What kind's he got?'

'How the hell should I know? I thought you could tell me.'

'Well, this is the first I've heard of it.'

'But Mum said she'd told you. You're a fucking liar, Sam.'

We were talking in circles, and he sounded way too upset to be listening to me anyway. I didn't know where to go with this. I just wanted it over. The only way I could think to get him off the phone probably wasn't the best, but I didn't care. I had to stop the yelling, I had to end the conversation.

'Look, Stephen,' I said, my tone as strong as his, 'I don't know anything, so I suggest instead of wasting time yelling at me, you ask Mum what's going on, because how the bloody hell would I know? I'm not psychic.'

I ended the call before he had the chance to reply, and then dropped the tainted phone into my bag on the floor of the car. I could feel the juddering spasms of the burgeoning sobs, and turned to look at Paul, his face grim and sober.

'Fuck.'

36

'Do you want me to come in?'

We were outside the flat. It was dark, cold, and the swirling mist of cloying drizzle just contributed further to my numbness. I stared out the car window, not yet ready to move, not quite capable of speech. I tried to breathe, but each exhalation lurched out of my body.

The enormity of what Stephen had said was filtering through the murk of my day and the persistent headache. Dad had cancer. My brain played a PowerPoint montage of Dad, the fit, strong, rugged southern farming man, morphing into Dad in the hospital bed last year, the heart monitor pads poking through the thatch of grey hair on his chest. Dad effortlessly tossing hay bales around like they were rugby balls, to Dad struggling with the stock gate last week. Dad, shirt off in the sun, muscles rippling, digging fence-post holes, to Dad last week looking lean, even thin, and, dare I think it, frail.

I had put it down to the fact he was getting older. I never imagined that super-heroes could get sick. With the rose-tinted eyes of love, I believed my dad could fend off freeze-rays, deflect bullets and was impervious to kryptonite.

Here he was proving to be very human after all, and the merest thought of a world without him in it opened a void of swirling nothingness, a vacuum that sucked out all warmth and light and left me quaking. My logical, calm self ceded to the hurt, devastated child, and I finally found the ability to speak.

'I don't want to be alone.'

37

Muscular arms enveloped me, his chest warm and strong against my back. Comfort took many forms. Was he asleep? I thought so. I could feel his breath against the back of my neck, it was slow, the tempo even. But he could have been like me, wide awake with his thoughts, pretending to be asleep so as not to disturb the other. My eyes were drawn to the crack of light from the hallway, peeping under the bedroom door. What was so very wrong with this? Why was I fighting it?

Paul, under his 'ladies' man' façade, was an old-fashioned kind of a gentleman. Of course, it was cleverly hidden behind a sharp wit and playful sense of humour, the same humour that had first attracted me — that and a seriously nice arse — but it was there all the same. He was the kind of man who was dedicated and who would protect, love, honour and cherish. So was that the problem? Deep down did I prefer the dangerous ones? The Han Solos? When I thought back to the men in my past, they seemed to fall into two distinct categories. There were the disasters: Cole had been one, but part of that was my fault. I was looking for comfort at the time, a bit like now, and look how all that ended. I could think of a couple of others whose system of values did not quite match mine, and those relationships had died a natural death after a brief but fun ride. Or I went for the steady Eddies. The Lockies, and perhaps now, the Pauls. I had been happy with Lockie, until he made clear his desire to have children; until he proposed. Lockie didn't understand my need to establish my career. At that point in my life I was still building it up, and the thought of children complicating things was unbearable. He took his misunderstanding and left. And now there was Paul. He too wanted something of me. Was he asking too much? It was too hard a question to answer, and not one to grapple with at one in the morning after a shit of a day. In many ways he reminded me of Dad, who was strong, determined and steady, especially in the light of my mother's temperament. He was the yin to her yang. Was Paul my yin? Thoughts of Dad flooded my mind again, and I started to replay the dreadful conversation I'd had with Stephen, which led to thinking about Dad with cancer, which led to thoughts of him dying, which led to my body shaking with the effort of hiding tears.

The arms drew me closer and Paul's concerned voice whispered in my ear: 'I'm sorry about your dad, Sam. I'm so sorry.'

38

I couldn't put this off any longer. Paul was in the shower, Maggs and Rudy had disappeared off to the farmers' market an hour ago. I had two extra strong cups of coffee on board and had made an attempt at food, although the gloopy remains of soggy Weet-Bix in the bowl in front of me clearly indicated where my appetite was at. It was 8.45 on a Saturday morning, which was a civilised kind of an hour, and it was as good a time as any.

I dialled the number before my nerve did a runner, and tried to think of an appropriate opening line while it rang. For once, I wouldn't have been upset if the answer machine kicked in. Alas, it didn't.

It wasn't the voice I expected.

'Hello?'

'Dad?'

'Sam.' I could hear the smile in his voice, and my resolve to be strong started to crumble.

'How are you?' It seemed such an inane question, given the circumstances, but it was all I could think of to say.

'Next best thing to dead, if you believe a word those quacks tell me.'

Dad could always be relied upon to make light of something. A strangled kind of laugh escaped me, and I heard his chuckle. It had his usual warmth, but I detected an edge that wasn't usually there.

'So, what Stephen said is true? It's cancer?' My voice broke completely with the last word, and I felt hot tears burn down my face.

'Ah, Pumpkin, don't cry,' he said. 'It's not all that bad.' It couldn't get much worse as far as I was concerned. 'You're as bad as your mother. You womenfolk turn on the waterworks at the drop of a hat.'

I couldn't remember my mother crying about anything, with the exception of once when she accidentally put the sewing machine needle through her fingernail, so I knew then and there the news wasn't good.

'What did they say?'

'Oh, they had some fandangle name for it, but basically I'm knackered. They said it's all around my organs so it's not something they can operate on.'

'Why didn't you say anything last week when I was down? You never mentioned you were sick.' Not even a whisper.

'I know, but we didn't want to worry you until we knew exactly what was going on, especially after you'd been hurt. It was supposed to be a rest for you, sweetheart, not a time to get you worrying about the old man.'

That was such a Dad thing to do. I couldn't imagine how Mum managed to keep it quiet though. My mind groped to find some logic to it all, the suddenness, it didn't seem right.

'You had all those tests last year and they didn't pick anything up. You had scans and everything. How can it be so far advanced?'

'It's just the way it is, Pumpkin. Nothing to be

done about it now.'

'But what about chemotherapy or radio-therapy?'

'They said there would be no benefits to it at this stage and it would just make me feel like crap. I couldn't be bothered with all that. What would be the point of feeling worse?'

'So they're just going to leave you?'

'Pretty much. Just treat the symptoms if it gets sore, and when it gets too much, I'll get your mum to take me down the back of the farm and put a bullet between me eyes, like the livestock, though I don't think she'll feed me to the dogs. Wouldn't want them to catch anything.' I couldn't help but laugh and he joined in. 'But seriously, Sam, I'll be okay. I think your mum's more upset about it than I am, but don't tell her I said that. You know how she likes everyone to think she's a scary ogre. We don't want to spoil that for her.'

He paused for a bit, but I couldn't find anything to say to fill the silence.

He gave a big sigh and suddenly sounded very tired. 'People with cancer can carry on for years, so I'm not going to waste my time worrying about it, and you shouldn't either.'

39

'What's with the limp?' Smithy asked when I walked into the squad room. I had seldom been so relieved to get back to work. After the events of the weekend I needed a murder enquiry-sized distraction from life, the universe and everything.

'Had an impromptu lesson in the laws of gravity,' I said. 'Mental note to self: Dodgy inner ear plus muddy bike track equals ouch.' I didn't mention that the burn from the graze and the ache from the bruise felt damn good.

'How many times do I have to tell you?' Smithy said in a mock-lecturing tone. 'Stay on the couch and you won't get hurt.'

'I know, I know. I'm a slow learner. You are truly the master.'

'I'm glad you realise the natural order of things. I didn't attain this fine level of manhood by unnecessary expenditure of energy. Why work to excess when 'enough' will do?' That was rich coming from a workaholic. He was as bad as my dad.

My cellphone rang. It rescued me from the flow-on effects of the dad thought. It wasn't someone already in my address book.

'Shephard.'

'Is that Samantha?' It was a woman's voice that I couldn't quite place.

'Yes?'

'Hi, it's Tamsin Paterson. I went out on the boat with you to retrieve the body the other day.' The mental image of it jumped into my head and my body gave a full-throttle shudder in response. How could I ever forget?

'Oh, hi Tamsin. Have you gone back to the boredom of drowning pigs' heads yet?'

Smithy gave me a querying look.

'Yes, thank God. After that mission, rotting pigs' heads seem tame. Pigs' heads good, people bad. Anyway, that's why I'm ringing. I've got a result for you on the amount of time the body was submerged. Seven days is what you're looking at.'

'Seven days. And how accurate is that? Plus or minus a day or two?'

'Oh, our research shows it's accurate to a day. But remember, our calculation relates to the time the body was submerged in water, so the victim could have been killed and dumped straight away, or the body could have been somewhere above water for a while — that I can't tell. But he was definitely in the water for seven days. Does that help?'

'Hugely, thanks.'

My mind flicked through what we knew about Clifford's last known whereabouts. The party at Aramoana had been nine days prior to the body being found. Clifford was alive on Sunday morning when he participated in a spot of looting. That left up to a day we needed to account for.

'Hey, good luck with your research. It's going to be damn useful for the police and I hope it

175

makes you world famous.'

'Thanks, and you're welcome. It would be nicer if it made me rich. Just call if there's anything else I can help with.'

It would hopefully be helping the prosecution in a court case. I wondered how new research like that stood up in the courts? I guessed there was only one way to find out.

'That sounded intriguing,' Smithy said.

'It was. That was Tamsin Paterson, the research student who went out with us on the boat to recover Clifford Stewart's body. According to her, our boy had been in the water for seven days. So, if you work backwards from when he was found on the Monday that means he was dumped in the sea on the Tuesday a week earlier. He was last seen on the Sunday morning, so there's one day unaccounted for.'

'Start with the party?'

'Yep.'

'Who shall we hassle first?'

'I bags ringing Jase. He'll tell me exactly whose party it was, or if he's too stoned to know, I can hassle Frog.'

'What makes you so sure Jase will cough up?' Smithy sounded sceptical.

'Because he's sick to death of seeing me.'

40

Hah, that had been easy. I'd phoned Jason and quietly asked if he'd like to tell me a few details over the phone, or if he'd prefer me to pop around for another visit, with a few of my colleagues. Of course, he'd sung like a canary. It had taken him a few moments to dredge up the name of the party's host from his addled brain, but when I finally got past the inevitable nickname — 'Chuck' (no points for guessing where that one originated from) — and even though he didn't know the guy's surname, the first name plus physical description was enough to nail it.

The answer surprised me, although it shouldn't have. Party boy was Felix Ford, he of the knockout punch.

Last time I'd clapped eyes on him he was in a courtroom, with his lawyer negotiating the case for diversion if he pleaded guilty.

It's a first-time offence, sir.

It was just the heat of the moment, sir.

He's very remorseful, sir.

Hasn't he suffered enough, sir?

Not in my book. I was still suffering tinnitus and dodgy balance, not to mention a lingering headache. And if he was that remorseful, why hadn't I received an apology? Even an embarrassed, half-hearted one would have been better than nothing. And I'd brought him back from the brink of death. I hadn't even had a thank-you for that. No, I wasn't feeling exactly charitable towards Felix Ford, so I'd been rather pleased when the judge said, 'Sorry buddy — beating the crap out of a police officer doesn't get you any favours', or words to that effect.

The long shot of all this was that I was pretty sure where to find him, because he was due back in court this morning. He'd decided to plead not guilty, seeing as he wasn't due any Brownie points for fessing up. So, consequently, he was going to waste a truckload of taxpayer dollars and try to pretend it never happened. Hah, justice.

I hopped on the phone to his lawyer, who, despite working for the enemy, was a formidable but fun kind of chick.

'Hi Meredith, Detective Constable Sam Shephard here.'

'Hi Sam, checking up on my client are you?'

'Yes and no. We need to ask him a few questions regarding another ongoing case and, seeing as he likes to have his lawyer present for everything, I thought I'd arrange a suitable time with you, seeing as you're busy with him this morning anyway.'

'Well, that's fine except for a couple of points.'

In my experience there were always a couple of points with a lawyer.

'Fire away.'

She laughed. 'You sound like you were expecting that.'

'You'd be disappointed if I wasn't.'

'True. Anyway, firstly, you can't do the

questioning, it will have to be someone else.'

'Can I be present, seeing as I'm on the team for this other enquiry?'

'No, I can't allow that. You'd intimidate my client.' They were the funniest words I'd heard in a long time. *I'd intimidate her client.* If anyone would and did feel intimidated, it would be me. Part of me was annoyed, part of me relieved.

'Okay, and the other point?'

'This one may be more challenging. He's done a no-show.'

'He's made an excuse, or just not turned up?'

'Not turned up for our pre-hearing meeting, and I can't get him on the phone. We're due in court in thirty-five minutes, so if he doesn't show before then, you guys will definitely have a valid reason to go looking for him.'

'Yeah, like a warrant.'

41

'So, what do we know about Felix Ford, other than the fact that he likes to take cheap shots at girls and hasn't turned up for court?' I asked, as Smithy and I headed back to the car.

We'd just paid a visit to Ford's address in Pine Hill Road, but it appeared that nobody was home, and hadn't been for a few days. There was an accumulation of junk mail in the letterbox, and from a peek through the kitchen window, a small accumulation of dishes on the bench. Judging from the newspapers still on the table, and the clothes hanging limp on the line, it looked as if he had left in a bit of a hurry. Other than the surface mess, the place was very well maintained. The lawn was mowed and the garden reasonably weed free, although admittedly the flowerbeds were barked for easy maintenance. Further to the easy-maintenance theme, they weren't strictly flowerbeds, but instead featured native tussocks and grasses, the good ole standby for those who like a more structural and textured look. Looking through all the other windows, we found that the house had three bedrooms: two with beds, although only one had a lived-in look, and one was set up with some gym equipment. That explained the power behind the punch. The lounge looked to have reasonable-quality furniture and what looked like a computer desk *sans* computer, but I couldn't quite see because of the angle I was looking from and my height, or lack of, even on tiptoes. It was in stark contrast to our victim's student hovel.

'We know he's a twenty-three-year-old who lives alone, no prior convictions, other than the one he'll get for 'taking cheap shots at girls'.' Smithy seemed to take pleasure in quoting me. 'He's an accountant by profession, works for MacLary Fergus, but he hasn't turned up there for two days.'

'Do you think that would give us enough to get a warrant to search the house? I saw what looked like a computer desk in the lounge, but couldn't tell if the computer was still there. I'm sure the tech guys would love to have a look at it if it was.'

'The fact that he's done a no-show for a court case, *and* conveniently disappeared when we started asking questions about Clifford Stewart and his connection to a certain party at Aramoana, should give sufficient cause.'

'Do you think Jason tipped him off?'

'That gormless wonder? No, it looks like Felix cleared out well before today. That circle of friends seem pretty good at keeping each other informed, so he probably figured out it was inevitable we'd get back to him sooner or later. You don't run unless you've got something major to hide.'

It made me feel more than a little uncomfortable to think that the man who assaulted me might have had something to do with Clifford Stewart turning up dead;

Clifford, who'd been beaten to death.

'Tiki tour to Aramoana next, then, while we're out and about?'

'Did you bring our picnic lunch?'

42

Last time I'd been out here it was hell in a handcart; today Aramoana was back to its tranquil best. The sunlight made the water glisten, seagulls wafted on the breeze and it was hard to imagine the chaos of a few weeks back. We cruised up to The Mole car park for a quick look before heading back to the settlement. The *Lauretia Express* was nowhere to be seen, having been refloated and berthed down the harbour at Port Chalmers, where they were getting her back to a state of seaworthiness. The beaches seemed pristine, all traces of flotsam gone, with only trumpet shells and swags of seaweed adorning the sand. The community clean-up day had been a success. The only tell-tale signs of the recent calamity were deep tyre ruts in the sand from the trucks needed to retrieve the beached containers, but they would disappear with the next storm. I could see two people and a projectile of fur I took to be a dog a few hundred metres down the spit. Other than that, the place seemed deserted.

I think that was what I loved about Aramoana: the solitude. It was also a place of contrasts. Like all seaside townships, it was at the whim of the Pacific weather. One moment all crystal and light, the next all moody and purple. Its murderous history would always wrap round it like a mantle, but it wore it with dignity, the weight adding to its sense of place, the memorial a poignant reminder of a black day.

The crib we pulled up to confirmed my suspicion about the party. Sheer proximity meant it had to be the same one that had kept me awake that notorious weekend — there couldn't be that many rip-snorter parties out here. Mum and Dad's friends, the Spillers, had a house one street over and about four doors down. I had the Spillers, or rather, the Spillers' dog Trixie, to thank for having been out at Aramoana that weekend in the first place. Trixie was a golden cocker spaniel, and, apart from being the canine equivalent of a dumb blonde, was lovely. Normally Bill and Nancy took her away with them when they took off for a weekend, but this time their hosts were allergic, so I got to doggiesit, by dint of being the only young and sort-of single person they knew. So in a roundabout kind of a way, I had Trixie to thank for a black eye and a hell of a hangover. I wouldn't hold it against her though.

According to the city council website this house was owned by Felix's parents, John and Alison Ford, who normally resided in Gore. I could understand why you'd want a beach bolthole if you had to live there, although surely something dinky in The Catlins would have been closer. Funny how everyone felt the need to desert Gore.

When Smithy had phoned them earlier, the Fords apparently hadn't heard from their son for several days. Well, that's what they said. They were well aware of his brush with the law and were very surprised he hadn't shown up for court. If it had been my parents, they'd have been lined up early in the back of the courtroom, Dad to support me, Mum to heckle.

Felix had free use of the crib on condition that he maintained it. I had to say he did a good job. Like his house in Pine Hill Road, the lawns were mown, the trees and shrubs tidy and there was a good supply of neatly stacked firewood in the lean-to. The crib was your Kiwi classic: small, creosoted-black weatherboard with white trim. A peek through the French doors into the living area showed a couple of old couches and armchairs complete with crocheted Peggy-square throws. A bookshelf had a reasonable collection of paperbacks and an obligatory pile of old *Reader's Digests*. The table looked vintage Formica, and the TV of a similar era. There were maps and pictures on the wall, including a flowery painting I sort of recognised, nick-nacks everywhere and an ugly horse statuette that looked bronze on the wooden, three-legged coffee table. It was the crib of my dreams.

'It all looks very tidy, don't you think?'

'The only evidence of a wild party, other than complaints from the neighbours, is a couple of large boxes of empties in that shed.' Smithy pointed to a matching black-and-white outbuilding next to the concrete water tank. Someone had painted a mural of a beach scene on the tank — sun umbrellas, kids in the surf, dog chasing a kite.

'The SOCOs might want to fingerprint those,' I said. At least that would be tangible evidence of who was at the party.'

'Good thinking, although the SOCOs might not agree.'

'They must have a new trainee to torment; that's the sort of job you guys would give me. Well, DI Johns would.' He was back from his course, but by the grace of God I'd managed to avoid him so far. I'd heard him yelling at some poor unfortunate, and that had been my cue to find something interesting to do downstairs. 'You know, this guy must be really fastidious, because I haven't seen a single cigarette butt anywhere on the grass, and I've never been to a party involving lots of beer that didn't have at least one or two people off for a puff.'

'And if Jason was there as well as our victim, there would have been an illegal puff or two as well, I'd have thought.'

'Could we get a warrant for this place attached to the other?' I asked. The living area was the only room we could see into; the others were obscured by seriously ugly net curtains.

'No need. The parents said they'd bring over the keys. I think they're a bit worried about the boy.'

43

We knocked on the door of a neighbouring house, but there was no reply so we shifted our attention to the house one over. This looked more promising, with a car in the driveway and a smudge of smoke emanating from the chimney. Again, this was your modest Kiwi crib. That was another of the things I loved about Aramoana: it hadn't been taken over by money-grubbing developers, so maintained that sleepy atmosphere and semi-deserted quality that was the whole point and pleasure of disappearing off to the beach. Dad would have loved it here.

The door swung open, and I was surprised when a familiar face greeted us along with a waft of what my chocolate-o-meter recognised as freshly baked cake.

'You're looking a bit better than last time I saw you,' the man with the walrus moustache said. He was dressed in short sleeves and I could see he had Popeye arms to go with the mo.

That wouldn't have been difficult. Last time he'd seen me I was KO'ed on the sand. 'Mr Gibbs, hello.' I reached up and brushed the hair from my cheek. Although the bruising had faded, there was still a vague numbness. 'I haven't had the chance to thank you for coming to my rescue the other week.'

He coughed, looking awkward. We all knew he'd been a little over the top in his defence of the constabulary, and he was going to suffer the consequences. 'Yeah, well, someone had to do something, didn't they?'

I almost apologised for the fact he was up for assault, but held my tongue. It wasn't appropriate, given the circumstances.

Before things got too uncomfortable Smithy got to the point. 'I'm sure you remember that weekend well,' he said. 'We're making enquiries about a party that was held a few doors over on the Saturday night.'

'Yes, I remember it very well.' Didn't we all. 'I rang noise control at two in the morning; we were getting sick of it by then. Not that it did any good. Selfish little shits. I mean, a party's a party — we all expect to put up with a bit of noise till midnight or so, that's only fair. But three a.m.?'

'Did you hear any fights or arguments?'

'Nah, just music and chatter. It was all very civilised in that respect.'

'So you weren't concerned about anyone's safety?'

'No, just the lack of sleep. Marie was here; she'll be able to tell you. I don't think she heard any fights.' He turned around and yelled down the hall. 'Marie? Love?' A homely-looking woman appeared. 'You know that party a few weeks back — the weekend when the ship ran aground — did you hear any fights?'

'No, just the usual noise and music. It all went on too long. Young people have no consideration. Iain had to ring noise control, but they didn't come.'

'Do you know Felix Ford? What can you tell

me about him?' Smithy asked.

Iain hesitated.

Smithy realised the source of his concern and clarified the line of questioning. 'It's to do with the party, not your case.'

'Oh, okay. Well, I used to think he seemed a nice young man until that weekend when he beat up the young lady here.'

'Did you normally see much of him?'

'Not really. The family only bought the crib a few years ago. Before that the Harrises were there for thirty years. He comes out some weekends, and I have to say, he keeps the place tidy.'

'Have you seen him recently?'

'No, not since . . . well, you know.' The muscles in his face tightened. The last time he saw him had long-lasting repercussions for everyone. 'What about you, love?' Iain said, turning to his wife.

'No, I haven't seen him either.' She looked pale and weary-worn. I supposed the impending court case was taking its toll on them both.

'So, do you know who came and tidied up after the party, then?'

'His parents did. I didn't think it would be appropriate to go and say hello, considering.' A wise move, I imagined. 'What's this about? It's obviously not about my case.'

'We're following up enquiries to do with the looting that occurred after the ship ran aground,' I said.

'Well, Missy, we both saw what young Felix was up to there, as well you know. There were a number of young men busy on the beach that morning. I'm sure a few would have been leftovers from the party.'

'There were a few residents, too, from what I recall.'

'Unfortunately, yes. Not everyone has a sense of decency, but some of us were trying to stop it.'

'And we do appreciate that.'

As we headed back to the car, Smithy said, 'Well, that didn't help with anything.'

'Should we even have been talking to him, considering the court case?' I asked.

'Dunedin's too small a place to get precious about conflict of interest and the like. For a supposedly big city, it has that small-town feature. Don't worry about it,' Smithy said. 'That cake smelt good though. Shit, I'm hungry.'

'No problem. Come with me. I know where we can cadge a cuppa.' It was time I said hi to the Spillers. 'Just watch out for the rabid guard dog.'

44

'Shephard?' The tone of the voice liquefied my innards.

'Yes, sir?'

'What the hell are you doing making enquiries into Felix Ford? And as for you, Malcolm Smith, you should bloody well know better, letting her within a mile of any of it. If his lawyer catches a whiff of this, she'll be milking police harassment and conflict-of-interest charges for all its worth.'

Despite the fact I'd talked to his lawyer and we'd come to an agreement, I still felt guilty. Smithy just looked frosty.

As Hurricane Arsehole stormed down the corridor, Smithy's voice stated what everyone was thinking: 'The bastard's back.'

45

'How did you get on with them?'

Smithy had just returned to the squad room from interviewing Felix's parents, John and Alison Ford. I'd caught a glimpse of them when they arrived, but had been careful to ensure I wasn't seen. John Ford resembled a younger version of my dad, which made me realise that, in a way, so did his son. We'd decided it was probably in everyone's best interests that I wasn't in on that interview. The Fords were well aware their beloved son had beaten the crap out of a female detective, and they also owed her one for the fact he was alive at all, but this wasn't the time or place for restorative justice and a group hug. We'd give any potential discomfort a big swerve. And DI Johns had made it abundantly clear I was not allowed within a mile of Felix Ford's case. I wasn't about to give him any ammunition for his anti-Sam regime.

'Felt sorry for them actually,' Smithy said as he dropped his bulk onto his chair. 'The missus looked on the verge of tears. If you think about it, it wasn't that long ago that their son was in hospital and they spent a few days thinking they'd lose him. Then he came right, and they had to deal with the little fact he'd assaulted an officer while trying to steal other people's goods. Now he hasn't shown up for court, so effectively they've lost him again.'

The words of Clifford Stewart's parents echoed in my ears: 'But he was a good boy, deep down, a really good boy.' Felix's parents were probably thinking the same thing and wondering where it had all gone wrong.

'It's been a bit of a roller-coaster ride for them,' I said. 'When did they last hear from him?'

'They talked on the phone on Friday, but they haven't been able to contact him since.'

'Did they say why they hadn't planned on coming up for the hearing today?' It seemed a bit odd to me that they hadn't intended to be there for their son, and that they only turned up now because he had gone AWOL.

'Yeah, I asked them about that. Apparently his sister just had her first baby — in Invercargill yesterday — so they were there to support her and meet their first grandchild.'

I watched Smithy's face closely for any sign of a tic or frown at the mention of babies. Nothing. Well, nothing physical. I thought I might have detected a tension, an undercurrent of something.

'They've being trying to get hold of him to tell him the good news, but he's not been at home, as we know, and isn't answering his cellphone.'

Christ, they'd had an up-and-down time. It was unfortunate their joy at being grandparents was overshadowed by the antics of their delinquent son.

'What did they say when you enquired about his relationship with Clifford Stewart?'

'They said the two of them were good friends,

back from school days, and that they couldn't imagine Felix ever doing Clifford any harm.' Well, he'd sure as hell harmed me. 'They were on the same cricket team and they were both involved in the young enterprise scheme for economics. They said Clifford was like part of the family when they were at school, and they both thought he was a lovely young man. Funny how everyone's on best behaviour for the friend's parents, eh? Although, they were worried about the influence he might have on their son after the drug conviction.'

'So they knew about that?'

'Yes, but they were quite emphatic that their Felix would never take drugs and couldn't possibly be involved with anything illegal like that.'

'Parents will always say that, though, won't they?'

46

Here we were, once again, winding our way along the narrow little road that clung to the edge of the harbour on the way out to Aramoana. As usual, Smithy was doing the driving. I had to admit, I was enjoying these little trips. The morning sun glinting off the water in the harbour, the myriad of little inlets nestled between the road and the railway line, the view across to the undulating hills of the peninsula, the little thrill I got every time I came around the bend on the road from Dunedin and onto George Street at Port Chalmers, and caught that first sight of the cranes, like strange mechanical giraffes guarding the docks. What was it about ports that awakened the gleeful child in me? Our trip was timed perfectly to see the arrival of a container ship. It had looked immense as it slid past Boiler Point, dwarfing the piles of containers and making the surrounding area look like a model whose craftsman had got the scale wrong. It had reminded me of the *Lauretta Express* stuck on The Mole, but without the unnatural tilt. She didn't quite cut the same spectacle berthed here at Port, minus her container load. I looked back and noticed a group of old boys with cameras. Like trainspotters, but with a far more picturesque hobby. Port Chalmers was a mecca for old sea dogs. The thought of sea dogs triggered more thoughts of

Dad, which then made me think about Paul. I sighed heavily. Why were the men in my life always so demanding?

The Fords didn't want to accompany us as we looked through their crib. Not that they knew I was going along for the ride. I'd questioned Smithy about whether he thought it was wise, considering the little lecture we'd received from the DI. Smithy's response had been, 'Fuck him.' The response had been so emphatic, I didn't bother arguing.

The Fords had told Smithy they'd stay on in town to track down their errant son, and of course they would accompany him back to the station if they found him. I believed they would. They had enough going on in their lives right now without adding aiding and abetting to the list. Tough love was exactly that, tough, and if more parents were prepared to dob in their children when they came up on the wrong side of the law, the country would be a better place.

I hoped they'd have more success than the CIB though. If you had a bit of cash on you, it was very easy to disappear in New Zealand, as long as you had enough sense to avoid leaving an electronic trail, by card or by cellphone. There were plenty of places to blend into. We didn't have the blanket big-brother-is-watching-you CCTV cameras keeping track of your every move like they did in Britain. If they tried that here there'd be public revolt and the civil-rights movement would be up in arms, and too right. Who needed that kind of claustrophobia? Only a few of Dunedin's trouble hotspots sported them:

Octagon and places on the university campus. We'd tried tracking Felix by his cellphone usage, but it must have been switched off — and his missed calls and messages from his parents, his workplace and his lawyer had not been downloaded. He clearly didn't want to be found.

We pulled up outside the crib, and I experienced another little pang as I admired its perfectness. That was on my 'one day' dream list, a little crib by the sea at Karitane or perhaps in The Catlins, near Curio Bay. It had been a quiet trip out, with Smithy lost in thought and driving on automatic pilot — not such a comfortable thing on that dreadful narrow road, but he got us there without a detour into the water.

'Smithy?' I said as we approached the French doors at the front. 'Someone's beaten us to it.' The windowpane at door-handle level had been smashed in. The pane had been knocked out entirely, so someone walking past on the road wouldn't have noticed unless they looked closely.

'Do you think they could still be in there?' I asked in a whisper.

'Police! Anybody in there!' Smithy yelled.

Silence.

'Nah,' he said.

I leaned over for a closer look. 'They can't have got in this way though, this is one of those old-fashioned locks that only operates with the key.'

Smithy pulled the key out of his pocket and dangled it in the air. And a big clunky key it was too. 'The door doesn't look forced,' he said, as he checked around the timber frame. 'Let's go and look at the back door first before we go in.'

It was hardly a surprise to see the same treatment had been given to the back door, although this was more obvious with a pane of frosted glass missing.

'This would have been point of entry,' Smithy said, with his head close to the gaping hole left by the burglar. 'This is a standard turn-the-handle-and-out-it-pops lock.' He pulled his head back and examined the window frame. 'Looks like they've been careful, too, no obvious traces of blood around the edges.'

'Not opportunists either. A smash-and-grabber wouldn't bother trying to hide the break-in.' I turned around and looked at the neighbouring houses. Bushes and trees obscured most of the windows that overlooked this property, so it was unlikely anyone had seen something. Also, it was midweek, which meant that all the weekenders would be toiling away at work in the city.

'Shall we?' I said. 'Or do we send in the SOCOs?'

'We're here now. Get the gloves.'

The crib was just as cute on the inside, enhanced with what looked like decades' worth of kitsch objects and nick-nacks no one wanted in their actual homes. I wondered how many lovely vases from Great-Aunt Betsy discreetly found their way to places like this. Whoever broke in here had been tidy about it. I looked around the lounge, trying to recall what I'd seen yesterday when I peeked through the window. It didn't smell too stuffy — the newly added ventilation system would have helped there — but it still had that distinctive old-house aroma I loved so much. They could bottle that and I'd be happy.

'TV and stereo are still here.'

'They're pretty old; no self-respecting burglar would touch anything less up-to-date than the latest flatscreen.'

'Microwave's still here, that's newer. They can't have been on an electronics hunt.'

'I don't know what they were looking for, then,' Smithy said, 'because as far as I can tell, nothing's moved or missing.'

There was something different about the lounge, though, I was sure of it, but I couldn't put my finger on it yet. I moved down the hallway to the rooms we couldn't peer into yesterday because of their awful net curtains. No crib of mine would ever have net curtains. Those things were a scourge on humanity. Privacy be damned; all they did was look butt ugly, collect dust and provide a fascinating climbing system for the cat.

There were two bedrooms down this end of the house. Both had double beds of dubious vintage and bedding with hand-me-down coverings from several home renovations ago. Recycle, recycle, recycle. Cribs were the perfect retirement home for all those replaced and surplus-to-requirements household items.

There was a bookcase in the end room that propped up a guitar and housed a library of reasonable-looking holiday reading — some Stephen Kings, Ian Rankins and some bloke-type books. It also held a collection of rocks, shells and tat. There was a tell-tale shiny line in the coating of dust on its surface.

'Smithy,' I called.

He wandered in to join me and I pointed to the bookcase.

'Something's been taken from here, check out the line in the dust. I'd guess a small picture of some kind.'

'Framed photo maybe — that would hold a five-by-seven, or slightly larger?'

'Who'd break into a house to nick a photo?'

'Could have been incriminating or could have been valuable, who knows? Gives us an idea of the sort of things to look out for now.'

I paid closer attention to the room, but there were no other signs in the dust. There was a double wardrobe on the other side of the bed. The Fords were lucky because most cribs I'd ever stayed in had zero storage. I took a look inside. There was an assortment of elderly coat hangers, only a few being used — by a towelling dressing gown, an above-the-knee wetsuit and a scraggy-looking coat. The shelf above the rail housed the entertainment — Monopoly, Scrabble, Battleships, Pictionary. It was the floor of the wardrobe that proved the most interesting, however. Cartons, larger cartons and spaces that a carton or two probably once occupied.

'Check this out,' I said. Smithy ambled over. 'There's a gap in the stacking there, and room for more in there. I wonder if they were filled yesterday? Do you think the burglar could have taken any?'

'Possibly could have. What's in the cartons?'

'I haven't looked, I didn't want to disturb it too much. I can reach the top one without moving anything.' I pulled up the flaps, which had been folded across each other, origami style. Seeing the contents, I laughed.

'What is it?' Smithy asked.

I stepped back so he could take a look. He laughed too.

'Little bugger had a bit of fun when the containers washed up, didn't he? Am I right in thinking those bits and pieces were on the list of goods missing from the insurance claims?'

'Certainly are,' I said. 'And I'd hazard a guess that these other ones were stolen too.'

They probably stockpiled the looted goods here until the heat died down, then planned to offload them. If this was Felix's room, his parents wouldn't go looking through the wardrobe unless they were after a board game, so storing it here would be a risk worth taking. Felix and Leo, and whoever else was with them, must have done several looting runs before I encountered Mr McFists on the beach. Trina said Leo had taken stuff, so it was likely some of his finds ended up here. A group effort perhaps?

'The parents cleaned up after the party, you'll have to ask them about the wardrobe.' I was sure they'd be thrilled to add stolen goods to the list of their son's misdemeanours.

It wasn't until we walked back through the lounge that it struck me what was missing in there compared to yesterday. The bookshelf find had clearly jogged my memory.

'There's a picture missing from in here; it was

201

on the wall over there, by the dining table. I remember seeing it; something with flowers. And there was a horse ornament on the coffee table.'

'Was it as ugly as the other things in here?' Smithy asked.

'Pretty much.'

47

No one in the neighbouring houses was home when we knocked on doors to enquire if they'd heard any breaking glass or seen any strange activities. Perhaps they'd gone back to their regular homes in Dunners; quite a few people did that, swapping between their Dunedin houses and Aramoana, and even cribs in Karitane or Waikouaiti, depending on work, the weather and whatever mood betook them. That would be a luxury I could learn to enjoy. Wasn't going to happen anytime soon, though, unless I found some rich sugar daddy to latch on to. Paul was only marginally more financial than I was, unless he was cleverly hiding something, so I was out of luck there, not that I wanted to latch.

'So what do you make of all this then?' I asked Smithy, when we were back in the ivory-and-brown granite tower that was Dunedin Central Police Station. Even though I'd been working here well over a year now, I still felt like I was walking into the Hilton or some other flash hotel whenever I crossed the threshold. The only difference was that the sleeping arrangements here were a little more basic than a five-star hotel.

'Huh?' He was still on another planet. Earth to Smithy. Come in, Smithy.

'Felix Ford doing a runner, his crib being broken into, the very same crib that hosted the party the weekend of the shipping accident, the same party that for a lot of people was the last live sighting of Clifford Stewart, deceased, and his flatmate Leo Walker, missing in action somewhere in Fiordland; the same crib that provided a nice hidey-hole for the stuff they looted from the containers on the beach. All connected? Or a couple of coincidences thrown in?'

I didn't do coincidences. There was always some connection, however tenuous, as far as I was concerned. Of course, that was just me. Most people I knew were perfectly happy with the idea of totally unrelated events colliding, and they slept well at night, so perhaps I should pare down my hyperactive sense of interconnectivity . . . . Nah. It was my job to be suspicious.

'He could have done it himself, broken in.'

'Who, Felix?' I said, amazed. 'Why? He had a key.'

'Needed some cash, went back to the bach' — Smithy's North Island roots were showing — 'to collect something to liquidate. Staged it as a break-in so as not to further disappoint Mummy and Daddy. I'd be a bit pissed off if he was my boy.'

'Nice theory, but it's a bit of a drive out to Aramoana and back, on a little road with not too many escape routes. Plus, he'd know damn well that the first thing the police would do when he didn't show for court was put a warrant out for his arrest, so there'd be a hunt on for his car.' People could be dumb, but I didn't think he'd be that dumb. Then again, he'd bashed a cop.

'True, but he could have borrowed someone else's car.'

'Why go to all that trouble? If he was short on cash he seems to have plenty of mates he could bludge a few bucks off. They'd probably hide him too. It would be a lot less risky than going back out to the crib and possibly getting caught in the act.'

'You'd just say you forgot your key and had to bust your way into the house.'

'Whose side are you on?' I asked.

'No one's side,' Smithy said with his equivalent of an eye roll. 'I just know you. You think that everything's related. In fact it could be complete chance. Some piece-of-shit burglar could very easily have decided to do over a few places at the beach. Give it a few days and, who knows, there may be other reports of breakins, especially with the weekend coming up and the townies heading out.'

'I suppose.' I stared out the window for a bit, looking down at people doing bizarre driving manoeuvres and dodging buses to get into the Farmers store car park.

'I wonder just how well Felix Ford knew Clifford Stewart.'

'In what respect? We know they were great mates, and at school together, everyone has said so.'

'I was just thinking about your comment about freeing up cash. If he knew where Clifford's marijuana patch was, he could go and pick some money. Actually no, he couldn't — wrong time of year — but what if he knew where Clifford stored it all? It wouldn't be hard to sell it on.' Money did grow on trees, well, bushes. My mind advanced a few steps down that 'let's suppose' route. 'Just throwing a few thoughts out there: Felix has done a runner from court, so maybe he was hiding something else? He could have coveted his mate's drug empire, bumped Clifford off, bundled him up in a wetsuit — he had some gear, did you see the short wetsuit in the wardrobe? — and dumped him out at sea.'

'Small problem with that theory,' Smithy said, left cheek drawing up into a smile.

'And that is?'

'All his party-going mates saw Clifford alive on the Sunday morning after the party, when they obviously went for a fun looting time down on the beach. Unless it's slipped your mind, young Felix then gave you a good doing over and ended up in hospital for a week. Bit hard for a comatose man to commit murder and stuff someone in a wetsuit, don't you think?'

'No need to be sarky,' I said. 'It was just a thought.'

And there I'd been accusing Smithy of being in la-la land with his mind off the job. I felt sickened and stupid. My own mind was occupied by way too many things at the moment. But having my life falling down around my ears was no excuse for such an unprofessional error. Thank Christ none of the others were in the room. You could imagine the flack if anyone else had heard that cock-up. Smithy must have noted my mortification.

'Hey, don't worry about it. We all make mistakes.'

48

'So, what do you know?' I asked Smithy.

I'd just whiled away my lunch break in the staff gym. After this morning's effort, I needed a little punishment. Running and cycling were my preferred choices for self-torture — pain was so much better in the great outdoors — but I supplemented them with some weight sessions at the gym. I might be little, but I would never be accused of being puny. In fact I would have bet I had a better power-to-weight ratio than any of the guys here, not that I'd challenge them on it. I'd hate to bruise their delicate egos.

'I know that when you leave the room everything happens,' he said.

That would be right, sometimes it seemed a lot went on behind my back. 'What do you mean?' I asked.

'Got word back from the SOCOs at the Fords' crib at Aramoana. The break-in was pretty clean. They found some prints, but my bet would be they belong to Felix and the family. And don't forget they had that big party, so there could be half of Dunedin's prints there. Oh, and speaking of SOCOs, they wanted to extend their warmest thanks to you for the suggestion of dusting all those beer bottles in the recycling bins.'

I felt a blush crawl up my face. Great, another fan club. I changed the subject. 'Did you let Felix's parents know about the break-in?' Smithy looked like he was enjoying my discomfort. I could do without being on the receiving end of his noxious mood.

'Yes. They weren't too happy to hear about it. I imagine they'd be in need of a liquid lunch after the time they'd had recently. But that's not the only piece of news that came in. There's something much more interesting.'

'And what would that be?'

'We now have a likely scene of crime for the murder of Clifford Stewart.' Wow, he was right. Things did happen when I left. Maybe I should take time out more often.

'Well, tell me then, don't leave me in suspense.'

'Felix Ford's house in Pine Hill.'

'Really?'

'Really.'

That was not what I expected to hear, and it did not bode well for Felix 'done-a-runner' Ford, even if he had a damn good alibi. 'But there weren't any obvious signs of a violent struggle or fight when we had our little recce. We could see into most places.'

'That's because there weren't any.'

'What do you mean?'

'It would appear that whoever did this cleaned up.'

'And that would be the same people or person who went to so much trouble to make his death look like a diving accident. That makes sense; they'd been thorough with the disposal of the body, so they'd be thorough about the scene of the crime. So in what part of the house was he attacked then?'

'There was trace evidence of blood on the lino in the entranceway, some on the carpet adjoining the lino, and on the walls. The carpet would have been the hardest to clean, but whoever it was, they made the effort.'

'Was there any sign of a break-in? The door wasn't forced,' I said.

'No, everything was secure.'

'So, either Clifford was already in the house and opened the door to whoever it was and let them in; or Clifford paid a visit to the house and was invited in, then assaulted in the entranceway. Either way, he must have known them.' My mind was whirring away.

'It's about now I'd like to have a little chat to Leo Walker,' Smithy said. 'DOC have contacted him, and he's on his way out, although the weather over there is foul, so it may take a while. I think he may have some explaining to do.'

'Yes, it sounds like it.' Despite his girlfriend's protestations. 'It's likely that one of Felix's mates has a key to his house — they might even use his gym equipment.' I thought about who else might have had access to the place. 'When Felix's parents found out he was in hospital, that week after the murder, surely they'd have been to his house to pick up some things to take to him, or even to stay while they were in town. It's not that far to the hospital from Pine Hill. It's likely they would have a key too, or that they would know where a spare was hidden.' Mum and Dad had a key to my place, just in case. I presumed most people's parents did. 'It would be useful to talk to them and see if they noticed anything unusual.'

'Yes, I'll get on to that. Reihana is out talking to the neighbours, to see if anyone can remember anything unusual. Which reminds me, I must get some chocolate.'

'Beaten you to it, but I did leave you a few bars. In the meantime, we have to try to figure out exactly how Clifford's murder connects back to Felix Ford, other than it happened at his house. And we have to ask ourselves if Felix did a runner because all leads were starting to point towards him,' I said, before Smithy chipped in with:

'Or was it just a coincidence?'

49

I seemed to be on the receiving end of a communication blackout from home. I was desperate to know what was going on with Dad, but neither of my parents rang me, and when I tried to ring them, it was inevitably Mum on the end of the phone. Any of my questions regarding Dad's health were deftly parried, and I was stung with the customary ripostes:

'You don't really care.

'You never come visit.

'Your antics will be the death of him.

'What are you doing with that nice young man?

'Are you going to marry him?

'Isn't it time you settled down and had a family like your brothers?

'Sheryl is lovely. Steve is so lucky to have a wife like that.

'At least they help us out.

'When are you going to get out of that job?'

These bouts always left me feeling tense and weary, and the most recent phone call had hurt more than most. I knew Mum was upset and stressed and worried, and lashing out at everyone, but all the same, as I put the receiver down the words that echoed around in my head were 'shame', 'hoped for more from you' and 'disappointment'. They burned as much as the tears.

50

'Sam, are you okay?' Maggie asked the moment I walked into the room, the concern in her voice perfectly proportional to how bad I must have looked. It was the disadvantage of having a transparent face, in all senses of the word.

'I've been pinged,' I said. 'Mum.'

Her face screwed into an 'ow' scowl. 'Was it bad?'

'I'd give it an eleven out of ten. She shoots to maim, not to kill.'

'That bad?'

'Worse.' What I needed was an escape from it all, and while the idea of a night out on the turps was appealing, it wasn't such a good scheme when I had to work in the morning. Mindless abandon for a few hours was a safer option. 'Do you want to see a movie tonight? I need to get out of the house for a bit and get my mother's voice out of my head.'

'What's on?'

'We'll have to check the newspaper, but I was thinking of something funny; nothing too dark. God knows I need a bit of a laugh.'

'Sounds great, but Rudy was going to swing by this evening. Do you want me to fob him off till another night?'

That would be ideal and I knew she would for me, but I couldn't ask that of Maggs. Mr Gorgeous-and-Foreign was far too lovely for me to have too many jealous pangs over him stealing my best friend, but I did allow myself the luxury of an inner groan.

'Drag him along too. I'm sure he's big enough and ugly enough to cope with two women on his arm.'

'He's French, it's what they do.'

★　★　★

The Octagon was something special by night. Sure, by day it had its charms, circled by architecture from the Gothic to the modern to the frivolous, and with Robbie Burns looking down, doing his best to look nonchalant under the garnish of seagull crap. But it was at night that it really came into its own: the spotlights throwing artistic shadows onto the ornate masonry of the Municipal Chambers and lighting up the foreboding steps and *frontis* of the glowering cathedral; the fairy lights glistening in the barren branches of the plane trees, making the avenue dance and seem alive in the midst of winter's leafless death.

The wildlife could be interesting too, although normally the worst of the drunken shenanigans didn't spill out from grand bar central until the wee hours. Judging by the commotion up ahead, though, a group had started early.

In a manner unfortunately common in this day and age, most people walked past pretending there wasn't really a group of four louts having a go at some poor individual. From this distance it looked like they were at the circling and shouting

214

abuse stage, but were leaning towards push and shove. The policewoman in me went on full alert, while the human in me thought, *This ain't right.* We were getting close enough now to hear snatches of conversation and the words 'cripple crap' and 'mutant' with f-word prefixes drifted on the breeze.

'Nice,' Rudy said as we neared. 'What will we do?'

One of the hoodie-wearing bodies shifted aside, and I got a glimpse of the target of their attentions. The hunched figure struck a chord of recognition.

'Shit, it's Spaz.'

'What? Do you know him?' Maggie asked.

'Yeah, I do. He's got cerebral palsy. Great of them to pick on the disabled guy. Really big and brave, aren't they? We've got to get him out of there.'

'You might have to pull out your police card and tell them to clear off.'

A quick scan around told me there weren't any other boys or girls in blue in the vicinity. If there had been it would never have got to this point. I looked at the situation and the amount of aggro involved and realised that one small female mufti trainee detective throwing her weight around was not going to be the smartest option.

'No,' Rudy said. 'That would not work. They are, how do you say, spoiling for a fight, yes?' Mr Frenchie had read the situation correctly; thuggery must be a universal language. I had a better idea, I hoped.

'Look, I'm going to go in there, and I need

you guys to follow my lead, okay? Just pretend you know him and play it by ear.' I took a big breath, smoothed down my Jacquard coat (thank God I'd gotten dressed up), strode forwards and called out, 'Hey, honey! There you are.' I walked between two of the thugs, straight up to a startled-looking Spaz, put my arms around his waist and kissed him squarely on the lips. 'We've been looking for you everywhere. We're going to be late.' I looked around at the faces of the gits, recognised two of them as station regulars; judging by their expressions, they recognised me. Which meant they recognised that I knew their parole conditions. 'Is there a problem here?'

Spaz clearly was not one to miss an opportunity because he dived in for another kiss before stuttering, 'No, no problem, sweetie.'

'Come on, you two, we'll be late; save that for later.' Maggie and Rudy, arm in arm, stepped in too, effectively blocking off the two idiots behind us.

I took the opportunity to grab Spaz by the arm and shuffle him off in the direction of the Rialto. The other two dip-shits stepped back and let us through, a look of incredulity on their faces. We must have been quite a sight — Mr and Mrs Tall and Gorgeous, arm in arm, Little Miss Me, looking pretty damn good, even if I did say so myself, and Spaz, on my arm, looking somewhat relieved, and dare I say it, smug.

As we got further down the street Spaz uttered with a lopsided grin, 'Thanks. Do you do rescue bonks too?'

'Don't push your luck, Sunshine.'

51

'Well, Sam. Suddenly you're everyone's best friend,' Smithy said, as I arrived in the office, ready for a fresh day of playing dodge-the-boss. 'That should make a nice change for you.'

Last night's Hollywood escape into Sandra Bullock-land had helped my mood somewhat, as had the amusing encounter with Spaz, but not enough for me to turn off my bullshit-o-meter. I looked at Smithy, trying to judge whether he was being genuine or making a bad attempt at irony. From my standpoint, he looked for real, although you could never quite be sure.

'Why?' I couldn't hide the suspicion in my voice. 'What's happened?'

'My, you are defensive this morning. Bearing in mind everything that's been going on in the Clifford Stewart case, and a few apparent . . . coincidences.' He winked at me as he said the c-word; quite an alarming sight on his craggy face. 'They sent out a sniffer dog to the beach house, on the off-chance, and the thing went berserk.'

'It found Clifford's plot, or store?' I asked. 'But we had a pretty good look around the house and didn't see anything obvious. And you couldn't even get underneath it. Did they fan out and do a search further into the neighbourhood or something?'

'Nope, this was better than that. You know

those cartons in the wardrobe — the ones we suspected came off the ship?'

'Something in those? Really?'

'Really. Quite sophisticated actually. Three cartons contained tins of paint, some an off-white neutral colour, nothing outstanding or eye-catching. The heroin was well-sealed and attached to the tin, down inside the paint.'

'So even if customs opened one up, they'd just see paint.'

Tricky. Would it have been picked up if it was x-rayed? Powder in paint? Paint was just powder suspended in thick goop, so maybe not. Or maybe they just got lucky. 'And the drug dog detected it despite the paint smell? That's incredible.'

'Actually, she scored two hits. The first time it was for a bag of weed hidden under the carpet in the wardrobe — someone's little beach-time supply. But then she kept going off, so they looked for something else.'

'There must be an amazing nose on that dog, because I know for a fact they've had some pretty bloody useless pooches over the years,' I said. I recalled one that could barely find his own food bowl before he was retired off to an amused and grateful family. Looked like this handler was on to a winner.

'Well you can imagine how proud Russ is about it; he's become insufferable. I'm guessing the two of them may get a few flights around the country when word gets out about her abilities.' Would they give a dog air points and a Koru Club membership?

'Heroin. Well, the plot thickens. I know we only had a cursory look at them, but from what I saw the tin labelling was professional; even the cartons were properly printed, not just affixed stickers. So someone rather organised I'd say — in both senses of the word — has gone to a lot of trouble to import a load of heroin. And I'm guessing they wouldn't go to that amount of trouble just for the three cartons we found in the wardrobe. There would have been a lot more in that shipment. Which means that, unless they were salvaged by our lot, there's probably a few more tins floating around out there.'

'The drug squad and customs are onto it. Thorne said they hadn't heard any rumours of a major delivery, so this import is a pretty tight operation, going from the twelve tins at the bach.'

'Crib,' I corrected.

'Bach, crib, whatever. Each four-litre tin had a hundred grams of heroin, so the twelve tins we found could have a street value up to three million bucks. Multiply that out by a few dozen more cartons, say, and that's a pretty tidy sum.'

'And a pretty good motive for murder?'

'One of the best.'

I thought about the timing here; it didn't quite stack up. 'According to the post-mortem, and the bacterial calculation, Clifford was killed two or three days after the ship stuck. Whoever this shipment belongs to, they would have had to react pretty quickly. And we're also assuming that Clifford had something to do with the drugs. They were found at Felix's crib, and just because they were good mates doesn't mean they were in on something together.'

'I'd have thought the fact his so-called mate has done a runner is a pretty good indication they were in on something together, and, gosh, now one of them is dead.' I could have done without Smithy's amateur theatrics attached to that last statement. 'Look, that ship foundering and the looting would have made the news all over the world. The sender would have known about it, and I'm pretty sure the recipient would be scrambling to make sure their delivery was safe. I bet once they discovered their shipment was one of those on the beach, they'd have been on to tracking it down pretty bloody fast,' he said.

'But how could they know so quickly? All of those containers, including the ones still on the ship, have been quarantined for weeks. Look how long it took you guys to even get started on sorting out inventories for the insurance claims. The murder happened too soon after the event for them to have known for sure their drug shipment was pilfered.'

'They might have driven out to Aramoana as soon as they heard, like half of Dunedin did. Then saw their container opened — they'd know the serial number. They might even have seen people carrying their stuff off, followed them and relieved them of their loads. Or Clifford somehow discovered the heroin in the paint; hell, he may have even been part of their organisation, saw an opportunity for some cash and tried to flog it off. Word gets around pretty quick. All he needed to do was try and sell it to the wrong people, then someone gave a whisper in someone else's ear and, hey presto, Clifford gets paid a little visit.' Smithy was just getting warmed up. This was the most animated I'd seen him for days. 'They want to know where the rest of it is, hence the beating the crap out of him for information.'

'But surely he wouldn't have held out for some drugs and a few bucks? Wouldn't he have just 'fessed up straight away? Why would they have to kill him?'

'Shit, Shep, you can be naïve sometimes. Don't underestimate these bastards. They probably had their fun, and they'd kill for less.'

52

'Detective Constable Shephard,' I answered. I was looking forward to the day I could drop the constable bit and just use the D title. God only knew I'd have earned it. There was a long pause on the phone, and I was just about to hang up, thinking it was some wrong-number loser, or someone put through to the wrong extension, when a distinctive swallowed voice said: 'Hello.'

No introduction was necessary. 'Hello, Spaz,' I said, still inwardly cringing at his nickname. I'd tried to call him by his given name, Cedric, the previous night, but he'd made it quite clear he would refuse to answer to it. He called it an abomination, which, given his speech difficulties, needed no further explanation.

'I need to see you,' he said. I could almost feel the effort required for him to hold a phone in position, let alone talk into it.

'Why? If you're looking for a date because of last night, don't even think it. I thought I'd made it pretty clear that was just to get you out of trouble.'

'No. It's about Felix. Nova. An hour.'

'Felix Ford?' I asked.

'What about Felix Ford?' a voice boomed from the doorway. My head spun around, I felt a lurch in my stomach. That man had a knack of appearing at exactly the wrong time. DI Johns looked like Thor, God of Thunder, on a bad day.

'I thought I had made it quite clear you were to stay away from anything to do with that young man. Do you need your bloody head read? How stupid can you be? What's so hard about following a simple instruction?' he said, his voice rising in volume with each word. I couldn't even look around the room for moral support; everyone else was off at lunch, so I stood there, phone in hand, gawping. 'Well?' he bellowed.

'It wasn't . . . I haven't . . . It isn't anything to do with the assault case, sir.'

'What then?'

'It's just someone downstairs getting back with some information for Smithy.' I figured my face was blushing enough, adding a blatant lie to the mix wouldn't be detectable amid the background glow. The shaking hands would be more difficult to explain. I lowered the phone to the desk.

'Well take a bloody number and get them to ring back. I don't want you so much as touching this. You are officially warned; you can expect the paperwork later.' He threw me one more lightning-bolt look, and then stormed off down the hallway.

I took a few deep breaths then raised the phone back to my ear. 'Hello, are you still there?'

All I could hear was a stream of staccato beeps.

53

'So, are you going to tell me what's going on?'

Curiosity had got the better of me, so I took a leap of faith and turned up at Nova within the hour. Told the boys in the office I was off to see the doctor about a gynaecological complaint; that way I knew there'd be no questions asked. Spaz had been waiting a while, judging by the empty coffee cup and cake crumbs. I was grateful he'd chosen the table down the back, by the door to the loo, and as far away from the windows looking out over The Octagon as possible. It would just be my luck for Dick Head Johns to decide to come here for a coffee and catch-up with the wife. I sat with my back to the corner, shoulder blades twitching.

'Felix,' he said, looking me in the eye with an intensity that made me wince.

'What about Felix?'

'He's in trouble.' Tell me something I didn't know.

'I am very well aware of that. He didn't show up for court, so there's a warrant out for his arrest. It looks a bit suspicious that he disappears just when his mate Clifford's body turns up, don't you think?'

'He needs your help.'

A snort escaped me before I could stop it. 'My help? You do realise I was the one on the receiving end of his fists? You know, the little

224

assault case he didn't turn up for — assaulting an officer. Me. See the scar? That pretty residual yellow is not jaundice, mate. Why on earth should I help him?' My voice must have got a little loud as the people at the next table turned to look.

He leaned forwards and shifted his gaze so it felt like it pierced right into my brain. 'Because you saved him. You saved me. You . . . ' he struggled to find the right word before falling back to the tried and true ' . . . save.' And gave a little shrug, like it was obvious.

Those three little statements sucked the air out of my sails, and in one of those 'clunk' moments in life, I realised he was absolutely right. If I thought about it, I'd spent my entire life trying to save things. Spiders and their webs from the scourge of Mum's vacuum cleaner, baby birds fallen from nests, half-dead hedgehogs, abandoned lambs, lame horses, and when it came to people, lame ducks. Sam Shephard, champion to the underdog. I was pragmatic about it. I was a farm girl after all and understood full well the circle of life and death — hell, I'd even killed dinner before today — but always, in the back of my mind, it was there. Policing was the perfect profession for someone like me: you got paid to save people, fix problems. And I knew in that moment, with absolute clarity, and against my better judgement, the same applied here.

I returned his gaze and sighed.

'What do you want me to do?'

54

My cover story worked perfectly as there were no awkward 'Where have you been?' questions when I got back to the office. No man on earth wanted the sacred feminine mystery shattered by an in-depth explanation of a woman's gynaecological problems. TMI — too much information. What I did walk back into, though, was an impromptu team meeting with DI Johns taking centre stage. He gave me a censuring look but there was no interrogation, so I guessed my colleagues had filled him in on my supposed whereabouts. The ruse had clearly worked too well as no one had bothered to text me about this little gathering; the courtesy would have been nice. Mind you, the mood here wasn't exactly warm. The crossed arms of the troops and the stare-em-down attitude of the boss made for an atmosphere you could carve. There must have been something in the water, because, impossible as it might seem, the DI had been even grumpier than usual this week. It was like he and Smithy were having a competition for most temperamental.

The whole crew for Operation Toroa — the bird name they'd given the Clifford Stewart case — was here, and also Billy Thorne from the drug squad and some bloke wearing a New Zealand Customs uniform. They must have received some new information, otherwise this would have been saved for the end-of-day briefing. I hoped I hadn't missed too much of it. Smithy would have to fill me in on any gaps later.

'As I was saying, now that DC Shephard has finally decided to join us' — he just couldn't resist, could he? — 'in light of news from Thorne's sources, we have to look at the real possibility that the discovery of the heroin shipment and the death of Clifford Stewart are related. As everyone is aware, Stewart had a prior conviction for possession for supply — for marijuana, not heroin; but it still shows a level of involvement in the industry. Drug squad is working with Customs to trace back the point of origin of the heroin shipment we've intercepted, and also its intended destination.'

I thought his use of the word 'intercepted' implied a level of prior knowledge on our part, instead of the reality behind the discovery — blind luck.

'ESR are also analysing the heroin to determine its origins. This looks like a large and organised operation that would have been planned well in advance. Their plans would have been thrown into total disarray by the shipwrecking and their stock being looted, and they'll go to any lengths to get it back.' He took a good stare at me before addressing Smithy. 'Malcolm, where does Felix Ford fit into this so far?'

Smithy remained where he was, propping up a wall. The uninterested expression that had occupied his face a moment earlier morphed into one of semi-attention. I could see the DI had also noticed Smithy's apparent lack of concern, and his scowl intensified.

'Ford, as you all know, is the custodian of the bach where the heroin was found yesterday,' Smithy said. 'We also have a warrant out for his arrest, after he failed to show at the court hearing for his assault against Detective Constable Shephard here.'

All eyes turned to me, and I dropped mine to the carpet. Despite the fact I'd been the victim, I could still feel the heat crawl up my face. Although, part of that might have had to do with what I'd just been up to and what I was planning for later this evening. Despite the unwanted attention, I could have kissed Smithy for the fact he hadn't put in the usual politically correct, crap word 'alleged' in front of the word 'assault', as we always had to do in public for the lawyers' benefit. I could vouch quite emphatically that it did happen.

'We also now know that Ford's Dunedin residence was the scene of Clifford Stewart's death, or the attack that caused it. Ford can't have been the assailant, as he was hospitalised at the time, but it is curious that both his residence and the property at Aramoana that he looked after have featured in this investigation. Felix Ford and Clifford Stewart were known to be good mates. They went to school together, and Stewart was at the party at the Fords' Aramoana bach the weekend of the shipping accident. We know a number of people from the party participated in the looting on the beach — and cartons, including those with the heroin inside, were found in storage at the bach. That Sunday is the last confirmed sighting of Stewart. He could have been back at his flat in Castle Street on the Monday, but the witness, his flatmate Jason Anderson, is uncertain and unreliable. It does fit in with the estimated time of death that he was still alive on the Monday — or for at least part of it — but he didn't turn up at work that day. His employers didn't pursue his absence, assuming he was ill. It should also be noted that Leo Walker, the other flatmate, has been absent since the Monday, too, apparently gone bush for DOC. He's since been contacted, and we're awaiting his extraction. It's not a large stretch of the imagination to think he might be involved in this somehow. Walker went to the same high school as Stewart and Ford, and, rather ironically, all three were in the same young enterprise group for their economics class. They manufactured and sold chocolate fudge.'

'Shephard,' DI Johns announced, causing us all to start.

'Sir?' My suspicion-o-meter immediately jumped into action at his acid tone of voice.

'You're off the case.'

'But, sir . . . ' I started to protest. Even my overdeveloped sense of doom when it came to the DI hadn't seen that one coming.

'But nothing. You're off. You aren't to have anything to do with it. There's too big a conflict of interest here. Felix Ford's lawyers would have a field day. As it is, they'll jump on the fact you went out to his crib at Aramoana, despite my making it very, very clear you could not be involved.'

I looked over at Smithy whose face mirrored my surprise, but also seethed with annoyance.

'No, I'm putting you on tidying up the thefts from the containers. Not the commercial ones — Billy's squad and Customs are tracking those for drug trafficking. I'm assigning you to the personal property of that family emigrating. Think of it as light duties while you fully recuperate.' There were times that man could look positively reptilian, and this was one of them. He oozed smug victory.

I recalled my earlier glee, feeling safe in the knowledge that it was not humanly possible for him to find a way to take me off this case when I was officer in charge of the body. I had underestimated him.

'And as for you, Malcolm Smith.' It would appear I was not his only prey today. Smithy was also in the firing line. 'You should have known better than to have taken her with you when you went out to the Aramoana crib. I had specifically said she was not to be involved, and you blatantly disregarded my order. What are you, bloody stupid?'

Silence fell on the room. It was all well and good the DI picking on an underling like me, but to pull up a senior detective, in front of the squad and visitors, was something else — let alone accusing him of being 'bloody stupid'. Oh, God. I'd seen the look on Smithy's face earlier. I hoped he had enough sense not to bite back. I looked over at him. He'd sucked in a big breath, but looked like he'd forgotten to let it go. But just when I thought the DI was nudging perilously close to crossing the line, he fair pole-vaulted across it.

'I don't know whether you're screwing her or what it is, but stop acting like she's your fucking girlfriend, or pet pony, and use your bloody brain. When this goes to court you're going to have a lot of explaining to do.'

'Jesus Christ.' I jumped to my feet and the words escaped my lips before I could stop them. Where was he getting this utter crap from? Smithy was the last person on earth I'd screw, actually second-to-last; the last would be the DI himself. I was about to vent my displeasure at his insinuation when a large and angry body torpedoed across the floor and grabbed the DI by the front of his shirt with both hands.

'How dare you make an accusation like that, you arrogant piece of shit? How fucking dare you.' Smithy's face twisted ugly with fury.

The DI wasn't about to take being man-handled kindly and punched his arms up through Smithy's, shrugging the other man off him and away, but in the process the action ripped the buttons from the top of his shirt.

He looked down at his front, then back at Smithy, the anger clear in his face. 'Well, if you're not fucking her, how do you explain breaking all the rules and behaving like a complete fuckwit? Huh? You're going to pay for this, Malcolm Smith, and the shirt. I should have got rid of you years ago, with your nasty, holier-than-thou, know-it-all attitude. I'll have your fucking badge.'

I looked desperately at the faces around me,

231

wasn't anyone going to say anything, do anything? The DI was way out of line, and had been disgusting and provocative, but everyone seemed to be stunned into inaction. I knew Smithy well enough to realise what the next step in this scenario was. It would involve fists, which wasn't going to be good for his career or for anyone involved on the receiving end. As his left arm reached out to resecure DI Johns by the neck, and as his right started to draw back, I jumped to my feet and launched myself into the space between them.

'Don't,' I yelled and yanked at Smithy's arm until it let go of the DI. 'Don't even think about it. Don't give him the excuse to fire you.'

I shoved Smithy as hard as I could, but he didn't budge an inch. I gave him another shove, and he reluctantly took a small step back. This time it was my turn for manhandling the DI. I poked my finger into his chest. 'You have no right making those kind of accusations, none at all, and I'll be writing a formal letter of complaint, mister. You do not talk to anyone like that, let alone in front of their colleagues.'

I removed my hand and then pointedly wiped it on my trousers before I redirected my attention to Smithy and started actively pushing him towards the door. Thank God, he took my cue and obliged, but with some belligerence and plenty of posturing on both his and the DI's behalf. Once out the door I grabbed him by the wrist and dragged him down the hall to the stairs.

'What the hell was that all about?' I asked,

after the heavy door had swung back into place. My voice echoed down the stairwell.

'He stepped way over the line,' Smithy said. His feet were stomping, his body twitching, muscles tensing like a petulant two-year-old ready to explode.

'Yes, he did, and he jumps over the line all the bloody time, but you've never gone off like that before.'

'You heard him. He accused me of fucking you. That was lower than low. That was fucking unforgivable.'

'Yes, and there was a room full of witnesses who would testify that he was being deliberately provocative, unreasonable and crude. But you came this close to punching him; this close to letting him get to you and fucking up your career, mate. Do you want him to sack you?' I leaned back against the handrail, looked at the agitated, seething mass of man in front of me, and lowered my tone. 'Look, this is about more than being dicked around by an arsehole, Smithy. You've been worse than a bear with a headache lately; you've been like a ticking time bomb. What's going on? Is this all about the baby? What's going on that is making you so damn upset?'

At the mention of the word 'baby', his eyes flared again, and he turned away, grabbing the rail, knuckles white with the tension. When he turned back there were tears in his eyes, but his chin jutted out and the look he gave me was not dissimilar to the one he had given DI Johns.

'Veronica doesn't want to have this baby. I

don't know what to think. I don't know what I'm supposed to feel.'

55

There were some days you wished you hadn't bothered coming into work, and this was rapidly turning into one. DI Johns had disappeared into his office, and Smithy had disappeared into the afternoon. Fat lot of good I was to him. I couldn't come up with a single word, consoling or otherwise. What did you say to a statement like that? Everyone else had buggered off out of the building, putting as much distance as they could between themselves and the grump fest, and who could blame them? I'd initially been glad to be the only one in the squad room and to be focusing my attention on something humdrum, as my new assignment now dictated. It was starting to wear thin though.

'Ah, Sam, there's a visitor for you.' Laurie from the reception desk poked her head around the corner of the door.

Any respite from the tedium of looking through files listing artefacts only people with money and questionable taste could afford was welcome. Of course my job was made all the more unpalatable by the knowledge everyone else was working on the good stuff, while I toiled at the bottom of the crap pile.

'Thanks. Who is it? Anyone I want to see?'

She laughed. 'Believe me, you'll want to see this one.'

That piqued my curiosity. I got out of my

chair and followed her down the hall. Even from a distance, and from the back view, my pulse shot up, and in a good way. Wide shoulders, narrow hips encased in what had to be a very expensive suit. Then he turned around.

'Jesus, I see what you mean,' I whispered.

'Oh, yeah.'

His eyes settled on me, and I felt a burning flush spread across my face. It went with the warm tingly feeling that had started in my belly and was heading south, and I was pretty sure the ole pupil dilation thing was happening too. I was experiencing a full-on Mills and Boon moment, and I had no idea who he was. All I knew was that he was hot, damn hot, in a nasty way — in a James-Bond-in-a-suit-oozing-sex kind of a way. My overwhelming urge was to drag him off somewhere private and shag his brains out. Instead I walked up to him, as calmly as I could for someone experiencing a blood rush to all sorts of private places, and reached out to shake his hand.

'Hi, I'm Detective Constable Sam Shephard. What can I do for you?'

The moment his skin touched mine it was like a circuit had closed and I could feel the flow of electrons whizzing through my body. He gave me a smile and a look that felt X-rated, and I visualised some of the things I could do for him, given half a chance.

'Detective Shephard. I'm Peter Trubridge. I believe you're working on the recovery of my collection and property from the container ship.' The cultured British accent only accentuated his

236

other attributes. He still grasped my hand in his warm grip. I secretly thanked DI Johns for the demotion.

My mind flicked through the details from the file on him and merged them with details from my adrenaline and oestrogen-fuelled observations. Married; bugger. Married with children; worse. Outrageous sexy flirt; definitely. Dangerous; absolutely. I reluctantly let go of his hand. My eyes flicked behind him to Laurie, who was making little fanning motions by her face and mouthing the word 'hot'.

'It's great to meet you, Peter. May I call you Peter?'

'Please.'

'I wasn't aware you'd arrived in Dunedin.'

'We flew in last night.' We, he said. Damn.

I'm sure it wasn't my imagination, but he was looking at me like I was the entrée, and he was famished. Wouldn't want to be his wife. I wondered if he made all women feel like that. Judging from the look on Laurie's face behind us, yes. But he did it without being slime-bally or leery, and left you feeling warm and in no doubt that you were desired. If all my encounters with Mr Peter Trubridge were going to be like this, I was going to end up being a twitching, incoherent, sexually frustrated mess.

Laurie was practically salivating on the reception counter, so I decided to put her out of her misery and take the eye-candy elsewhere. Although I briefly debated the dangers of putting myself in an enclosed room with him, I was prepared to risk it.

'Would you like to come down to one of the interview rooms, and we can discuss or progress.'

'That would be appreciated. After you.'

I walked ahead of him down the hallway, acutely aware of the swing of my hips and imagining his eyes noting the shape of my body. I led him into the nearest interview room, invited him to take a seat, then excused myself to retrieve the files.

Man alive. I took a moment to compose myself. I recalled an episode of The X-Files where the merest touch of the alien-cleverly-disguised-as-man rendered women helpless to his attentions and entrapped in hormone-overload. This is what it must have felt like for Scully, having to do her job and ignore the overwhelming need to jump his bones. I seemed to recall from the episode that all of the women he shagged ended up dead, though.

I don't think I'd ever experienced such a visceral reaction to a man before. Sure, I could appreciate the manliness of many, and Paul could certainly spin my wheels, but this was something else. Paul. I felt a little pang of guilt for my adulterous thoughts. I was supposedly with Paul, and I was in love with him, but why didn't he ever make me feel like this? What did it say about me that I could have such a reaction to a complete stranger?

56

'What am I doing, Maggs?'

She looked at me, realised I wasn't talking about eating a Modak's cinnamon pinwheel, and sought clarification. 'I'll need a little more context, Sam, before I can solve all your problems.'

I'd called an emergency summit after my encounter with Mr Oh-My-God. 'Paul,' I said.

'Oh,' she said, and set down her coffee. 'I thought you sorted that out the other night.'

'Well we did, sort of, but something else has got me thinking.'

'And I'm guessing that thinking is not a good thing?'

'Have you ever met someone who makes you ache inside, who, with just a look, melts you completely, takes your breath away, leaves you a gasping, boneless mess?'

'I take it we're not talking about Paul.'

'No.'

'Is there someone else? Have you been holding out on me?'

'No, there's no one else, and you know very well I can't keep anything from you. But, I met someone today who did just that. It was amazing. It was, to coin an American phrase, Fourth of July fireworks: enough chemistry to ignite the world; breathtaking, shocking.' I went all warm just thinking about it.

'And the object of your desire?'

'It doesn't matter really — unobtainable, married, way out of my league anyway. But still, it was there, and I felt it, and I've never felt like that with Paul.'

'Oh, so what we're really talking about here is the old lust versus love debate?'

'I guess so, although that's rather simplistic. This guy is amazing, he's got it all. But, like I said, he's unobtainable, even if he did flirt outrageously.'

'Oh, one of those.'

'One of what?'

'The sex-on-legs-and-he-knows-it variety.'

'Yes, but not in a yucky way.'

'They exist?'

'Believe me, if you met him you'd understand.'

'So, back to the point. Why has this affected how you feel about Paul?'

'Well, it's made me wonder where the fireworks are.'

'Honey, I share a flat with you. Believe me, there are fireworks.'

'Oops, sorry,' I said, feeling a little embarrassed. 'But that's not what I mean. I'm just thinking — worrying — that with Paul I've somehow settled for second best, shortchanged myself somehow, because it's easy, and he pursued me, and I haven't had to risk anything. I don't think he's the love of my life.'

Maggie took a slow sip of her coffee, probably corralling her thoughts before she told me off for being a stupid cow. 'Maybe he's not the love of your life.'

Not the response I had anticipated. 'So you agree with me?'

'Absolutely . . . ' she paused ' . . . not.' She looked at me, with a hint of sadness in her eyes, and I wondered what was coming. 'You know I love you, Sam, and I'm your biggest cheerleader, and that I'd tell you if you were making a mistake.'

'Yes?' My voice did that suspicious rise at the end.

'You're making a mistake.'

I flopped back into the black couch.

'You have this strange notion that romance is all about fireworks and shooting stars, grand gestures and vast true loves. But love is far more insidious than that; it is something that needs nurturing and care so it can flourish. It may start out as something small and seemingly bland, but, given a chance and the right environment, it will bloom.'

'Okay, enough of the botany lecture.' I almost added a comment about it being rich coming from someone with a not-too-flash track record — current relationship not-withstanding — but decided against being petty.

'I'm not finished yet. Paul is a fine, fine man, Sam. He adores you and is breaking all of his rules for you. It wasn't that long ago that you were telling me how he was the ladies' man, flirting with all and sundry. He was the one who was hot, and knew it, and knew how to push all the right buttons. He made the ladies swoon and got them all flustered, and got you flustered too, I might add. Hell, I think he's hot, and I'd have him. But, he's chosen you. You, Sam.'

'Yeah, but . . . '

'No buts. Do you think he's hot?'

'Well, yes.'

'Do you enjoy his company? Can you talk about anything?'

'Yes.'

'Is he your second-best friend?'

'Yes.' I smiled at Maggie's correct presumption.

'Does he rock in the sack?'

'Yes.'

'There you go; I fail to see the problem. Actually, I do see the problem: it's you, and your astronomically high and unreasonable expectations. This is not Hollywood, Sam, this is life, and in real life love takes time. And given time and a chance, yes, it can involve fire and sparks.' The earth mother was on a roll. 'But it is what you make of it, and bring to it. Paul is a gem, and when the universe throws you precious gems, you don't throw them back in its face. No, you say 'thank you very much' and you treasure them.'

I looked down at my hands, couldn't bring myself to look Maggs in the eye. She was probably right. And sure, it sounded good in theory, but this was real life, my screwed-up real life, and though my heart tended to agree with her, my brain was not quite so convinced.

57

This was like some clandestine moment from a D-grade movie. I was in the heart of the industrial area down by the docks, the dark punctuated only by the occasional feeble street light. Dunedin had turned it on — adding just the right amount of mist and drizzle to the miserable atmosphere and making me wonder when the Mafiosi and the machine guns would show up. I half expected to hear some mournful foghorn roll out. Instead all I could hear was the wet swish of cars on the nearby main road. *What the hell are you doing here?* I said to myself. I turned off the engine but remained in the car with that unusual confliction of feeling over-cooked by the heater, yet chilled to the core.

Was this worth my job? In a moment of sheer histrionics I wondered if this was worth my life?

'Don't be so bloody pathetic.' I got out of the car and felt the cold, moist air wrap around my body. A quick look up and down the street showed it to be deserted, so I crossed the road and began to check the numbers before finding the right one and pressing the buzzer. You'd never have known it was here if you weren't looking for it. I was pretty sure an apartment here wasn't strictly legal or zoned under the city's district plan.

'Yes?' An echoey voice enquired over the intercom.

'It's Sam Shephard,' I said into the box.

There was a burrlike buzz and a sharp click that jolted my frazzled nerves. I pushed open the door. So far, so Maxwell Smart. My eyes winced at the flood of light. I stepped through and then closed the door behind me with a clunk. It was a narrow little entranceway with a precipitous set of stairs extending up to a small landing. I climbed on up and knocked on the internal door. There was still time to back out of this. I could turn around, head straight back down those stairs and walk away, make one phone call and put it all right.

Before I had time to chicken out, though, the door opened inwards and there was Spaz, the guy who got me into this mess. He looked both relieved and apprehensive to see me.

'Thank you,' he said and gestured for me to enter.

I noted a small but comfortable-looking flat with minimalist furniture, but maximalist books. It must have been Spaz's home but I couldn't understand for the life of me why he'd opt to live up a flight of stairs when he struggled to even walk. Either he was incredibly astute, or he'd developed the skill of mind-reading, as he said, 'Good view and I like a challenge.'

I was about to make a rude comment back, when Felix Ford walked into the room from what I guessed was the bathroom, judging by the flushing noise that followed him. He spotted me and froze, poised as if he was ready to bolt. The sight of him got my fight-or-flight mechanism on full alert too. After my mini freak-out the last time I'd entered a flat alone, I'd taken the precaution of wearing my stab-proof vest under my coat. I loathed the thing, and it made breathing an effort, but considering the circumstances I could put up with squashed tits. We eyed each other warily, waiting to see who would speak first.

Spaz broke the impasse. 'You going to arrest him?' There was the million-dollar question. This could all be tidied up here and now if I did. Would they let me? Once again I wondered what the hell I was doing here.

'By rights I should. But no, I want to hear what he's got to say first.'

I walked over to an armchair and perched on the edge of the seat. Felix sat, also perched, on the armchair opposite me, a coffee table separating us. Spaz sat on the couch, like a ref in the middle.

I was about to say *Well get on with it then*, when Felix blurted out: 'I'm sorry.' He ran his hands through his hair. 'Jesus, I'm really sorry. I didn't mean to hit you like that.'

I felt a swell of shock and confusion rush through me. Finally, an apology, and, daft as it may seem, hearing him utter those simple words caused a fundamental shift in my mind and being. It washed away some of the apprehension at being here, and it washed away my inhibitions too.

'Well, you bloody well did,' I yelled. 'What were you thinking? What could possibly have possessed you to hit anyone, let alone a woman, let alone a police officer?' The flood of pent-up anger and hurt spilt out and I couldn't stop the tide. It drove me back to my feet and I couldn't stop the tears either. 'I did not deserve that. I was just doing my job, and you chose to disregard me; you chose to carry on plundering; you chose to bloody well knock me out. I was concussed and ill. God, I was ill. I had to have a week off work. I'm still giddy now, and I've got a permanent headache, and I had stitches. See here?' I pointed to my eyebrow. 'I'll always carry that scar and all because you couldn't keep your fucking fists to yourself. And over what? What, I ask you? A box of stolen goods? Do you realise you've completely screwed your life and your future over a crap carton of . . . of . . . crap?' I stood there, pointing at him, gasping with the force of the tirade.

He sat there looking like a stunned mullet. There was a charged silence.

'That went well.' I turned and looked at Spaz with his deadpan face, and was amazed to hear a laugh burst out of me, then another. It was pretty ridiculous wasn't it? Me breaking all the rules — being in contact, unbeknown to my superiors, with a fugitive who was on assault charges against me and a suspect in a murder case. Here I was giving him a good bollocking. My mother would have been proud. Well, she'd have been proud of the telling-off bit, but not the skulking around behind everyone's back.

I wiped away the tears, sat down, and this time slouched back into the chair.

'Yeah, well, I am sorry — truly — to you, and also for the way the whole business has screwed up my life. If ever someone wished they could turn back the clock, that would be me.' Felix sat back into his chair too and leaned against the armrest, his head in his hand and a look of complete misery on his face. I felt a momentary twinge of pity for him. 'I should never have done that — any of it — because look what happened: I nearly got myself killed; I did get my best friend killed; and I hope I haven't got the other one killed, and now I think the bastards are out to get me.'

'Wait a moment,' I said, not quite believing what I was hearing. We'd had our suspicions, but I never thought I'd be here for a confession. 'What do you mean you got your best friend killed? What have you got to do with Clifford's death?'

He sat up straight, sighed and looked me in the eye. 'Everything, I think.'

58

'Sorry? You'll need to explain yourself. Start from the beginning.'

Felix took a few moments to collect his thoughts. 'Well, you know how the ship ended up on the rocks, and the containers washed up on the beach? Well, a few of us thought we might retrieve a few things from them. You know, find something interesting, maybe sell it, make a few dollars.'

'Steal things you mean?' I asked.

'No, not stealing, it was finders keepers, salvage rights.'

'I'd challenge you to find a judge who'd agree with you there.'

Spaz cleared his throat. He was right, it wasn't the time to nit-pick.

'Sorry,' I said. 'Go on.'

'Well, we got quite a few boxes and took them back to the crib. My folks have a place at Aramoana and we'd had a party there the night before. A few of us had stayed over rather than go all the way back to Dunners. That's why we were out there in the first place.'

'I'm well aware of that bit,' I said. 'Your bloody party kept me up half the night.'

He looked surprised.

'Yeah, I'd been staying out at Aramoana too. Why do you think I was on the beach in civvies at that ungodly hour? The police recovered the

248

rest of the boxes you had hidden in your wardrobe, by the way, and a little stash of something else that shouldn't have been there.'

'Shit, did they?' He knew exactly what I was talking about and assumed the weary look of someone wondering what the hell else can go wrong. Unfortunately for him, the answer to that little thought was 'plenty'.

'So what else happened that morning, Felix?'

'Well, we did a few runs down to the beach, then Leo and Clifford decided to take some boxes into town early, before the police blocked off the road. They were going to take them to their flat. We thought we'd leave the rest at the crib for a bit, until all the fuss died down.'

'Sorry, I thought you just said there was nothing wrong with taking it. Why the secrecy then? Still finders keepers, huh?' I asked.

Spaz gave the coffee table a kick. Admonished again. When I looked at him he was giving me an 'ease up, lady' stare.

I rolled my eyes. 'So what was in the boxes?'

'There wasn't anything really valuable: some nick-nacks, ornaments, pictures, some old books, stuff from a house by the looks, and lots of paint.'

Paint, of the super-duper variety, with a kick. I held my tongue, and waited to see what he would divulge about it.

'We thought we might get a bit of money for some of the stuff, so Leo and Clifford took several boxes with them to list, and we were going to get rid of some of the stuff with a friend in the second-hand business.'

'List?'

'On Free-Market.' I raised my eyebrows. The internet trading website: online auctions, receiver's heaven.

'What day was this?'

'Well, we had planned to meet up at my house in town and do all the online things that Sunday afternoon, but then I went back to the beach to try to score some more goods, and then, well, you know what happened.'

My hand reached up and brushed across my eyebrow. I sure as hell knew what happened. I noticed his hand had automatic-piloted up to his head too.

'So, what do you think any of this has to do with Clifford's death?'

'Well, I didn't hear from either of them at all after that day. Not even when I was in hospital, which was weird because they were mates, you know? I can understand them taking a few days to find out, 'cos I was the last one left at the crib, and it took the police a day or so to get hold of my parents. Still, I thought they'd have visited me. But not even a text. When I got out, I rang up their flatmate, Jase. He's the most useless prick you've ever met.' I could second that. 'And he hadn't seen them for ages either. He didn't seem too worried about it, but I thought it was odd. It wasn't like them.'

'I've met Jase. He seemed too permanently stoned to worry about anything.'

'Yeah, you got that right. When I asked, he remembered them bringing some boxes home, but said they'd taken them away again.'

'Why would they do that?' I asked.

'You've seen their flat, right?'

'The words 'infested rat hole' jump to mind.'

He smiled at my understatement. 'We had this little business going, right, with Free-Market. Most stuff we sold we sent off in the post, but sometimes local people want to pick up rather than pay freight. We couldn't have them pick things up from that flat, they'd get suspicious, so we'd always do any pick-ups from my place.'

That made sense. By my recollection, Felix's house was well maintained and in a reputable suburb. It wasn't likely to make a would-be purchaser take one look and run a mile, unlike the other hovel, which would have had the buyer reporting the listing immediately. It did beg a question though.

'Can you tell me why on earth they'd choose to live in that rubbish-tip hole in studentville and with a moron like Jase?'

He shrugged his shoulders. 'Rent was cheap. They both did a few papers at uni and poly and . . . ' he hesitated for a moment ' . . . it was close to Clifford's other business.'

It didn't take a rocket scientist to guess what the other business was. Felix, it would seem, was not going to hold anything back. He must have decided I was his best route to salvation.

'And that would be Clifford's little pot sideline?' Pot, grass, electric puha, marijuana — call it what you wanted, it was illegal.

'Yeah. Students are good customers, and Jase had a number of friends in need, shall we say.'

Ah, networking. I was sure their Otago Boys'

High School economics teacher would have been so proud. It was young enterprise at its best. And we all knew how much the NORML activists liked campaigning to legalise marijuana on campus, with their regular light-ups. It was the perfect place to blend in with your customer base. But it was all rather small-time on the scale of criminal activities.

'You still haven't said why you think this has anything to do with Clifford's murder and Leo's disappearance.' I decided not to let him know right now that Leo was safe and sound. The man was on a roll, and I wasn't going to slow the flow.

'It has to. I can't think of any other explanation for it. We never had any problems until we found this stuff. Life was sweet, and then suddenly, wham, all this shit happens. And there's another thing: when I got out of hospital I found my flat had been broken into.'

'Did you report it to the police?' I asked.

'Well, no, I didn't.'

'Why not? Surely your parents would have noticed? They came over, didn't they, helped you get settled back in? Wouldn't they have reported it?'

'The thing is, it wasn't broken into as such — no broken windows, jimmied locks or anything like that — but there was no sign of any of those boxes, and my computer was gone. The guys wouldn't have taken it — it was a proper PC, not a laptop, and they had their own. I didn't actually tell Mum and Dad, because they were worried enough already. I couldn't report the missing boxes, because technically I'd stolen them.' Oh, he admitted it was theft now. 'And I didn't report the computer because, well, you know, the police weren't very fond of me, and I didn't want to draw any more attention to myself.'

That was probably wise, all things considered. 'Did you notice anything else about the flat, anything at all?'

'A few things seemed to have been moved slightly, and it smelt a bit odd.'

'How odd?'

'I don't know how to describe it; different.'

It was time to divulge some other information he wasn't aware of. 'What if I was to tell you that forensics have decided your Pine Hill Road house was the most likely scene of Clifford's death.'

'No way, that's not possible. Jesus!' He stood up and started pacing backwards and forwards across the room, his hands clutching at his hair.

'There were traces of blood spatter evidence. Someone had gone out of their way to clean up, so these traces weren't visible to the naked eye, but we've got equipment that can point them out. It's probably what forensics could smell, though, that alerted them to the right spot, cleaning products or damp carpet. It looks like he was beaten to death in your hallway entrance.'

'Surely you can't think it was me?' he asked, almost pleading.

'No, of course not. You were unconscious in hospital — you've got what everyone considers the most rock-solid alibi in history. What I do need to know is whether you can think of anyone

253

who would do this to him, and to be straightforward about it. Do you think Leo could have done this to him?'

I'd thought he looked shocked before. 'Leo? No. No way, man. They were good mates. No bloody way.'

I looked at him, could see how uncomfortable he was under my gaze. He turned away and went back to pacing the room.

'You want to know what I really think, or what really worries me?' he asked.

'Please, fire away.'

'I'm thinking, if Leo has disappeared, what if he's been knocked off too, and his body just hasn't been found yet? What if he's dead too?' When I looked at his distraught face, I had to put him out of that little piece of misery. He hadn't finished yet, though. 'And, I'm wondering if I'm next.' I looked up, surprised.

'Is that what your disappearing is about, and not showing up for court? You're worried about your safety?'

'Well, yeah, that's part of it, and I just freaked out, you know? I've never been in this much trouble, ever. And it all just seemed to be getting worse and worse. I didn't know what to do and I panicked.' All of a sudden he seemed very young and very vulnerable, and it was hard to equate the guy who saw fit to punch me one over some loot with the strung-out, nervous wreck before me now. I tried not to feel sorry for him.

'The justice system has to catch up with you eventually, Felix. You know that, don't you?' He nodded reluctantly. 'And if you're truly worried

254

about your safety, if you hand yourself in, we can take measures to protect you.'

'I can't. I can't do that. Not right now. Not yet.' He turned his head away, but not before I saw the tears in his eyes.

'And you don't need to worry yourself about Leo,' I said. 'We know where he is. He's alive and well and quite safe.'

The pacing stopped and he finally slouched back into the couch. 'But . . . '

'He'd been bush for DOC and has only just made his way out. He's probably being interviewed as we speak. The thing is, we do have to look seriously at his involvement here.' I was pretty sure, in light of the heroin discovery, which I wasn't about to share, and the testimony from Trina, that Leo was not in the picture, but I wanted to hear it from Felix.

'I can tell you, categorically, he would never harm Clifford. They were like brothers, you know?' He added a quiet postscript: 'We all were.' I was tending to believe him.

'So, you really think the stolen stuff from the ship is what this is all about? That it all started with that?' I asked.

'Yeah, it's the only thing that makes any sense.' If only he knew.

'Did Clifford or Leo have a key to your place?'

'Yeah, so they would have let themselves in. They probably did the Free-Market listings there, started without me. My digital camera was missing too, but I presumed they had borrowed it, to photograph the other stuff. Anyway, doing the listings at my place was better than at their flat, because Jase could be a nosey bastard, and really annoying, so it wouldn't surprise me if they got sick of him and shifted camp.'

'Do you remember the Free-Market username and password you guys use?'

'Why?' This was not the time to be coy.

'We can look online here and see exactly what they listed and if anyone placed a bid. Or have you already checked that out with Spaz?'

'No, I haven't.' He looked a little embarrassed.

'What's the problem, then?'

'Our username is 'cathnadam'.'

'Who are Cath and Adam?'

'No one. We just decided to choose a name that looked a bit mumsy-dadsy, you know? A couple selling off their junk, so it would look more legit.'

'As opposed to 'ripoffartists!' or something like that?'

'Yeah.' He laughed. It sounded thin and strained. 'The problem is, though, I can't remember the password. I've tried to think of it, but nothing. There are a few things I can't remember since I was out, you know. My computer at home was set up to log on automatically each time, so I didn't have to think about the password, and now that's gone too.'

'What about your email? There would be a record of sold items on there.' Every time I'd bought something from Free-Market, my inbox had been inundated with 'you have won an auction *blah, blah*' or payment instructions.

'I can't remember that password either.'

'You could contact your provider and get it, or

a replacement password.'

'Well I would, but I'm in hiding, remember?'

Good point.

'I can help.' We hadn't heard from Spaz for so long it was a shock to hear him speak.

'How?' I asked.

'Free-Market password.'

'You know that?' Felix asked. 'How do you know that?'

'Watched you. Memorised it. We can check it out.' He gestured over to his little corner of technology, which looked pretty highend.

From the outside people might have thought he looked harmless, but they'd have underestimated the man. On the inside he was as cunning as a shithouse rat.

I decided I was really starting to like Spaz.

59

There was that familiar frisson in the air at work that told me DI Johns was still in his little mood after yesterday's events. When the big guys tiptoed around him, you knew it was bad. I was keeping as low a profile as possible. It was easy to hide behind a computer when you were my size.

My brief was to go through the insurance claim for the Trubridge family. I was surprised I was even allowed near it, seeing as it was distantly connected to the Clifford Stewart case, but courtesy of being short-staffed due to winter coughs and colds, and DI Johns' personal need to let me know my station in life, it was my privilege. The task was made somewhat easier by the fact Peter Trubridge, as well as being a lust bucket, was a hard-core collector, and had photos and provenance for the more expensive or significant items in his collection. Fortunately for him, he was also vaguely paranoid and had taken the precaution of splitting his collection in half, so one container was on the *Lauretta Express*, and the other on a different ship due in later this week. Well, it was part paranoia, and partly because they had a hell of a lot of stuff.

The superstars of his collection were air-freighted separately again; you know, the little Picasso, the Rembrandt, and something revolting and pickled by Damien Hirst. Don't know how they would have managed to get that past biosecurity. Imagine if that had smashed and ended up on Aramoana beach. Urgh. They say art's subjective, but there wasn't any way in hell I'd have a semi-dissected and smelly looking fish on my lounge wall. Fish were for eating, preferably battered, with tartare sauce and a lot of chips.

After a few hours staring at a godzillion auction pictures, I'd stumbled across several items that had once been safely ensconced in a shipping container. Fortunately the Free-Market guys were usually very helpful; when your reputation rode on being a site for the legal and proper trading of goods, it paid to co-operate with the police. You didn't want the police ticking the box with the sad face and the poor rating, so, consequently, they had a dedicated liaison person just for us.

I particularly liked the creative writing accompanying some of the sale notices: 'We're shifting off-shore, everything must go,' or, 'Selling on behalf of my grandmother who is going into a rest home,' or, my personal favourite, 'Estate items'. If only they knew that someone was dead and that some items put up for sale were the reason for it. Some of the auctions had closed, some were current, all were illegal.

Being the paranoid type, I made sure I buried any dead certs from the cathnadam consortium among general searched or Googled items, just in case anyone decided to check on what I'd been up to. My butt seemed to be a regular target, so I thought it best to keep it covered.

As far as I could tell, Shark-face Super Grump had now left the building and it was just Smithy, Reihana and me holding the fort. It was time to show my hand. I thought I'd go for the wide-eyed and innocent approach; I was sure they'd fall for it. Then I gave myself a sudden reality check. How did it get to the point where I was wilfully hiding the whereabouts of a criminal and filtering only relevant information to my colleagues? This could very well cost me my job. But in my heart of hearts, I knew I was doing the right thing. It passed the acid test for me, which was what Dad would do if he was in this situation. He would have looked out for the little guy too. The sharp realisation that one day soon I would not have Dad's wisdom and reassurance to draw on hit like a blow to the chest. I took a deep breath, and put my fifth-form acting skills to the test.

'Hey, Smithy?'

'Yeah?' You'd never know there had been a dust-up yesterday. If he was going to pretend everything was okay, so could I.

'You know how DI Johns said I'm not supposed to have anything to do with the Clifford Stewart or Felix Ford cases?'

'Yes?' The desired level of suspicion was in his voice.

'Well, I've found something here that may be of interest to you.'

As anticipated, Smithy and Reihana came and peered over my shoulder at the computer screen.

'I've been trawling through Free-Market for

these insurance claims, and I came across a few items that look very familiar.'

I flicked up the appropriate page and listened with satisfaction as the expected gasps came from behind my shoulder.

'These listings for the paint appeared the day of the ship grounding, so I'm guessing the cans were looted and the offenders wanted to flick them off as soon as possible. Do you want me to check with our Free-Market liaison person to see who the vendor was and the purchaser? It looks like they bought it on the 'buy now' option.'

'No, no, we'll do that,' Smithy said. 'Even though you were just doing what he asked, I don't think the boss would appreciate you finding this, so how about we keep that aspect to ourselves?'

Yeah, like I needed to be told. 'Suits me fine. I've got enough to do and I don't need any more crap from him.' So far, so good.

I dropped the next little pearler. 'There's more,' I said, trying not to smile as the infomercial catch phrase 'but wait, there's more' flicked through my brain and the image of a set of steak knives floated around. 'I found it because I was following this listing.' I clicked up the auction page for a small bronze horse sculpture. I tapped the provenance folder page for the object. 'Firstly, I'm sure this is one of the things that was missing from the Aramoana crib after the break-in. If you look at the provenance it was one of a matching pair, and the two are worth a shitload of money. From the date of the listing, this isn't the one taken in the break-in, so it must be the other one, stolen from the beach. I clicked the 'see my other listings' link and found quite an array of goods from the Trubridges' shipping container, and also — *ta-dah* — lots more paint. The vendor's names are 'cathnadam'. They're address-verified, so it might be time for you guys to pay them a little visit when Free-Market coughs up the address.'

'Great job, Sam.' I enjoyed the praise from Smithy, even if it was ill-gotten. 'Email me through the links and I'll get onto it right away.'

Somehow I didn't think 'Cath and Adam' would be setting out the tea and bikkies.

60

It's amazing how you can seem absorbed in your work and still manage to listen in on a telephone conversation. Most of the time I hated being in an open-plan office. They are so incredibly noisy, and they would have to be the most unproductive places on the planet; in fact, scientific tests had proved it. Between the phones ringing, people talking and continuous comings and goings, it was a wonder any work got done. And then there was the whole computer thing or, more specifically, the typing thing. I had learned how to tune out most noise, but Reihana's typing had been the hardest to overcome. I had never heard anyone tap a computer keyboard so hard. It was more a thump than a tap. Each key strike seemed to take to the air, then explode, the force emanating out like little shock waves. I could swear it shook the desks. And of course it was slow. He was of the two-finger-and-no-long-term-memory-of-where-the-keys-were school of typing, so not only did I have to endure the noise, I had to live with the knowledge that whatever he was doing was going to take him three times longer than it would a normal human being. There had been numerous occasions where I couldn't take it anymore and I'd wanted to rip the keyboard out of its USB port and ram it down Reihana's throat. On those occasions I'd taken myself off for a little walk to prevent bloodshed on his part or hysterical screaming and a subsequent appointment with the station shrink on mine. So far I'd avoided having to kill him, but only because I didn't want to have to explain to his wife that their kids were fatherless because he couldn't type. Nowadays my response had simmered down to teeth grinding. But today I could put all the teeth gnashing aside because claustrophobic close proximity had its uses.

After my little cathnadam revelation this morning, there had been numerous phone calls from the other desks, and the general level of excitement had been climbing. It reached its climax when Smithy set down the phone with so much force I feared for its life.

'Sam, it's official, I think I love you.'

An interesting choice of words, after yesterday, I thought. I raised an eyebrow and gave him a look. 'That's nice, Smithy, but I think Veronica would have something to say about that. Not to mention Paul.' He gave a 'yeah, yeah' wave as he came over to elaborate. Not that he'd give a toss about Paul.

'Cathnadam's address turns out to be rather interesting,' he said, while doing a rugged impersonation of the cat with the cream.

'How interesting?'

'Extremely interesting. In fact, it happens to be the very same address as your friend Felix Ford. And the very same address where young Clifford Stewart met his untimely end.'

'Really?' Even I was impressed by my acting skills.

'Really. So they're not some couple getting rid of a few things from the junk room. Looks like it's just a front for his stolen-goods disposal scheme.'

'That's a cunning ploy, isn't it? Let people think it's all mumsy-dadsy and above board.' I plagiarised Felix's words. 'I wonder how long it's been going on?'

'According to their records, cathnadam have been trading for well over a year, with ninety-seven point eight per cent positive feedback. There were twenty-two items listed on the afternoon of the boat grounding. Fast mover, young Felix; saw an opportunity and wanted to clear his stock as quickly as possible, I imagine. Eight cans of paint, and fourteen items that will have most likely come from your manifest there, Sam.'

Thank you, Smithy. He'd delivered the perfect opening for my next pitch. It was a bit of a concern though. Smithy wasn't as unaffected by everything yesterday as he was making out, and the home-front situation must have been bad. Because normally he'd never make that kind of mistake, especially as I'd done the exact same thing a few days ago. I was shameless enough to take advantage of his faux pas.

'There's a little problem with all that,' I said.

'Such as?'

'Such as on the afternoon of the boat grounding, Felix Ford was in a coma in hospital. Remember?' I indicated the yellowing souvenir on my face. 'It would have been a bit hard for him to be conducting business.'

'Shit. You're right.' He looked a little deflated.

Reihana took up the logical train of thought: 'Which means that his little cathnadam business must have been in partnership with others. Either his business partners are ruthless and cold-hearted, and carried on without him while he was hospitalised, or they were unaware of his little health issue.'

'I'd like to think the latter, but you never know these days,' Smithy said. 'So who exactly are the partners, then?'

'Given the friendship between Felix Ford and our murder vic, I would hazard a guess that Clifford Stewart was one,' I said. 'And considering he's the dead one, you have to wonder if it was him who did the listings, and came a cropper because of them. What about Leo Walker? Surely he'd have been in on it too. What did he say when you interviewed him?'

'Slight delay there: crap weather in Fiordland delayed them tramping out, so we're not expecting him until later today. But I agree with you there, given their schooling history he'd be a likely candidate for the second-hand goods scheme.'

'What did the Free-Market guys say about the purchasers?' I asked.

'The paint, all eight cans of it, was sold using the 'buy now' option by someone going under the name 'Dun297'. The purchase was made at ten thirty-five that evening, so I suspect the drug importers realised their shipment was inadvertently waylaid and were pretty quick to start recovering their goods. That's very fast work on their part, but then Free-Market would be an obvious place to start looking.'

'And it doesn't take much imagination to realise they may have been a little anxious about it all and called around promptly to pick up their purchases, and also to have a little chat with the vendor to find out whether he had any more. The fact that a beaten-up body turned up in the harbour has to make the possibility of a drug-related killing very high.'

'It sure as hell does,' Smithy said. 'Free-Market has provided the details of the purchaser, but I doubt they'll be genuine or easily traceable. This import operation is too sophisticated for them to be that stupid. I'll get onto the Internet provider to get a record of the email correspondence. Hopefully it's still on the server and we can track things from there. We'll be needing a lot more of the drug squad's services though.'

'Did they give you a list of purchasers for the other items?' I asked.

'Not over the phone. They didn't detail them at all, and I didn't ask specifically because I was more interested in the paint, sorry. But they're going to email through a full report for me soon. Then you'll be able to chase up some more of your exciting insurance job.' Smithy did sarcastic well.

'I take it that means you're not going to reward me for providing the breakthrough by letting me help out on the enquiry?'

Reihana snorted.

Smithy was pretty close to it too. 'Not in a

267

million, Shep,' he said. 'It's not worth my job, or yours.'

61

Billy Thorne, the drug-squad man, was in a bit of a lather. He'd been talking with a few of his more intrepid contacts. These weren't your Joe-Average low-life scavengers or parasites. These were people who made the Mob wince, who took private enterprise to a whole new level. Speaking of wincing, DI Johns was in the room, so I was down the back, doing my very best impression of an inanimate object. It was a surprise he hadn't asked me to leave the meeting to make coffee, or fetch muffins, or something else suitably demeaning. I'm sure it wasn't an oversight. My suspicion-o-meter told me my presence would have been somehow strategic.

Billy addressed the group: 'It would appear that we have a new player in the import market. My gang contacts were emphatic they knew nothing about this import, but they were intrigued. In fact, if they could figure out who was behind it I imagine they'd be keen to muscle in on the act. We'll be keeping a close watch on them in case they try to intercept any other paint that turns up. But they were the easy ones to deal with. Another of my contacts seemed a little bitter that something of this scale could have been happening under his nose when he knew nothing about it. Not even a whisper. I imagine there will be a bit of behind-the-scenes enquiring going on there. That could be useful for us.'

'So, are you thinking new players in the local market? Or that Dunedin was just a transit stop for distribution elsewhere?' Smithy said.

'I'd say Dunedin was merely a transit stop. Normally there'd be word on the street of a delivery. A bit of pre-emptive marketing, as it were, to generate business and anticipation, but in this instance there's been nothing. The other curious thing is that the drug of choice is heroin, which is pretty rare round here nowadays. That suggests Dunedin wasn't the final destination. Round here it's mostly methamphetamine, or its manufacturing ingredients, especially in the gang circles.'

'So if it's new players, they're proving to be good at keeping a secret. We have no idea of the level of ruthlessness within their organisation?' That was DI Johns. Billy Thorne was one of the few people the DI always treated with respect. Had to wonder what Billy had over him.

'No, we don't; they're an unknown quantity. If it had been the big-business guys, I'd have no doubt whatsoever they'd be prepared to torture and kill to reclaim their goods. But all we have is a strong suspicion that the death of Clifford Stewart was at the hands of the people expecting a delivery of heroin smuggled in paint cans. A suspicion based on timing and no hard evidence. They appear to be very organised and, as you said, secretive. The shipment was despatched from China. The miles of paperwork required for customs and the importation of goods was in correct order. Naturally, most of it will be counterfeit, but for the purposes of getting the goods into the country, they dotted the i's and crossed the t's. If the shipping order is correct, after we deduct the cartons that remained on the beach and weren't stolen, there are another twenty-four cans unaccounted for. The shipment was for a gross of paint tins.' My brain had to dredge out the figure 144. 'Of course, to put customs off, not all of those may have been carrying heroin, but it is a huge shipment overall. It's entirely possible we have a new Asian group on our hands. I've got Auckland, Wellington and Christchurch squads with their ears to the ground, in case they were the ultimate destination. Also, it's possible the importers may have spread their risk. The major centres have flagged this as urgent and are also looking closely at shipments into their ports.'

'And what have you got on the paint shipment delivery address here?' asked DI Johns.

'The PO Box number provided was for a non-existent import company with a non-existent premises in Ward Street.'

My ears pricked up at that. Spaz's flat was in Ward Street. I was dying to ask what was at the given address, but the presence of Dick Head Johns in the room inspired me to keep my mouth shut. Instead I mentally projected every thought wave and vibe I could at Billy to cough up that information voluntarily.

'Cellphone contact number was for a pre-paid. Majority of calls for that number have been through the Dunedin central tower, or neighbouring. Calls logged to and from have all been pre-pay phones. These people are careful.'

'And none of the calls were to or from Clifford Stewart or Felix Ford?' Okay, the DI hadn't forgotten me. He stabbed me with a look as he mentioned Felix's name.

'Negative. Or to Leo Walker, the other flatmate.'

Leo had finally come to light and had spent a not-too-pleasant afternoon under Smithy and Reihana's scrutiny. The upshot was that he vowed not to have known anything about Clifford's death until he had been contacted and hauled out of the bush. He was not a happy camper, in any sense of the word. He also corroborated Felix's story that he and Clifford had left Felix to it at Aramoana to take some boxes into town. He said they'd first taken them to the Castle Street flat, but then decided Jase was being a nosey pain in the arse, so took them to the Pine Hill Road house instead. Leo had helped Clifford do some of the listings for Free-Market, but had then gone on to Trina's place as promised. He claimed Clifford was alive and well when he left. He also said he and Clifford had no idea Felix had come to grief and had been fighting for his life in hospital, otherwise they would have been in to see him straight away.

'What was at the Ward Street address?' My thought waves must have deflected and been absorbed by Smithy. God bless Smithy.

'Panel beaters.'

Spaz lived above a panel beater in Ward Street. This was a bit too much of a coincidence for me. Not that I could imagine Spaz being the mastermind behind a drug-import business, although if I'd learned anything from my interactions with young Spaz, it was not to underestimate him. One thing I was certain of, though, considering the concern he showed for his mate Felix: I couldn't picture him arranging the death of his mate Clifford. Still, it was probably time for another little chat.

'And the Free-Market follow-up? Smithy?' DI Johns asked.

'We've accessed email records from the cathnadam account,' Smithy said. 'The purchase of the paint and subsequent communications about pick-up and payment were made through a gmail address. Untraceable. The purchaser called themselves John in the emails and had arranged to pay cash and pick up at nine-thirty on the Monday morning, which is incredibly quick. Spun a nice little story about the mates coming around to paint the house, hence the urgency. There was more email correspondence from buyers of other items, some of the jumble-sale stuff. One had arranged for cash and pick up next morning too.' That had been in the report Smithy gave me, and I was following it up for my fun insurance caper. 'Can't picture anyone killing Clifford Stewart for a few ugly ornaments though,' Smithy said. 'The last time someone logged into the cathnadam account from the home computer was the Monday afternoon at three-sixteen, so we would have to presume this was Clifford, meaning that, at that point at least, he was still alive. But then we had an interesting situation last night. After two weeks of inactivity, someone logged into the account remotely at about eight o'clock.' I felt a cold wave spread from the top of my scalp and break in the pit of my stomach. 'Whoever it was, they seem to have gone to spectacular lengths to decoy and deflect detection, but we've got the IT boffins working on it.'

Shit. I had to warn Spaz.

62

These clandestine, mist-shrouded meetings were starting to seem normal. That wasn't a good thing for a girl planning a long career in the CIB. What the hell was I thinking? Actually, I knew pretty well what I was thinking. I was thinking that I was too far in to back out now. Damned if I did and damned if I didn't. My only hope was that Smithy and the drug squad found Clifford's killer quickly, so that interest in Felix Ford would subside to the point where he was regarded simply as another courthouse no-show, and a few months added to his inevitable prison term. I was yet to figure out how on earth I would be able to convince the guys it was in all of our best interests if my employers didn't know about my role in all of this. The irrational, anxious female in me didn't find it hard to imagine Sam Shephard doing a prison term for aiding and abetting, or at the very least getting her arse kicked to some one-horse backwater. And considering what had happened in the last one-horse backwater I'd worked in, it wasn't something I wanted to revisit. The familiar throb beneath my right temple demanded to be rubbed. It didn't respond favourably to the attention.

Despite expecting it, I still jumped when the door clicked open. I took another few scopes up and down the street before walking in and up the stairs. It was Felix who opened the inner door. He had haversacks under his eyes and looked like he hadn't slept in a week. He was probably thinking the same about me. Spaz was parked in the armchair.

'Gentlemen.'

'Detective,' Spaz said.

Felix mumbled something and wandered back to perch on the edge of the couch. He looked poised for action, ready to run. They were scared of me, or at least Felix was; nothing fazed Spaz, probably. Although, when I'd phoned to say we needed to meet, it took some work to convince them it wasn't so I could arrest them.

I decided to forgo the social niceties. 'Okay, I'm not going to beat around the bush, here. Two things.' They looked dubious. 'Firstly, the police have noticed your login to the cathnadam account. They've got the IT geeks on your trail.'

Spaz paled a little before tossing out some bravado. 'No prob, I'm good.'

'No one's that good. They'll track you down.'

'Betcha not.'

'But what if they do, Spaz?' Felix's voice had the edge of someone who was going to need clean underwear soon. 'They'll find me here and arrest me and I can't go to jail. I can't.'

He should have thought about that before he took a swipe at me. But that ball was already rolling and the terrain was downhill all the way. Something in me still felt compelled to fix his problems, though.

'Would your parents hide you?'

He looked down at the floor. 'I couldn't ask

them to do that. I'd get them in trouble too.' So he did have some common decency after all.

'Have you got someone else you can trust whose house you can crash at?'

'No, don't trust a lot of people. Just Spaz, really, and you now.' I hoped to God he wasn't alluding to crashing at my place, because that was never going to happen. Not even I was that stupid. Feelings of responsibility only went so far.

'What about your family, Spaz? Would they consider it?'

'No. Too strait-laced, too Christian.'

'You might want to make yourself a little scarce too, then. If the police track down your computer, you could be in a lot of trouble.'

'Like you?'

I didn't need reminding of that. 'If you think you're going to use my involvement here as some kind of leverage, just remember I'm the only person who has a shit show of keeping us all out of prison, so you can keep your smart-arse comments to yourself and use that brain of yours to find some solutions here.' He'd pressed the wrong buttons this time. 'And while we're on the subject of you, would you mind telling me what the hell it is that you actually do? Because I've got a murder enquiry for your friend that looks suspiciously like a drug hit because of an ill-timed theft of a few cans of paint containing heroin that were supposed to be destined for some now very pissed-off people, who just happened to list their street address as the panel-beater's workshop directly under where you live. So what do you know about that, Spaz, huh?'

By the time I'd got to the end of my mini-rant I was towering over him, as best as someone just over five feet could tower. Shock registered on his face, but I couldn't figure out whether it was guilty shock or 'no way' shock.

'Nothing. I know nothing about that.' His stammer was even worse than usual and he had to wipe at his face to remove the spittle.

'So you're telling me that this is all just a coincidence? That your friends just happened to steal the cartons of paint off that boat, the same cartons that just happened to be destined for a business address below your flat?'

'Yes.'

'That's a pretty sophisticated computer set-up you've got there.' I turned my attention to his work station. 'A lot of technology involved. It must cost a bit to buy gear like that. That's your thing isn't it? Computers? Your friends told me you were some kind of genius. Bet you do a bit of hacking into places — places you shouldn't be. You've got your own wireless network. What about the other businesses around here? They got networks too? Have you snuck past their security, gone for a peek into their systems, discovered a few things that could be of use to you and your friends here? Like a shipment of drugs that your friend Clifford was in just the right industry to distribute and earn some big dollars for you all?' I didn't know where all this was coming from, it was just spouting out of my mouth, but in a sick kind of way it was making

278

some sense. 'Of course you couldn't possibly make a bloody great container ship get stuck on rocks, but, if you knew the goods were on board, it might explain why your friends were so keen to loot the containers, and why Felix here was prepared to bash the crap out of an officer to make off with his box.' By the time I got to the reference to Felix I was building up a fair head of steam. 'But then, if you're half as clever as they say you are, who's not to say you couldn't remotely hack into the shipboard computers and put it off course? Perhaps you planned the whole bloody thing.'

Silence hung in the air as what I said sunk in. It was probably in the realms of science fiction or James Bond movies, but nowadays, you never knew. If a handful of Somalians could hijack an oil tanker on sheer audacity and a few firearms, who was to say someone with the technological know-how and means couldn't pull off a similar feat.

Spaz lurched to his feet, now towering over me, and uttered, 'No fuckin' way.' He put his hands on my shoulders, got his face up close and locked eyes. 'Not involved. We had no idea about the heroin. That was a fluke.' He was so emphatic, and his eyes bored into mine in such a way, I believed him.

I sighed and started nodding, and Spaz dropped back down into the chair. Felix had drawn up his legs and was hugging his knees. Both were silent.

'Well, your fluke has obviously pissed off some very scary people, because you didn't get to see what they did to your mate. I did, and it's something that will probably haunt my dreams for the rest of my life. So if you know anything, even the slightest little thing about these bastards, you need to tell me. They will stop at nothing — *nothing* — to reclaim their goods. And who knows, the police might not be the worst creatures trying to track you guys down right now.'

63

The sight of the vehicle parked on the street outside my house made me want to keep on driving, so I did. After an evening of scaring the crap out of a felon and an accessory, not to mention myself, the last person I wanted to face was Paul. He hadn't mentioned he was coming up, and, considering I was very late home, he hadn't texted to find out where I was. What was he doing here then?

I had no idea where I was going to go. What I really wanted was the couch, a Milo, Toffee Pops and a book to escape into, but the presence of Paul's car put paid to that. Ah, bloody hell. I did a u-ey on Kenmure Road and headed back to the house. I couldn't run away from this forever. There was no point in being wimpy and pathetic about it.

When I walked into the lounge, Paul was sitting on the couch with a bottle of Speights in his hand, and Maggie was in the armchair with a glass of red.

'Well,' she said, as she stood up. 'That's my cue to go do some study. Nice to see you, Paul. I took the liberty of pouring you one, Sam.' She pointed to a glassful of wine on the coffee table. She must have been psychic. 'So, if you'll excuse me.' She made a gracious retreat.

'Thanks, Maggs.'

I went over and gave Paul a cursory kiss, then

grabbed my wine, sat down in the armchair and took a substantial swig. Paul gave me a bemused look.

'So what's up?' I said, returning his look. 'Why are you here?'

'Lovely to see you too, Sam. You know why I'm here.'

'I thought I made it clear I need a little headspace right now. You didn't warn me you were coming.' Like some advance cyclone-alert system.

'If I did, you would have made some excuse for me not to, and I'm not the kind of person to leave important issues to a few text messages and grumpy phone calls.'

Yeah, he was the type of person to face them, damn it. Unlike me. He was right about the excuse, but I didn't think I'd been that grumpy on the phone.

'So we could start again with my asking you how your day was? Apparently that's what polite people do.'

I laughed. 'I'm not polite.' I didn't really think he'd want to know how my day had gone. Considering most of it had been based on half-truths, lies and deception, it wasn't the best footing for a conversation that would inevitably turn towards the state of the nation, as it were. 'But seriously, Paul, what is it you want? Because I'm tired, and this isn't the best time, if I'm honest.'

'That's precisely what I would like,' he said, looking at me with affection and a hint of vulnerability. 'Some honesty from you, because, let's face it, you haven't exactly been forthcoming.'

'Oh?' I took another big swig. Part of me thought I should take offence at that comment, but the other part of me felt too tired and couldn't muster up the energy.

'You've been on the run since I told you about my job application. And yes, I will admit here and now I made a monumental cock-up dropping it on you when I did.'

A laugh slipped out of me. 'I am sorry about that.' It was hard to get angry with someone so damn-well earnest.

'So here's the thing. How about you just tell me what you actually want. I'm a big boy; I can handle it. Let's quit this beating around the bush. For better or for worse.'

A 'now or never' moment. Great. I wondered if the phone would go this time. I seem to be always rescued by the phone. I looked at it, waiting, but nothing happened. Damn. I took a swig that ended at the bottom of the glass. When in doubt, answer a question with a question. He did it often enough.

I turned back to him. 'Well, what do you want, Paul? In your perfect world, what would you want, huh?' That sounded a little facetious, it wasn't really meant to be.

'It would just make you more freaked out.'

'Tell me. Come on, hit me with it.'

I knew exactly what he'd say.

He took a deep breath, a swig of beer, flashed me with one of his charming and fatalistic smiles and launched in. 'In a perfect world it would be friendship, marriage, lots of great sex, overseas travel, a great working relationship, and eventually babies.' He gave me a salute with his bottle.

'You don't ask for much.'

'Apparently I do. That seems to be the problem. But this isn't a perfect world, especially with you.'

I raised my eyebrows.

'Sorry, that didn't quite come out right.' He seemed to be scrambling for words. 'I realise, with you, there won't be marriage, and most likely not babies, so I would be very satisfied with friendship, lots of great sex, overseas travel and the fabulous working relationship part.' I went to interject. 'And before you explode — you asked.'

I went to say something else but he beat me to it again.

'And before you get all high and mighty on me, at the end of the day, I quite fancy you and it's you I want to be with. You. Stroppy, passionate, slightly nutty you. All the other stuff is by the by. God help me, I happen to love you, your company, quirks, tendencies to get uppity and panicky, commitment-phobia, warts and all. Can't help it. So there you go. It's on the table. You can take it or leave it. But if you're going to take it, can we get on with the lots of great sex bit please?'

For once in my life I couldn't find anything to say.

64

There was something about antiques shops I found unsettling. From an aesthetic standpoint, sure, some of the items were beautiful, but it was almost like they carried with them the ghosts of past lives, a certain heaviness or burden. You'd never find them at my place. Besides the fact I couldn't afford them, they'd seem like a little pocket of sadness lurking in the corner. I'd stick to cheap and cheerful. Consequently, this was the first time I'd actually set foot in Curio Antiques at Port Chalmers. The first thing that struck me was the smell. It was more refined than the old-stuff smell at Cash for Crap, with a hint of furniture polish and old leather, but it was there all the same. The second, and more remarkable thing, was the rather familiar face behind the counter.

'Hello, Mr Gibbs, I didn't realise you worked here.'

'Detective Shephard.' He came around and shook my hand.

I didn't correct him on my rank, in fact I very much liked the sound of it. He wasn't as apprehensive as he'd been when I'd last seen him at his crib at Aramoana.

'How are you feeling now? Everything on the mend?'

'Much better, thanks. What about yourself? Have they given you an indication of when your court case will be?' I took the don't-beat-about-the-bush approach.

'There's such a backlog that it's unlikely to be before next year. I still can't believe it's going to trial. A man tries to help an officer down, and look what happens. The law's an ass.'

'You won't get any argument there from me,' I said.

I was just grateful he'd bothered to come to my rescue. How many people nowadays would just stand by and watch while someone had a go? Most, I would think, and cases like this would ensure it stayed that way. In fact, half of them would be busy recording it on their phones to upload onto their social media accounts, expressing their disgust at what society had become. Wouldn't occur to them they were part of the problem. All in all I felt thankful to Iain Gibbs. Sure, he'd gotten way too carried away, and he was lucky Felix Ford didn't die, but all the same, it was another instance of someone being punished for being the good Samaritan.

'Is this your store? I didn't realise you were in the antiques trade.'

'Been in the business for over twenty-five years. Pretty good way to make a living, and fascinating with it. If you're into history or art, I couldn't think of anything better. I've got things in this store that are over three hundred years old; they're older than our nation.' I could see by the enthusiasm on his face it was a bit of a passion. 'Were you looking for something in particular?'

I was, but it wasn't something for my house. 'Yes, but I'm here on police business. Actually it's to do with the shipping accident, and that weekend. I've been visiting all the antiques stores around Dunedin, working on the recovery of some items stolen from the household goods of a collector. Needless to say, he'd quite like them back. I'd be grateful if you would take a look through this portfolio of goods to see if any have been offered to you.' I waved the folder I was holding. 'And also we'd like you to keep an eye out in case someone comes in trying to sell any of them.'

'Sure, I can do that.' I handed the folder over and he started flicking through the pages. 'Nice collection here,' he said. 'Quite eclectic. Did they lose the lot?'

'Some boxes were recovered on the beach, and the larger furniture items were too big to make off with.' Although some people had made a valiant attempt at carting off a massive sideboard, but all they succeeded in doing was scratching it to buggery with the sand. 'You may remember the skull the old lady found on the beach that caused a bit of excitement? That was part of this collection too, so he certainly had a bit of variety. We estimate there would be over a million's-worth missing.'

'Ouch,' he said. 'That's a substantial collection. Have you managed to recover anything?'

'Yes, I've located several things through online traders. I'm hoping this little trip around the dealers will bring a few more articles to light. Anything look familiar?'

287

'Not so far,' he said as he leafed through the pages.

I went for a little wander around the shop while he kept looking. I almost laughed out loud when I saw the most enormous harmonica I'd ever laid eyes on. Gawd, the small ones were bad enough. Imagine the noise that came out of that thing. I walked quickly past a dark-timbered, ornate clock that gave me the heebie-jeebies, and finally found a cabinet of fine bone-china cups and saucers that brought back memories of frilly tea with Nana. Our farming crockery was far more utilitarian than that. You didn't serve up fine china teacups to farm workers with hands the size of footballs. It had been Dad's mum who put on the fancy teas, bless her. Even though she was a farmer's wife, she said there were some standards that needed to be maintained, and frilly tea was one of them. Looking back I think she suspected I never got to enjoy playing tea parties with Mum and was trying to make up for it. Nana was special like that. That brought another face into my consciousness, and I experienced the familiar lurch as I wondered how Dad was.

'There's nothing here that's come into the shop, I'm afraid, but I'll certainly keep an eye out for you if anything does. Have you got a card?'

I pulled out my police business card, then grabbed a pen from the counter and scribbled my work email address on the back. 'I'd appreciate that. Like I said, this family's lost a lot, so it would be good to recover as much as we can. Some of it's very valuable, but Joe-average looter probably won't know that. I've got the second-hand marts to trot around too, so it's going to be a long day.'

'Have fun,' he said, 'and good to see you looking a bit better.'

'Yeah, thank heavens. Wish the headache would go though.'

That was three antique shops down, a squillion to go. Why on earth wasn't a uniformed officer doing this legwork? I could have been put to far better use elsewhere. Actually, I knew damn well why. DI Johns had to have his little power games and was the master when it came to strategic condescension.

Reality sucked.

65

I walked out the door into the teeth of the howling southerly and was so intent on assuming the hunch-over-and-protect-myself-from-the-wind pose, I walked headlong into a rather broad chest. The chest smelt of myrrh and wood and warm spices, and when I looked up I saw it was attached to Mr Peter Trubridge himself.

'Detective Constable Shephard, watch yourself there, now.' He braced me by the shoulders to steady me. 'We must stop meeting like this.' The voice and the close contact had its predictable effect on my endocrine system.

'Yes, we must, people will talk,' I said and gave what felt like one of those pathetic, nervous girl laughs. It didn't seem so cold any more.

'Where are you off to in such a hurry?' I was quite disappointed when he let go of my shoulders and left me to stand on my own two feet.

'Duty calls, people to see, crooks to catch, that kind of thing.' I reached up and brushed the wayward, wind-assisted, loose strands of hair off my face. It was a futile gesture.

'Working hard on my case, I hope.' He reached out and wiped aside a strand that had eluded me. His action seemed unconscious and natural, but the effect on me was somewhat shocking.

'Actually, I am. Yes, exactly that. I'm working

hard on your case, of course I am.' I sounded babblier than a besotted teenager. I tried to slow my speech down and lower the tone. Now I sounded stilted rather than silly. 'I'm visiting. All the local antiques dealers. And second-hand places. Seeing if they've had any items turn up. From your inventory.'

'Well, I'd better not hold you up from your work then, had I? You have a good day, Detective.'

I will now, I thought.

I walked a little further down the street, my mind still preoccupied with the feeling of his hands and the smell of him. I had a momentary pang of guilt about my body's reaction and mental disloyalty to Paul, especially considering he'd stayed the previous night. But then I thought, how bloody stupid, there's nothing wrong with window-shopping, as long as you look and don't touch. And I just had to look. I couldn't resist any longer, the carnal creature in me just had to turn around and appreciate the view. I wasn't disappointed and caught his very nice derriere in action as it entered Curio Antiques. Well that was curious; maybe he was already looking to fill the gaps in his lost collection. I supposed if that was your thing, it was your thing. But I was intrigued. I was going to have to check it out now. But how? Peeking around the corner would be a bit obvious. I could do the old 'I left something behind' ruse in order to go back into the shop and see what was going on, but I was afraid that would look a bit like I was a stalker. So I took the 'oops, I meant to go this way' approach instead. I hoped to hell no one was watching. It felt like one of those smile-you're-on-candid-camera moments. I waited until I was halfway along the shop front before I turned my head to have a surreptitious gawk in the window.

They were embracing like old friends.

66

After a day of wandering around old junk shops, I was all antiqued out. It had gotten to the point where the continued exposure to the aroma of advanced age had given me a thumping headache and my skin was crawling with imagined dust mites or borer, and I had an overwhelming desire to wash its lingering taint off my body. But, alas, there was one more to go on today's quota before I could call it quits and head back to the relative sanctuary of my clean-smelling, deliciously modern workplace. I stood outside my target, took several breaths to psych myself up and physically propelled myself through the door.

The eyes of the poor guy behind the counter nearly bugged out of his head, even more so than usual, at my Krameresque entrance. Frog didn't look that delighted to see me. Cash for Crap had lost none of its charm since my last visit, and neither had Frog. His demeanour and colour palette remained the same; only the print on the black T-shirt had changed. This time it was a band by the unlikely name of My Chemical Romance. I thought it was a bit sad to think the only way to shore up a romance was to add chemicals, but hey, I was hardly the one to profess authority in the love department.

'Hello, Josiah, is your boss in today?' I asked.

'No, he's away until Monday.'

'So it's you in charge today, is it?'

The poor guy blushed, and I wondered at the owner's wisdom at putting someone in charge of his business who dressed like that and acted a little immature. The only compelling reason I could think of for his employment was that there was a spot of nepotism involved.

'Er, yes.'

'Well, maybe you can help me, then. I'm not here to talk about Clifford's case today.' His shoulders relaxed a fraction at that news. 'I'm here on other business. You remember the containers that washed up at Aramoana the weekend of the party we talked about.'

They hunched back up. 'Yes?' The timorous tone in his voice confirmed for me that Frog was the friend in the second-hand business Felix had alluded to.

'I'm in the process of tracking down some belongings stolen from one of those containers, so I need you to have a look through this portfolio and see if you recognise any of the goods.'

His face was by now suffused with a charming red, so I was guessing a number of the goods were likely to have gone through here, or still were here. With that in mind, I thought a little tour was in order.

'How about you have a look through the folder there, while I take a little look around the shop? Then we can compare notes.'

Frog looked slightly relieved that I wasn't going to hover over his shoulder like a blowfly; he didn't seem like the type to function well

294

under pressure. But he still had a hint of panic in his eyes; at least, from what I could tell, considering his fringe mostly covered them up and he wasn't making any eye contact anyway.

By the time I got to the end of the first aisle there were three items I recognised from the portfolio. In fact, I was seriously thinking of shuffling the other customers out and closing the doors, when a turn around the end and into the next aisle clinched it for me.

'Shit.'

I pulled out my cellphone and pulled up the contact name.

'Smithy?'

'Yeah, what?'

'You're going to want to get down to Cash for Crap right now, and bring your friends.'

'Why?'

'Let's just say you might want to do a spot of painting.'

Frog looked mortified when I started ushering the customers out, then spun the 'open' sign to 'closed' and locked us in.

'What did you find?' he asked.

'Enough of the articles from that,' I said, tapping the folder, 'to be of concern, and enough cans of a certain kind of paint to be dangerous.'

He gave me a baffled look.

'Some of my colleagues are going to come down soon and will want to know where it all came from, so I hope for your sake you are going to be exceedingly co-operative. Do I make myself clear?'

'Am I going to be in trouble?' he asked.

'That depends on the level of your involvement and how helpful you are to the police.'

Frog added scared to his repertoire of demeanours.

'I don't think I can impress upon you enough how much it is in your best interest to be co-operative.'

The kid didn't know what was going to hit him when Smithy and the gang arrived, so I thought I'd occupy his time and get some ticks off the list in my caseload.

'While we're waiting, what did you recognise from the folder? You've been here full-time for the last two weeks?'

'Yeah, Monday to Friday, with my cousin on for half-days on Saturdays and Sundays.'

'And the boss has been away all this time?'

'Yeah.'

I bet the boys couldn't believe their luck having a no-questions-asked outlet for their acquisitions. The timing couldn't have been more perfect. I imagined Frog would have been promised a cut of the proceeds, and everyone would have been happy. Though, when I thought about it, Clifford must have been the one to drop the stuff around, otherwise Leo would presumably have mentioned it when he was being interviewed. It did say a little something about the nature of Frog, though. He'd kept the stock on the shelves, trying to flog it off even after he found out his mate had been killed. Maybe he wasn't as sensible as I'd picked. I wondered if he was planning to clear the unsold items off the shelf come Sunday, before his boss came back, and then flog them off on Free-Market.

'Okay, Frog, level with me. Are you going to show me which of these items you tried to flog off?'

He had enough gumption to realise there was no point trying to hide anything from me, so he pointed out the items I saw, plus a few extras.

'So some of these items have come in and been sold already?'

'Yes, a few have already gone.'

'And do you keep records of who you sold things to?'

'Urm . . . no.'

'Not even the till-paper trail, or credit-card or electronic records?'

He seemed to be suddenly fascinated with his shoes. 'I didn't exactly put those ones through the till,' he said eventually. A weighty silence followed.

'So you were collecting money for those on behalf of . . . ?'

He read my look enough to know I was onto his game. 'Clifford, Leo and Felix.' As suspected.

'But it was Clifford that dropped these things in to you, not Leo?'

He gave me a how-did-you-know-that look. 'Yeah, it was Clifford.'

'And you kept them out for sale despite Clifford being killed?'

Frog didn't answer.

'How did the customers pay?' I figured that if they'd used a card it would have left an audit trail.

'Well there was one guy mainly, four or five

days ago, and he paid cash, so I didn't have to worry about that.'

'What did he buy?'

Frog pointed out several items in the folder, whose insurance value totted up to well over forty thousand dollars.

'And how much did he pay?'

Frog dropped his eyes and mumbled. He must have been doing the mental arithmetic too.

'Sorry, what was that you said?'

'About a hundred.'

'A hundred what?'

'Dollars.'

I felt the beginnings of a giggle start around boot level, and by the time it burst out of my mouth it was a full-on guffaw. 'Jesus bloody Christ, you sold forty-thousand-dollars-worth of prime goods for a hundred bucks?'

It was like a scene from *Antiques Roadshow*, except in reverse and gone feral. The guy who found these things, he must have recognised them for what they were worth if he'd picked out the gems from the rest of the crap. He must have been laughing all the way to the bank.

'And what else have you sold for a song?' I asked.

'Well, I flicked off some of the paint.'

At that, I stopped laughing real fast. 'When, and how much?'

He must have detected the change in my voice, because an edge of caution replaced the resignation. 'Yesterday. Some guys came in and bought up all the tins we had out; there were eight I think.'

'Can you remember what these men looked like? Do you have them on security tape?'

'We haven't got security. My uncle keeps meaning to get around to it, but hasn't yet.' I was right about the family ties. 'They were quite rough, and I didn't like the look of them. They asked me if there were any more, but I told them no, that was it. They wanted to know where we got it from, so I just said I didn't know, that I just worked here.'

His scary-o-meter probably saved him from a nasty fate; that and perhaps the presence of other customers, and therefore witnesses. It paid to listen to that small paranoid voice called instinct.

'And they haven't been back today?' I suddenly felt glad I'd locked the doors until Smithy got here.

'No.'

'Would you recognise them again if we showed you some photos?'

'I think so.'

'Okay, that's good.' If he could pick someone from photos it would be an immense break in the case. 'You're in for a busy afternoon at the station I'm afraid.'

It was with quite a sense of relief that I spotted the unmarked car pull up outside, with Smithy's bulk behind the wheel. Once they got into the building, my involvement would once again end. I thought I might as well try and get my money's worth before that happened. 'Was there anything else you wanted to tell me?'

'That other guy, who bought the ornaments, I did recognise him.'

That got my full attention.

'It was that guy who looks like a walrus with the antique shop out at Port Chalmers.'

67

Cash for Crap had turned into the equivalent of a three-ringed circus, and I was right about Frog: the poor guy had the look of someone in sensory overload, desperately wishing he was elsewhere. In an attempt to jog his memory Billy Thorne was busy filling him in on how fortunate he was to still be breathing. As a general technique for improving recall, it sucked, and Frog looked like he was about to break down altogether.

'Do they have to be so harsh?' I said to Smithy, who was in the cheap seats with me.

'Yes.' He didn't elaborate further.

'Frog said he might recognise the people who bought the paint from photos. I don't know that what Billy's doing to him is going to help any. But you know Frog did recognise a chap who came in and brought up some of the collectables and antiques from my insurance file.'

'Well, you're lucky then.'

I turned and stared at Smithy, then gave him a good thump on the arm.

'Ow, what was that for?' he said, rubbing it and giving me the evils.

'That's for being so bloody grumpy. Cut it out.'

'I'm not being grumpy,' he said. 'I'm always like this.'

'You bloody well are not. You're worse than a

petulant two-year-old. If you were a bit smaller I'd stick you in time out. How's it going with Veronica?'

'None of your business.'

'Well, I'm making it my business.'

'No you're bloody not, so fuck off.'

His vehemence shut me up. After a few minutes of uncomfortable silence, he must have realised that statement ranked pretty high on the rude-o-meter.

'So what were you saying about this idiot recognising someone?' It was a nice change of subject. I took it.

'Frog told me a chap had been in three or four days ago and purchased several items from my portfolio — several very expensive items — and he paid the grand sum of a hundred bucks cash.'

'Wish I could get that lucky.'

'Luck has nothing to do with it. The man just happens to be in the antiques business, and just happens to be my Mr Iain Gibbs.'

That prompted raised eyebrows. 'He's a greedy bastard then.'

'Yeah, and he's a lying greedy bastard, because I was in his shop earlier in the day and showed him the portfolio, including the items he purchased from here for a pittance. He looked me straight in the eye and told me he hadn't seen any of them.'

'Do you get the feeling he's milking the situation for all it's worth?'

'I sure as hell do. And what makes it worse is that I saw him greet Peter Trubridge like they were long-lost friends. My suspicious little mind is thinking, 'Hello, what's going on here then. Are the two of them having a quiet little scam against the insurance company on the side?'. You know, buying back what they can for next-to-nothing and claiming the full value of the loss from the company?'

'Funny that your mind works exactly like mine.'

'I'll take that as a compliment. Face it, we're sick and twisted. It's an occupational hazard,' I said.

'So what are you going to do about it?' he asked.

I took this as a sign I had carte blanche to act as I saw fit on this one. 'I'm thinking that between Frog's testimony and mine, I have good cause to get a warrant to search Gibbs's business and houses for receiving stolen goods. Do you want to come along for the ride?'

'Nah, thanks all the same; I think we'll have our hands full chasing up this lead to the bastard who knocked off Clifford Stewart. It looks like Billy's put the wind up this guy enough and is ready to take him down to the station.'

Even from this distance it was clear Frog's eyes were bloodshot and his nose colour co-ordinated. Poor kid.

'Great work, Sam, spotting that paint.'

'I take it that despite being the one who did the spotting, I have to leave the party now?'

'Sorry, you know the stakes and the rules. But you've handed us the break we needed. Even Dickhead Johns will have to admit that.'

303

68

Iain Gibbs' Saint Clair home looked the perfect venue to showcase a collection of antiques. It was what real-estate agents politely described as a 'gentleman's residence', which was jargon for a big old house that needed a ton of work done and a pile of money thrown at it, which leaked like a sieve and in which you froze your arse off in winter. This beauty was double-storied red brick, slatetile roof, with leadlight windows and a stunning conservatory that just begged for afternoon gin and tonics while you looked out at the stunning view down the length of St Clair beach to St Kilda. The waves were rolling in spectacularly today, sending flumes of spray into the air, courtesy of a high tide, large swell and some serious wind. The home was set in grounds with mature, if slightly overgrown, trees, including my favourite, kowhai, and the ubiquitous cabbage tree — those hardy buggers would certainly handle the salt-spray environment here. The long, curved driveway meandered up from the street to an expansive levelled lawn; the overall effect was stately and grand.

The main house seemed the logical place to serve the warrant, as the antique shop would be closed today. The majority of shops in Port Chalmers didn't open on a Monday or Tuesday, and some even gave Wednesday a miss too, much to the consternation of visitors and locals alike.

For some strange reason they thought the normal rules of commerce didn't apply and their customers would admire them for their ladylike and gentlemanly hours. In reality, it just pissed everyone off. They didn't even bother to open up for the many cruise ships that berthed at the port, including foreign customers with bulging wallets. God only knew how they made a living. But hey, perhaps seeing as so many of them had galleries and were so used to being starving artists, it didn't occur to them they could trade like normal people, and get to make and eat a crust.

Just to make sure, earlier I'd phoned John Farquhar, the Port Chalmers cop, and he'd gone out for a little recce to confirm the Gibbses weren't at the Aramoana crib or in the antiques shop. So my first place to sting Iain Gibbs for being a greedy, lying bastard and possessor of stolen goods would be in the sanctity of his home. I liked that thought. I was also looking forward to interviewing him about the involvement of Peter Trubridge in all this. Were the two of them in cahoots? Part of me hoped not; I was enjoying my little fantasies about Trubridge. I didn't want them tainted with the stink of petty crime.

It was pretty obvious there were people home at 'Frantok', as the polished brass plate proclaimed the house was named. I always thought it odd that people would name their home like it was a family pet. It was a gloomy kind of a day, so there were lights on in the downstairs rooms, and a curl of smoke emanated from one of the four impressive brick chimneys.

To be honest I was disappointed Smithy hadn't wanted to come out and join me in the fun, but I supposed they had bigger fish to fry. They were chasing up the big murder/ internationally connected drug bust of the year, while I was chasing the latest in what felt like a continuous stream of greedy old codgers. Whether it was ripping off hospitals for millions, or the bloke down the road for a couple of bucks, people's greed and lack of common decency continued to amaze me. Didn't their parents teach them the difference between right and wrong? Mine sure as hell did. My mother still took great pains to correct me on any minor deviations I might take from the straight and narrow, or her view of it. Just as well she had no idea of some of the things I'd been up to lately. Although I think Dad would have secretly approved. The little knife twisted in my gut at the thought of him.

'We'd better get on with it, then.'

I had company for this task in the form of a couple of constables. They were male and a foot taller than me, which suited me fine. I wasn't intimidated by Iain Gibbs, but after the unexpected thumping I got from Felix Ford, I wasn't about to take any chances and was pleased to have a little brawn at my side.

Marie Gibbs opened the door, and, at the sight of me and my side dishes, her eyes widened. A waft of eau de chocolate cake greeted us again. It made me wonder if they had the scent canned like air freshener, or if they were just serious cake-eaters.

'Hello, Mrs Gibbs. I was wanting a word with Iain please, if I may?'

'Oh, yes, of course.' She scuttled off to find him.

'There isn't a back entrance to this property, so we shouldn't have to worry about him doing a runner. If he does, it's your job to play catch,' I said to the boys. We'd done our research; Google Earth could be very handy.

But I needn't have worried as Iain Gibbs soon came to the door tailed by his wife, but he appeared rather wary.

'Is there something I can help you with?' he asked.

There certainly was. 'Iain Gibbs,' I said, 'I have a warrant to search your house for stolen goods from the grounding of the *Lauretia Express*. I also have a separate warrant to search both your business premises and your Aramoana residence.'

His tone changed from polite enquiry to pissed-off defensive in an instant. 'On what grounds? What kind of crap is this?' He took on the look of a wrongly accused schoolboy, but I wasn't fooled for an instant. 'You aren't coming anywhere near my place. You wait till I speak to my lawyer. What kind of gratitude is this?' He now changed it to wounded hero. 'After everything I did to help you, and all the crap I've had to go through because of it, you've got the cheek to stand there and accuse me of stealing? I don't believe this.'

My peripheral vision caught the movement of

the officers flanking me as they edged forwards. I didn't think there was any menace in his voice, more indignation.

'You are most welcome to call your lawyer, but the terms of our warrant means we can enter now. If you prevent us from doing so, you can be arrested for obstruction.'

He stood there like a huffing train building up steam, with Mrs Gibbs behind him, gawping like a goldfish. Her gawping made a perfect counterpoint to his huffing.

I dropped the formal speak for a moment. 'Look, Mr Gibbs, when I came to your shop and showed you the portfolio the other day, you lied to me. You claimed you hadn't seen any of the items in it, yet I have a witness who says you purchased several of those very same items from him several days prior. And if it had been by chance that you wandered into the shop and just happened to only pick out items from the looted container, then you had the opportunity to tell me about them when I asked. But no, you looked me dead in the eye and told me you had not seen any of them. Let's be straight about this. You lied.' The last two words were emphatic. The realisation he'd been sprung brought the huffing and puffing to an abrupt halt.

His sudden change in demeanour didn't go unnoticed by his wife, who was now looking at him, puzzled. 'What is she saying, Iain?' She came up alongside him and pulled at his sleeve, trying to catch his attention. 'Is that true?'

'Quiet, Marie,' he said, swatting away her hand while looking straight at me. 'It's got nothing to do with you.' She looked crestfallen, but remained by his side.

'So may we come in?' I asked. 'Or are you going to make this difficult?'

69

The lounge had a very cheerful glow, from a vintage candelabra that dropped gracefully from an ornate plaster ceiling rose and the golden flickers of light dancing in the fireplace. The room exuded warmth and charm. Its owner did not. Especially after I pointed out a small carved Chinese lacquerware bowl and lid, displayed on a sideboard with other oriental objects, which, if my memory served me right, was valued at around twenty thousand dollars. It was one of the things he picked up for twenty bucks at Cash for Crap. When I drew his attention to it, he suggested to his wife she might like to go and ring the lawyer after all. It was probably a good idea.

We moved around the ground floor, comparing items we were uncertain of with pictures in the portfolio, photographing anything that provided *Bingo!* moments. There had been eleven of those so far. Iain Gibbs had been a busy boy. He must have been doing the rounds of the second-hand stores, hoping bargains would pop up. It made me wonder why Marie Gibbs didn't question where these things came from. Did she choose to ignore them? Or, more likely, having been in the business for such a long time, the *objets d'art* in the house rotated with those in the shop on a regular basis, so no questions were asked. That was, of course, assuming she hadn't been trotting around the used-goods marts picking up the steals too.

It also made me wonder, seeing as Iain Gibbs knew exactly what to buy, if he'd already seen the customs manifest and knew what was in it. Was he such good friends with Peter Trubridge that he had been provided with a copy in advance, like a kind of insurance policy? An off-site backup. Those would be questions for later.

I wandered up the stairs, my hand running up the smooth wooden balustrade, admiring the gilt-framed paintings and maritime etchings that lined the sides. Port Chalmers seemed to inspire the need in people associated with the place to carry reminders of the sea on their walls. The landing had a display cabinet that was a work of art in its own right. It reminded me of the original Otago Museum ones — up in the animal attic; one of my favourite haunts. The resemblance wasn't just in the cabinetry; it was the contents too: it was filled with taxidermist's art. Iain Gibbs, it seemed, also had a thing for birds.

It was his office I was hunting out. A businessman like him would no doubt have a suitable office space, and I suspected a few of the articles I was looking for would still be in there awaiting classification, or designation, or simply to avoid prying eyes. The first room on the right hit pay dirt. It was exactly what I imagined the office of an antiques collector and peddler would be. A leather armchair dimpled with buttons; a large wooden, leather-topped desk with one of those green glass oblong-shaped desk lamps. The

311

built-in shelves were packed with old books, collectables and ornaments as well as more modern-day accompaniments: cardboard document boxes, lever arch files, cellphone chargers. There were two computers, one set up on a separate desk across the end of the elegant one to form an L-shaped work station, and another on the floor waiting for a new home, perhaps after an upgrade. The whole thing reminded me of another office from another time, full of creepy old things, and I shuddered.

I had hoped there would be more items from the Trubridge collection up here, but my first look didn't set off any alarm bells. That was disappointing, but there were still numerous cupboards and drawers that could hide away his contraband. I decided to start with the large, red Chinese-style cupboard — a wedding cabinet I think it was called — down the end of the room. I pulled the doors open and *Bingo*! The items we'd discovered downstairs were displayed in plain sight, so he must have felt happy enough to explain those acquisitions to any curious parties. *Picked them up at the junk shop, stellar find, lucky me, huh? Stolen? Really? I never knew?* I was sure he'd be convincing. The ones in this cupboard, though, must have been the ones he couldn't explain away quite so easily.

'Oh, Iain, you've been a busy boy,' I said out loud.

'Found what you were looking for then?' His voice came from behind me.

I was glad my pelvic floor muscles were strong.

I spun around. 'Jesus Christ, you shouldn't sneak up on a girl like that.'

He was about level with the desk lamp and, judging by his mid-step poise, must have just entered the room. 'I'm sorry, I didn't mean to give you a fright,' he said and stopped where he was.

'Yeah, well, I wish you'd announced yourself. Anyway, didn't I tell you to stay downstairs?'

He didn't reply.

'I see you did a spot of online shopping as well as canvassing the second-hand shops.'

Hidden safely in the cupboard, among some other things I recognised, was an ugly bronze horse ornament. The same horse ornament that had been listed by Clifford Stewart on Free-Market and purchased as a 'buy now' by John03. I now knew who John was, and realised he may have been one of the last people to see Clifford alive before his little visit from the drug lords. If that was the case, he may well have valuable information for the case.

'Look, Iain. The fact you even have these things in your possession means you must have purchased them off Free-Market from Clifford Stewart, the young man who was murdered a few weeks ago.'

I pointed out the bronze horse. A wary expression crossed his face.

'You may be able to help us in our murder investigation. What time exactly on the Monday morning — Monday the thirty-first of August — did you arrange the pick-up?'

Again, he said nothing.

'Look, I know you must be the online trader, John03, on Free-Market, and all it would take would be one look at your computer over there to confirm it for me. It means you arranged the pickup for the Monday morning, which means other than the killer or killers, you may have been the last person to see Clifford Stewart alive. So if I were you, considering you're already looking at prosecution for possession of stolen goods, I would start getting very co-operative right about now.'

He hesitated a moment before answering. 'Well, I couldn't say exactly, it was a few weeks ago.' At least he had the sense to admit it. 'I think it was early-ish, around eight-thirty.' Which confirmed the time arranged in the post-sale email correspondence I'd seen and meant he was there an hour before the paint purchasers were due.

'Did he happen to mention any of the other things he had for sale on Free-Market and if he was expecting other buyers?'

'Well, no. I didn't stay long or talk, just picked up the horses and left.'

Something twinged in my mind. Horses? Plural? There had only been one bronze horse for sale on the listing. The other horse from that pair had been stolen from Felix Ford's Aramoana Crib.

It was another lie.

A little chill started working its way down my spine. My eyes flicked over to where the end of an ugly floral painting stuck out from behind another framed piece of art. His eyes followed my eyes and an infusion of red rushed into his cheeks. My eyes then flicked to the computer on the floor. One of those had been stolen recently: Felix Ford's. Did we have this all wrong? Did Clifford Stewart's problems start with a visit from the antiques man rather than the drug dealers? Surely not? Not over an ugly bronze horse.

When my eyes flicked back to his, the look on Iain Gibbs's face caused my chill to plummet into a full-on freeze.

I knew.

He knew I knew.

My eyes darted now to the door, the only exit to this room, on the far side of a large and now desperate-looking man, a desperate man who began to take steps towards me, his hands spread in supplication, entreating.

'I can explain,' he said. 'Just let me explain.'

He could do all the explaining he wanted to later, down at the station. For now he needed to stand back.

'You stop right there,' I said. 'Don't you take one more step,' I said, my voice raised, but still he moved forwards.

'Don't you bloody well dare.'

The image of the mess this man had made of Clifford Stewart and Felix Ford leapt into my mind, and I knew I had to get attention and fast. I opened my mouth to let out a scream for help, when Iain Gibbs threw himself across the gap between us, faster than I would have ever imagined possible, and fastened his hands firmly around my throat, the force of it throwing us both back into the Chinese cabinet, the bang reverberating through my back.

Please let them have heard that downstairs. My hands instinctively raised to my throat, tearing at his fingers, but his grip held firm, and I felt the heat of his breath on my skin, his face right up against mine, so close his eyes had merged into one cycloptic giant. He had lifted me right off my feet, and I tried to bring my knee up to get him in the groin, but he was too close. When he realised what I was trying to do, his grip tightened all the more.

Pepper spray, I had to get to my pepper spray. It was in my pocket, but when my hand groped for it I realised it was so wedged between me and the cabinet, there was no way I could pull it loose. Tinges of red edged into my vision. I could hear the roar of blood in my ears, feel the ache as my chest strained for breath. *Think, Sam, think.* But it was hard to concentrate with the pain of his fingers clawing into my throat, my own body weight adding to their strangulation. My right hand groped behind me, hit the cabinet, hit the cabinet shelf, felt along, grasping for something, anything, to use. It closed around the cold solidity of metal legs, equine legs, and in one immense and desperate movement I swung my arm up and around, and struck as hard as I could at the back of my attacker's head. The force hit his head into mine and he jerked back in surprise, his hands releasing their grip momentarily, enough for me to suck in a breath before they tightened again.

'You fucking little bitch,' he said through

gritted teeth, and he shoved me back hard against the cupboard and redoubled his efforts.

But I still had the horse in my hand and this time I aimed for the side of his head, for something more vulnerable, and again swung the horse in a great sideways arc that connected directly with his ear. This time he screamed in pain and let go of me, pulling back, shock consuming his face, his hand flying up to his ear, blood squirting out between his fingers.

My feet hit the ground and I immediately struck out again, this time at his exposed face, I wasn't about to give him a chance to regroup. The horse's rump connected with his nose with a satisfying crunch before his other hand could come up to protect it. With both of his hands now covering his face he left himself exposed, so I drove my knee hard up into his balls, felt their softness mash against his pelvic bone, then took a second shot at them with my foot as he fell backwards towards the ground.

'Sam?' I heard urgent voices calling and footsteps pounding up the stairs.

The cavalry was coming but I wasn't finished with this bastard yet. I whipped the pepper spray out of my pocket and gave him a blast full in the face as he lay there groaning on the floor. He screamed.

The boys burst through the door to find Iain Gibbs curled in foetal position on the floor, and me standing there, horse in one hand, pepper spray in the other. I stepped over him and walked towards my men, my own eyes streaming from the effects of the spray.

I stopped, turned back and took one more parting shot: 'You messed with the wrong girl, you fucking piece of shit.'

70

Iain Gibbs was looking very much the worse for wear. He had been tended to by the on-call doctor and had a row of stitches across the bridge of his nose and another set holding his earlobe together. Bruising accompanied the handiwork. It was quite gratifying what damage an ugly metal horse could do.

'That officer, she pepper-sprayed me when I was down and incapacitated. I mean, look at me,' he said, pointing to his face. 'It was unnecessary use of force. That's police brutality.' He was whinging like a four-year-old.

I rubbed gently at the livid bruises on my throat, and swallowed. It hurt. In fact, my neck and head felt like someone had forcibly tried to separate them using one of those medieval torture devices. There would be a few physio visits in order, that was for sure. DI Johns noticed the gesture. We were watching Iain Gibbs being interviewed by Smithy and Reihana, from the cheap seats in the next room.

'Did you really pepper-spray him while he was down?' he asked, looking straight ahead through the one-way mirror.

I felt my alarm-monitoring system go on full alert. The last thing I felt like right now was a lecture from him. But I also realised the foundations were being laid for the inevitable internal enquiry should Iain Gibbs decide to make a formal complaint. The honest truth of the matter was that I shouldn't have sprayed him. And any lie would come back to bite me. It was ammunition served on a plate for the DI's anti-Sam campaign, which seemed to be in full swing at the moment.

'Yes — ' I said.

But before I could justify my actions any further the DI interrupted me. 'Then you must have felt you were still under great personal danger,' he said. His eyes remained fixed on the man in the next room.

'Yes, sir.' I felt my eyes mist up and I had to look away. It was quite possibly the kindest thing he had ever said to me.

Now the game was up and Iain Gibbs had clearly demonstrated for the third time his propensity towards violence, he didn't pretend innocence, but he did play the 'I didn't mean to kill him' card.

'He wouldn't tell me where the other horse was, or even if he'd seen it, and when I kept pressing him about it, he got all mouthy and told me to piss off, and he was about to shut the door on me, so I just shoved my foot in the way and pushed the door back. But it hit him square in the face and he fell backwards, and he must have fallen heavily because I heard his head hit the floor really hard.'

'So, what did you do then?' Smithy asked. It seemed such a benign question.

'Well, I went into the house to make sure he was all right, but he was lying there on the floor, and he was twitching and frothing at the mouth like he was having some kind of a fit, then he just stopped breathing.'

'And it didn't occur to you to call an ambulance?'

'I was in such a panic, I couldn't think what to do.'

'You could have done CPR.'

'I know. I know that looking back, but I just panicked.' He looked distraught, and if you didn't know better, you could almost buy into it.

'And that panic involved cleaning up the evidence, stealing the goods and his computer, then stuffing your victim in a wetsuit and dumping his body at sea?'

As it turned out, Iain Gibbs happened to own a boat, although he didn't keep it at Aramoana. Instead he had an old boatshed at Hooper's Inlet, on the other side of the peninsula — somewhere nice and remote where his activities would have gone unnoticed. ESR forensic scientists would be out there going over the boat and shed as soon as they arrived from Christchurch. We were all pretty certain what they'd find. He used to dive a bit too, according to his now shell-shocked wife, and kept his gear out in the boatshed now he wasn't using it. I did wonder about her. I wondered if a little more probing and gentle questioning would reveal the true source of Marie Gibbs's timidity. I could guess what or who it was.

'You see, Iain, we have a few problems with your little story, and the largest one is this: have you heard of blood-spatter analysis?'

He shook his head. Another lie, I was sure.

Everyone who had ever seen a CSI programme or watched crime on UKTV would know what blood-spatter analysis was. Smithy maintained a level, even reasonable, tone of voice that seemed in stark contrast with his size and battle-hardened face. The resultant juxtaposition was quite menacing.

'Here's the thing,' he said. 'You took the time to clean up the blood, but you can never get all of it. You'll always miss some, and even though you can't see it, there is always some trace left behind. And those traces told us that Clifford Stewart suffered not one, but many blows, and they even told us that two of those blows were while he was on the ground, which means they were most likely caused by your foot.' Smithy noted the look of surprise on Iain Gibbs' face, but maintained the same, almost light tone. 'Yes, we can tell that, and we can tell you dragged his body for a little bit before you realised you were making a bigger mess and found something to wrap him up in. So your little story is looking a bit shaky now, isn't it?' He started to pour on some grit. 'And where it all completely falls apart for you, I'm afraid, is that you said he hit his head on the door, but, and this is a big but, there was absolutely no blood or skin evidence on the edge of the door. You lied to us again, Mr Gibbs. And you know what? I don't take too kindly to being lied to.'

Iain Gibbs knew he had met his match, physically and strategically. His posture changed from someone on the edge of his seat, ready to plead his case, to someone who realised it was pointless. He was being called to account, and payment was due.

71

The back-patting and congratulating were over. For all of us, these moments in a case were always underpinned with sadness. Sure we'd identified a killer, but it didn't bring Clifford Stewart back. I'd kept my promise to his parents, and in particular Marlene, his mum, and found who did this to him. But the simple fact of the matter was she had lost her son, and the future they had looked forward to — for him and with him — remained stolen.

Like any major, or even minor, case, it still had to have its day in court, so our job wasn't over with Smithy and Reihana escorting Iain Gibbs down to the cells, chucking him in and slamming the door. There was plenty of work left to do and a mile of reports to write. Unfortunately, the criminal justice system seemed to have an insatiable appetite for paper. My report would have to be very carefully worded and now was as good a time as any to start.

The phone rang on the desk next door and I reached over and picked it up.

'Shephard,' I said.

'Can I speak to Detective Smith, please?'

He was still busy performing his task downstairs and was no doubt taking great pleasure in it.

'He's busy at the moment. Can I take a message or get him to call you back?' Add receptionist to my job description.

'It's Anthony Wilder here, from Free-Market. He wanted us to notify him if there was any activity on a particular account, and I was ringing to inform him of a few new listings that were loaded last night.' There was only one account I could think of that would warrant that kind of monitoring.

'Was that the cathnadam account we've been tracking?'

'Yes, it was. The listings went up around seven-thirty p.m.'

'What was listed?'

'The listing — well, twelve separate listings actually — were for more of those four-litre tins of paint, as well as some old books. The paint has already sold as a buy-now purchase, sold this morning around eleven.'

'And the buyer's name?'

'Dun297.'

Shit.

'That's the same buyer as last time.'

I knew the drug-squad guys were inching closer to the purchasers of the paint. They had executed a number of search warrants around town, but unfortunately they hadn't, as yet, coughed up the heroin. We needed to intercept these people, and not just because they were drug dealers, and therefore by default the lowest scum on the planet, down there below toe-jam and cockroach shit. According to the email correspondence and times arranged, these people would have come to the house after Clifford Stewart had been murdered. They may have witnessed Iain Gibbs in the act of cleaning up, or removing the body. Or, just as likely, they found no one home, so walked in and helped themselves to the paint. It would have still been there, as Iain Gibbs would have had no use for it. He was more interested in pricey but ugly horse statuettes and the like. The paint people could be witnesses to the murder or its clean-up, or at least narrow down the time of death for us, before we threw them in jail and melted down the key.

'What email address was used by the seller?' I asked.

'The same as last time.'

'Great, and you're emailing all this information through to Detective Smith?'

'Already done.'

'Brilliant, thanks a lot.'

Well that certainly made life interesting. We'd have to get straight on to the email provider and find out the pick-up arrangements for that paint. Who the hell was selling it at this stage in the game? Whoever it was, they had no idea who they were inviting to their house.

Smithy would be back at any moment, and as soon as I brought him up to speed, he would be off after the scent like a shot. But before he came back I needed to make one little phone call.

'Detective Shephard.'

So he'd programmed my cellphone number into his phone; I must have rated highly in his world. I hadn't returned the favour.

'Spaz,' I said. 'I need to be quick, so I'll make this really simple for you. Please tell me you and

Felix weren't stupid enough to list some paint and Aramoana stuff on Free-Market last night. You're not that daft are you?'

'No way.'

'Thank God for that.' I'd grown fond of Spaz, so felt relieved it wasn't him. I also realised Spaz's skills could come in handy right now. 'Can you quickly check the cathnadam email account for me? There should be an email about a Free-Market purchase made last night from a Dun297.'

'Sure, give me a minute.'

'Haven't got a minute, otherwise questions will be asked.'

'Gotcha.' I could hear movement, and also a background conversation with Felix that went along the lines of: 'You didn't stick anything on Free-Market?' 'No way, never touching it ever again.'

Felix was still there. He must have had a lot of faith in Spaz's anti-detection techniques, or he couldn't find anywhere else to go. I'd tell them the good news for them, and bad news for Iain Gibbs, in person, later.

'Got it. Email sent at eleven fifteen this morning. Asked for pick-up at three p.m. today.'

I looked at my watch: it was just before two. There was time to organise a welcoming committee. I heard a sharp intake of breath.

'What is it, Spaz?'

'Found who your idiot is. Address for pick-up is the flat in Castle Street.'

Bloody hell.

'Jase,' we said, in unison.

72

'Reihana, you and I will go right now and pay a little visit to Jase. We'll brief him and remove him from the premises as quickly as possible,' Smithy said as he pulled on his jacket. 'The Armed Offenders Squad have been notified and are gearing up. It could take them up to half an hour to get mobilised and down there. Shit, this could be tight. We don't have a lot of time.'

I instinctively looked at my watch. It was 2.05 p.m. Fifty minutes until show time. They were going to set it up as a wee trap, so instead of young Jason answering the door when Dun297 knocked, they'd get the full reception committee. I just hoped the crims didn't turn up early.

'What do you want me to do?' I asked. 'I could bring Jase back to the station for you, then you could stay and watch the fun.'

'Sorry Shep, you're not along for this ride,' Smithy said with a tone that didn't invite argument. He could be bloody scary when he was in serious mode.

Why was I never allowed along for the exciting stuff? I'd say it was because I was a woman, and small with it, and it was their misguided need to protect me. They'd say it was for my own good because some sod had tried to strangle me to death this morning. Whatever the reason, once again I'd be left holding the fort. Mind you, there could be an advantage to that. It meant I could invest a little energy in covering my butt. Time was too short to wait for the correct channels to spew out information, so I'd taken the plunge and risked it all for a perpetually stoned, stupid piece of shit with a really bad hair-do. Now I could make the correct phone call, get the info and make it all look legit, as long as no one examined the times too carefully. Actually, I could even get around that if I got the Internet provider to email the information to me, then I could forward it to Smithy's email address and just tweak a few digits in the process. I gave myself a mental check. Jesus, when did I turn into the conniving bad girl? Tampering with the information? But no, this wasn't bad-girl stuff; it was all for the right cause. I was using my powers for good, not evil, if you called trying to save a dumb-nut like Jase good.

Time dragged when you weren't having fun. 2.22 p.m. I was sure it was 2.21 when I checked five minutes ago. I'd made the right phone call, and was suitably impressed when they followed my request immediately and sent through the info. The email had been corrected and forwarded through to Smithy's inbox, for perusal at his leisure. In the light of everything else going on, I was certain no one would check.

I'd also been putting some thought into how on earth Jase would have got his hands on the paint. He had been at the party at Aramoana, but had supposedly left in the small hours, and hadn't spent the night. Well, that was what he said. He may have lied. I was rapidly beginning to realise people did that, and often. He could have been there in the morning, collected his own treasures, then kept them somewhere safe until the fuss had died down. No one had mentioned his being at the crib in the morning, but then Jase was like a pesky blowfly; everyone knew he was there, thought he was disgusting, and gave him a swat occasionally, but other than that, they ignored him, and he faded into the background. The only other way I could think of that would give him the opportunity to acquire goods was when Clifford and Leo came back to the flat on the Sunday morning with their loot. Jase had said they brought some cartons in, and then took them away again. But what if they didn't take them all? What if they hid a few away? Everyone said Jase was a nosey bastard; he may have seen them stash the boxes or had discovered them afterwards. The SOCOs had been through the flat very thoroughly the day we identified Clifford Stewart, but the terms of reference were different at that stage in the investigation — we didn't know about the extra-special qualities of certain tins of paint back then. So any paint they may have found, say in a cupboard or under the house, in the context of the general mess and squalor, may have just looked like something the landlord had dropped off to do some optimistic fixing up. Every flat I had ever lived in had a pile of paint cans lurking in some shed or cupboard, along with plastic lightshades and a few part-rolls of wallpaper. Leo Walker hadn't mentioned leaving cartons at Castle Street in his interview, but then, the specific question had not been posed, and he was pretty upset at the time.

The sound of someone running down the hall broke me out of my navel-gazing. That was weird; people generally didn't run around here. A body in blue flew past in the direction of the boss's office. It was Nate, one of my minders from that morning, and the glimpse of his face told me something serious was up. I got out of my chair and raced after him.

'Where is he?' he said, panting, when he came out of the DI's office.

'No idea. What's up?'

'The shit has hit the fan in a big way. Castle Street flat, shots fired.'

I felt the impact of his words hit me square in the chest. 'Smithy and Reihana are there. What happened?'

He shook his head. '111 call from neighbours. Don't know details. Can't get hold of the boys.'

'Jesus. Are you going down there?'

In answer he broke into a run.

I turned and ran after him.

73

You'd have thought the circus had come to town. Our squad car had been let through the roadblock on the corner of Castle Street and Dundas Street, but we'd had to manoeuvre through a sea of gawping students to do so. Some even had cans of beer in their hands. What did they think this was — a bloody sideshow? As we crawled up to the cordon of police cars and ambulances, we passed more students being evacuated out of the area, their faces harried and anxious, their fear emphasised by the flashes of blue and red from the emergency vehicles. They didn't share the almost jovial air of the idiots by the roadblock. It was all a bit different when you'd been plucked from your flat by the police and told to hoof it because of mad men with guns; not so funny then.

'Isn't the Armed Offenders Squad here yet?'

'Doesn't look like it, but they can't be far away.'

That was the only downside to having a specific squad. It took time to call in the various members, get them kitted up and armed and to the scene in a co-ordinated fashion. It wasn't an immediate response. Sometimes I thought it would be easier if the regular force were armed, like they were overseas, but then again, there was something to be said for the police being viewed as part of the community, rather than something dangerous and to be feared.

I'd spent the time during the car race down here trying to get Smithy and Reihana on their cellphones. No luck. Nothing. My belly felt full of lead.

We got out of the car and moved up to the safe forward point where officers were gathered. The ambulance staff were there too. Everyone was standing around waiting, while our colleagues — while Smithy and Reihana — could be in there, lying injured or dying. Why wasn't anyone doing anything?

The flat was halfway along the block, about a hundred metres from where we were standing, sheltered behind vehicles. From here I could just make out the front porch, but the angle prevented a better view. I looked further up the road and saw there was a similar cordon where Castle Street bisected Howe Street.

'Isn't anyone going in?' I asked a familiar figure.

We now knew where DI Johns was. He must have been one of the first to arrive.

'No,' he said. He didn't even bother to look at me.

No? He was just going to leave it at no?

'Why not?' I asked.

The usual tetchiness crept into his voice. 'We've secured the perimeter, but we don't know what's going on in the house. It's too risky. We have to wait for AOS, their ETA is ten minutes.'

That was ten minutes too long as far as I was concerned. And that was ten minutes until they got here. It didn't take into account the time needed to assess the situation and act, so who knew how long before it was declared safe? Meanwhile, they could be dying in there.

I pressed on. 'They could be hurt though.'

'I know that.' He began to sound seriously irritated. 'But we can't put others in danger until we know it is safe.'

'But it's Smithy and Reihana.' My voice must have carried my desperation, because he turned and looked at me then, breaking his concentration away from the house.

'I know, Shephard. Believe me, I know. But I can't risk anyone else.'

'But — '

'That's enough.' Clearly the end of the conversation, as far as he was concerned.

But how the hell could they know it wasn't safe to go in if nobody checked it out? For all they knew, the offenders could have taken off and been miles away. Sure, they couldn't get anyone on their cells, or the flat's phone, but there hadn't been any more shots fired since the first report. So what was the fucking problem? Jase. I needed to try and get hold of Jase.

I pulled my phone out, scrolled down my messages till I reached the right one, and then hit call back. I moved back several metres away from my colleagues, so I would be away from prying ears and so I could hear clearly.

'Spaz,' I said, sharp. 'I need Jase's cellphone number and I need it right now.'

Spaz fired a string of numbers back at me real fast and without question. I wrote them on my hand, not trusting my memory when my brain was saturated with adrenaline, then hung up on him.

The phone took an agonising eight rings before it was answered.

'Jase? Jase, is that you?' I pressed my hand over my other ear and leaned forwards, straining to hear.

There was no response, but I could make out breathing — shuddery laboured breathing — on the other end. A wave of goosebumps circumnavigated my body.

'Jase, it's Detective Shephard. Do you remember me?'

Just breathing.

'Now you listen to me. I know you're hurt — I can hear you're hurt — but if I'm going to be able to help you, I need to know if the people who did this have gone. Have they left the flat?'

All I could hear was breathing. I was just about to repeat myself when I heard a tight little 'yes'.

Thank God, but I had to confirm it. This wasn't the time for a misunderstanding. I started walking back towards DI Johns.

'So you're telling me they are no longer in the house and have gone.'

I could almost feel the effort it was taking him. He had to be in a bad way. 'Yes.'

The next question was the one I couldn't bear to ask. By this stage I was back next to the DI and I pulled at his sleeve to get his attention. He was about to swat me away when he heard my question.

'And are the two detectives who came to see

you, are they hurt?'

There was another big pause, before a sob and a 'yes'.

'He said yes.' I relayed the information to DI Johns. 'This is Jason, he's in the house there with them, they are all badly' — my voice cracked as I said the word — 'hurt, but he says the offenders have left the house. We have to go in. Now!'

The DI looked at me, the tussle between concern and wariness apparent on his face, and I knew in an instant he wasn't going to give the order. He was hamstrung by protocol.

By this point I was beyond being patient, reasonable or respectful. I grabbed him by the top of his vest and started shaking it. 'For God's sake, it's our guys in there. They could be dying for all we know. If we wait, they could be fucking dead.'

Everyone turned to look, and a pocket of silence hung there, repelling even the background sound of police sirens.

'We can't,' he said, the spell broken. 'We have to wait.'

'Well, fuck you,' I yelled. It was too much to bear. How could we just sit back and wait while our colleagues, our friends, bled to death? Before I was even aware of having consciously made a decision, my feet had taken off, sprinting in the direction of the flat. I felt a hand grasp out, trying to stop me, but I was too quick.

'Stop her!' came the cry, but it was too late. I was out of there.

'Jason, I'm coming,' I yelled into my phone, before pushing it into my pocket as I ran.

It felt like mere seconds before I was at the front door of the house. Caution be damned. Jason surely wouldn't lie when his life depended on it. I pulled at the door, but it was locked. It was one of those old wooden ones set into a doorframe with rectangles of coloured glass down each side. I backed up to the glass nearest the handle, pulled my right arm forwards, and gave the glass a good fast whack with the back of my elbow. It shattered and I felt a sting as a broken shard caught my flesh. The junk mail had made a reappearance on the porch, so I grabbed a few pieces, wrapped them around my hand, then punched out the remaining glass so I could reach through and turn the door handle.

The hallway was deserted, but I could see blood on the walls and floor, and my worst fears were realised.

'Smithy?' I yelled out as I raced down towards the kitchen and living area. I could see legs lying across the doorway.

'Jase? Jason?'

His face contorted into relief and tears as I bent down to check on him. He was bleeding from the abdomen and the shoulder. He was still clutching his cellphone. He must have dragged himself across to where it was charging to get to it. My eyes followed the trail of blood to where he'd been.

'Oh, Jesus.'

I crawled over on all fours to where Smithy lay on the floor, still, in a pool of blood. The path of his fall was signposted by the red, sticky smear down the wall.

'No, no, no, no,' I kept uttering to myself as my hands pulled at his collar and tie. They groped for his throat, and I prayed for a pulse. I felt a fluttering beneath my fingers. 'Oh, thank God,' I uttered. It was faint, but it was there.

But there was still someone missing. My eyes hunted around before they finally found the prone, familiar black-clothed form hidden behind the chair legs on the other side of the table. Reihana. Even from here I could see his hair was matted with blood, and with something else I didn't want to think about. I crawled around towards him, and the closer I got the more apparent was the devastation, until I reached the point where it was clear there was nothing that could be done. The fears I'd been suppressing rose up with the bile, and the tears that I'd been holding back burst free and scalded their way down my face.

Epilogue

'Here's trouble,' I said as Smithy limped into the squad room.

The limp was going to be a permanent fixture seeing as the bastards with the guns had decided to try and remove one of his kneecaps. Shooting him through the shoulder and in the chest hadn't been enough, apparently.

'Missed you all so much, I begged them to let me back,' he said, a half-smile rearranging the crags on his face.

I watched as his eyes moved to Reihana's empty desk, and the smile slumped. Although a month had passed, we all still pitched in to keep a vase of something on his desk. This time it was gerberas.

'He'd have hated the poncy flowers. You know that, don't you?'

Despite the passage of time, I felt the familiar welling of tears, and my voice was a bit choked when I gave the reply, 'That's why we're doing it, to piss him off.'

Smithy snorted a laugh, headed towards his desk, then lowered himself into the chair. He'd had a lot to contend with recently between the long road to recovery and a difficult decision made on the family front, so it was great to see him here. I couldn't help but wonder what the atmosphere was going to be like next week when Reihana's desk and position was filled. Some people didn't take well to change, and this one was going to be difficult for the both of us. I don't think Paul could have foreseen that he would have ended up working in the same squad room as me, let alone the next desk, but due to this unforeseen vacancy, he'd been shuffled from a starting rotation in narcotics to homicide. And considering Smithy seemed to hate his guts, it remained to be seen how successful that arrangement was going to be. Not to mention our relationship situation. Paul and I were still yet to figure out exactly what 'us' was going to entail. For the moment, thank God, it involved being under different roofs.

Smithy started tapping his fingers on the table surface, then turned to me and in a moment of *déja vu* said: 'So, what's happening, what do you know?'

I leaned back in my chair, fingers interlaced behind my head. 'Nothing exciting. Just working on the prosecution of some low-life scum-buckets who decided to shoot up some of my mates. Don't think the boss will let you help out on that one.' I decided not to mention the new team member.

It was amazing how the publicity around an officer killed in the line of duty, especially a family man, could cough up the right bits of information to lead to the culprits. Not even the hardest of businesspeople wanted to be suspected as cop killers — it tended to make their lives very difficult — so naturally the information had come from the killers' competitors. All the groups under suspicion had been falling over themselves to dob each other in, so we had been inundated with information and misinformation. As a result there had been a lot of raids on properties, a lot of individuals dragged in for questioning and a lot of manpower invested into the hunt. For once the civil libertarians had kept quiet about the scattergun approach to finding the culprits. But so far it had been a frustrating exercise. These organisations protected their hierarchy well, so consequently we had the small fry at the low end of the food chain, the kind of low-level intelligence, low-skilled, low-life individuals who would take a cop's kneecap out for sport. The type who were dumb enough to leave their fingerprints and DNA all over the crime scene. Their superiors were far cleverer than that. The way they were organised was reminiscent of closed terrorist cells, so the underlings, or contractors, worked without knowledge of who was calling the shots. But we all knew who the king-pin arsehole was that ordered this, and we were all bloody determined to make him pay for squandering Reihana's life, and maiming Smithy's. His time would come, he could count on that, because I wasn't the only one around here who was making this personal. He may have thought he was Teflon Man, but by God we were going to make sure he paid the price. We would get our evidence and when we did, no amount of being lawyered-up would help him.

The dispensable bastards who turned up early to their Free-Market pick-up appointment at Jase's were enjoying remand time under the government's hospitality. Another one enjoying — or enduring, as was more likely the case — some prison time was Felix Ford, who had finally realised it was time to hand himself in. His parents brought him in to the station the week after the shootings, keeping their word they would hand over their son. So far he was keeping his word that he wouldn't mention my involvement in his break for emancipation. Spaz, Felix and I came to an agreement that it wasn't in any of our best interests to share that information. Now I had to hope they both continued to see it that way. I knew you reaped what you sowed — Dad had always drummed that into me, and I'd colluded with these two with the best of intentions — but still, it wasn't a comfortable sensation having that hanging over my head like some unexploded bomb.

One consolation to all this was Jase lived to see another day. I highly doubted he'd have an epiphany and see this experience as a second chance at life and an opportunity to straighten himself out. Somehow my mental image of him was always going to be accompanied with a joint or a bong, and with a severely drooping eyelid.

The other person warming a cell was Iain Gibbs. Good bloody job, too. I could not for the life of me understand how he would kill someone for ugly ornaments like those horses. Surely greed only went so far. It also made me question the motivation behind his intervention on my behalf out at Aramoana that fateful day. Somehow I didn't think it was just to help the damsel in distress. As it turned out, he'd been ripping off his friend Peter Trubridge too. It would appear it wasn't some opportunistic insurance-fraud scheme. Peter had been horrified to find out what his so-called friend had been up to. Yes, he'd forwarded copies of his manifest to Iain for safekeeping, so Iain Gibbs knew exactly what was on that ship, and that the pair of bronze horses was worth more than his entire superannuation savings. And that was the thing: sure there was a lucrative market in stolen art, but New Zealand was a small place, so offloading it here would be near impossible. It would seem Iain Gibbs needed to possess things, to have them, hold them, admire them, own them. So much so he killed for them, and with his own bare hands. He killed Clifford Stewart. He almost killed Felix Ford. He tried to kill me. It made me wonder who else had suffered his attentions? I knew of at least one. I had bumped into Marie Gibbs a few days after he was jailed. It was the most relaxed I'd ever seen her.

'Shep.' I was pulled back to reality.

'Yes, Smithy.'

'Thanks.'

I looked up at him, saw the tight, earnest expression on his face and his glistening eyes. 'You're welcome,' I said quietly.

'I got you a little present.' He reached into his coat pocket and handed me a tennis-ball-sized parcel wrapped in purple tissue paper. It was quite weighty for its size.

'You shouldn't have,' I said, feeling really quite pleased that he had.

'You deserve it,' he said and gave me a wink.

I peeled back the layers of purple until there, resting in my hand, was a miniature black, and extremely ugly, metal horse. I cracked up laughing, made a pretend swing at his head with it, which he duly ducked, and then plonked it down with a clunk on the wooden desk.

The cheeky bugger.

'You most *definitely* shouldn't have.'

Acknowlegements

You can have a lot of fun with science, and I was fortunate to do postgraduate study at the Sir John Walsh Research Institute — a hotbed of novel and sometimes gruesome research, including into marine decomposition, using pigs heads! A huge thank-you to Dr Gemma Dickson for letting me make use of her research, and to the late Professor Jules Kieser — we had some pretty wild discussions!

Another fun part of this novel was delving into maritime history and all things shipping. I am immensely appreciative of the time I spent with Dunedin historian, the late Ian Church. He was very generous with his time and knowledge, and he told a ripping yarn.

And where would I be without my wonderful crew at Team Orenda. I am eternally grateful to Karen Sullivan for taking a punt on this gal from the other side of the world, and still utterly delighted at her 'make it more Kiwi' attitude — music to this NZ gal's ears. Thanks to West Camel for his fabulous editorial eye, Mark Swan for those amazing covers, and the whole team for your incredible support and belief in me.

And of course I wouldn't be able to do this without the support and jollying along of my family. I'm sure having a writer in the house can be a tad interesting at times! Love you all heaps, xxx.

Containment is dedicated to my gorgeous mum, Heather, who passed away in 2017. Miss you so much, Petal xxx.